# THE VISTA
## -A Journey
### of a Bacha Bazi boy

## C. R. SHEA

### INSPIRED BY TRUE EVENTS

ISBN: 978-1-4834-9318-3 (sc)
ISBN: 978-1-4834-9383-1 (hc)
ISBN: 978-1-4834-9317-6 (e)

Library of Congress Control Number: 2018913103

Lulu Publishing Services rev. date: 12/12/2018

*This story is dedicated to the abused young innocent "Bacha Bazi Boys".*
*God bless their souls!*

# ABOUT THE AUTHOR

C. R. Shea of The Vista was born and raised in Minnesota through the 60s and 70s. Enlisting in the Navy he was stationed out of San Diego during the 80s, assigned to a squadron aboard the flight deck of the aircraft carrier "Kitty Hawk."

Along with his service the author had four Uncles in the US Army, one Uncle in the Air Force, and one Uncle that served in the US Marines in Iwo Jima, during WWII.

The authors female cousin served in Vietnam from 1969-1970. She became one of the first female Drill Sergeants in 1972, graduating at the top of her Drill Sergeant school. She was featured on the cover of "Army Magazine" in 1972.

*The Author's father with 9 years of service in the Air Force was killed in the line of duty in South Korea in 1956 during the Korean War.*

This wonderfully crafted story reflects the patriotism and pride of the military men and women, but also enlightens the readers on the abuse and cruelty of certain cultures around the world, in the exploitation of young innocent children. Inspired by true events, this story will have you on the edge of your seat.

THE VISTA

A Journey
of a Bacha Bazi boy

BY C.R. SHEA

INSPIRED BY TRUE EVENTS

# THE VISTA - JOURNEY OF THE BACHA BAZI BOYS

Afghanistan, called the crossroads of central Asia, has had a turbulent history. It has evolved from Arab rule to Genghis Khan, to eventually the European influence, which brought more conflict in the late 1800s.

It wasn't until 1973 that prime minister Daoud abolished monarchy, abrogated the 1964 Constitution, and declared Afghanistan a Republic. His new attempts for social reforms failed and the Constitution was promulgated in 1977.

In 1978, after the Soviet invasion, a treaty of cooperation with Afghanistan was signed and the Soviet military numbers increased. The regime was now dependent upon the Soviets. As insurgency spread, the Afghan Army began to collapse.

After the invasion, the Karmal Regime, which was backed by Soviet troops was unable to establish authority. A majority of the Afghan people opposed the communist regime, actively and passively. Afghan soldiers made it impossible for the regime to become established, which lead to the demise of the Soviet takeover.

Afghan's population was now over 28 million people, most living outside the country, in Pakistan and Iran. There were more than nine ethnic groups and their religion was mostly Sunni Muslim. They spoke primarily Dari or Afghan Farsi. Afghanistan has survived decades of war, poverty, and many foreign and domestic regimes. The people of Afghanistan have been strong, resourceful, and resilient, while living with the nightmare of war and constant instability.

This story is about another dark side of Afghanistan, the lives of the Bacha Bazi Boys. Young boys forced into dance and sex slavery by the successful businessman and the warlords of the region. This time-honored tradition condemned by human rights activists continues today. The United States military and its allies have tried to make a difference.

# CONTENTS

## PART ONE
### THE MISSION

## PART TWO
### THE MOUNTAINS

# PART THREE
## THE CAVES

# PART ONE
## THE MISSION

# CHAPTER 1
# THE EXPLOSION

The year was 2003 in Kabul, Afghanistan.

My name is Mike, and I'm a US Army Staff Sergeant with eight years prior service in the Navy, aboard the aircraft carrier U.S.S. *Kitty Hawk*. Upon re-enlistment with the Army due to my prior military experience, I was assigned lead of my first squad. Following the 9/11 attacks, my squad was in the middle of some of the most intense fighting in the region, with a high rate of civilian and military casualties.

Up until this point, I had been stationed in Kabul for almost a year. It was a bright sunny day out on patrol as I drove the foothills east of Kabul, focused on the surroundings ahead. It was hard to believe that at any moment we could be engaged in gunfire. In the back seat were two new recruits from California, both just out of boot camp. Bud, a Sergeant was in the front seat next to me; he's been with my unit now for nearly ten months.

As we headed deeper into the foothills outside Kabul, I could hear the groan of the Humvee as we navigated through tight turns, dry dusty terrain, and steep ravines. I glanced back at the two newbies, noticing their look of fear and bewilderment as they nervously scanned the terrain around us. They were holding on tightly to their M16s as if the guns were some invisible protective shield. The tighter they held on, the more they felt a false sense of security.

*I will have to keep a close eye on these two,* I noted to myself. The added responsibility of babysitting wasn't what I wanted today.

Bud was engaged in conversation with himself droning on about his heat rash outbreak—I listened to his words, but his words sounded muffled. All I could think about was the temperature, the dust, and the constant sweating. It was late in the afternoon and nearing one hundred degrees.

For a brief moment, I imagined a tall cold glass of beer. *Keep a watchful eye,* I reminded myself. Patrol was never a time to daydream.

*Pop! Pop!*

As we drove over the next ridge, we heard gunshots down in the foothills ahead.

I pulled over and shut down the Humvee. We listened intently, getting a fix on what direction it was coming from. Bud was already in position with his high-powered binoculars scanning the valley, I noticed the newbies' hesitation as I barked an order for them to get out. As Bud evaluated the situation in the valley, I herded the other two to take cover behind a large boulder.

Bud glanced back at me as I knelt down next to him. Looking through my own binoculars, I noticed what looked like ten to fifteen men in synchronized movement, about one hundred thirty meters down the valley. It was getting later in the day, so the shadows were playing tricks with my vision. The new guys huddled together behind a boulder.

We decided to move in closer.

"Looks like another Taliban cell," I whispered to Bud. He nodded in agreement. I ordered the other two to stay back, take cover, and keep an eye out. If there was any movement from behind, they were to alert me by clicking the radio button once—but absolutely no voice communication. We moved into position hidden behind a few boulders and noticed the group of men surrounding someone lying on the ground. We were about the span of one football field away.

As we got closer to the men, I recognized the group through the binoculars as one of the Taliban cells we had been after for the last few months. My heart was racing. I knew from our Intel this was one of the Taliban cells that had been eluding the Americans by going back and forth over the mountains of Pakistan and Afghanistan.

Suddenly, Bud motioned for me to *look now!* as he pointed aggressively. I swung my binoculars in the direction of his finger and focused on the shadowy figure of a man curled up on the ground. It appeared to be a soldier. I couldn't make out from which country, but he lay on his right side with his hands bound behind his back, a rag stuffed in his mouth. Blood ran down the corners of his eyes.

As Bud glanced over my way, I knew all too well he wanted to go in guns blazing—but I motioned for him to hold up. We had to see what was going on, and I as glanced back over the trail we had just left, I had the feeling we were being watched; we couldn't afford to act too soon.

We kept watching. In the middle of the group, a small fire was burning, and as the flames grew higher, it lit up the darkening valley. I could see that the soldier on the ground was one of our own: an American soldier.

One of the men had a torch-like stick burning with a red glow on the end. The man positioned himself over the American soldier, raising the burning stick high above his head with hatred in his eyes. Then he came down with full force and jammed the burning stick into the right eye of the soldier. Cheers went out from the men as the American soldier screamed in pain and horror, choking on his own blood.

Bud and I looked at each other with horror, our adrenaline pumping. I knew we were both fighting the impulse to rush to rescue one of our own, but we knew we were outnumbered. The distance back to the Humvee made it nearly impossible without getting shot to hell. All the men in the group had rifles slung over their shoulders; I noticed one with a RPG launcher. I motioned for Bud to retreat, but we both were frozen in our tracks, watching the disgusting spectacle before us.

The Taliban took turns kicking and stomping on the American soldier. Another hand rose up holding a pesh-kabz knife with an 11-inch blade that glistened in the firelight. The knife-wielder pulled the soldier to his feet by his hair, and the soldier moaned in pain—I knew he must be nearly passing out from the brutality of the torture he had just endured, but he was defiant.

The knife-wielder pulled the soldier's head back with his left hand. With his right hand, he put the knife blade to the soldier's throat and began a cutting motion. The American issued a blood curdling scream that was followed by a muffled guttural sound as his head was slowly severed from his body. Intentionally, the butcher elaborately gestured in saw-like motions as if to add to the sick amusement for the rest of the men.

At that moment, the radio clicked. I motioned Bud to *move out*. Without drawing attention to our position, we slowly backed out of the valley, keeping an eye on the men and the slaughter taking place. I witnessed the gruesome sight of the soldier's head being held high in the fire-lit darkness. At a safe distance, we turned up the trail and headed back to the Humvee.

*Pop! Pop! Pop!*

More gunfire. I looked up to the Humvee and saw our newbies aiming at another area. More insurgents must be ahead—and now the beheading group of Taliban knew we were there.

We ran to the Humvee, hearing sounds of the butchers pursuing us. Gunshots could be heard as the two new guys engaged in gunfire.

I heard a loud scream: "I'm hit! I'm hit! Shit I'm Hit!"

Darkness had completely fallen, but we could see the flash of light coming from the gunfire ahead. I realized that two more Taliban soldiers were behind a ridge ahead pinning down the new guys. As we rounded a huge boulder, we lit up the night, firing back at the Taliban and forcing them to take cover.

One of the newbies was shot, sprawled out on the ground. We moved quickly to help him into the Humvee, then sped off in a rain of gunfire. Leaning out of the Humvee, Bud took his best shots at the angry mob. Trying to get my bearings in the midst of gunfire, darkness, and confusion, I did all I could to navigate the winding sandy trail—nearly rolling over the Humvee.

After several minutes, we finally made it out of the valley onto open road. I looked back at the hit soldier with his head on Bud's lap. Bud had applied pressure over the gaping chest wound to slow the bleeding.

*Boom!*

There was no notice of the explosion whatsoever; suddenly, the Humvee was flying through the air, the IED explosion so loud it was deafening. Everything faded to black...

...When I finally came to, who knows how long we had been there? I heard nothing—complete silence in the darkness.

I called out to Bud, but there was no response. As I looked around the Humvee at the mangled twisted metal, I saw that the force of the

IED had hit the passenger side toward the back where my three soldiers had been sitting. The explosion had ripped through the Humvee, killing Bud and the other two instantly.

I was lying on my back in the mangled mess of metal and flesh, blood everywhere. I looked down at my left leg and saw that it was wedged in the metal debris—half ripped off just below the knee.

Next to the jagged metal, I saw my leg bone as I passed out.

# CHAPTER 2
# CHICKEN STREET

That black moment in 2003 where I broke my leg and lost three good men faded away into 2004 as I was forced to rest and do hours of demanding rehab that kept me away from active duty with my squad. During those months of rehab, anxiety filled me most days. I was wanting to get back out there and finish what we'd started, and I missed the adrenaline rush of tracking, hunting, and capturing those ruthless animals: the Taliban. The beheading, my injury, and the loss of my men that day was a memory that followed me relentlessly.

*The Taliban relish in the suffering of innocent people without any remorse!* I would often think. *They're soulless men without any compassion whatsoever!* And it would never fail to infuriate me.

One year passed in grueling therapy, but I was determined to get back on my feet again. Nothing would stop me in getting back to my squad. After a clean bill of heath I was back on the ground in Afghanistan just one year after my broken leg had left me incapacitated.

It was a hot sweltering August in 2004 when I was finally able to return to duty. I went back to Kabul with a new squad that consisted of ten soldiers, and we were given orders to perform the same tasks I'd left behind a year ago.

Back out on patrol with two of my men: Tex and Big Joe. The rest of my unit were back at base for weaponry training. "Sweet Home Alabama" was blaring from Tex's stereo earbuds. I spent two tours with Tex in the Navy on the aircraft carrier U.S.S. *Kitty Hawk CV 63*.

Big Joe came to my unit just after I was assigned the squad before the explosion a year ago. He was 6'6" and 290 lbs, and he was constantly ribbing Tex, who was six inches smaller and barely weighed 175 lbs soaking wet. The three of us were extremely devoted patriots, and we had developed a relationship like brothers who were watching each other's backs at all times.

"Sweet Home Alabama!" sang Tex playfully. I rolled my eyes. The music from Tex's earbuds was so loud, it became a distraction, but I dismissed it as we continued toward the center of the market area. Big Joe, who had an insatiable appetite, was constantly eating something; at the moment, it was sunflower seeds.

It was a hot day around 1300 hours as our patrol took us through the market on Chicken Street. Chicken Street, one of the primary market areas in downtown Kabul, was an open market with nearly a hundred vendors—everything from goat heads to intricate handmade toys were available for Afghani people to add some comfort and normalcy to their lives.

Throughout the past year while I was enduring rehab, our soldiers have been successfully regaining some control of the Kabul area—forcing the Taliban into the surrounding mountain ranges in to hiding. The locals have not only endured another bloody war, but had been resourceful in the ability to create business in the midst of so much bloodshed and hardship.

Chicken Street became a popular market area, beginning to flourish the last few years as American soldiers stayed diligent in the fight against the Taliban around the markets. Today, Chicken Street was already bustling even though it was earlier in the market day.

As we drove deeper into the market, we decided to park the humvee and walk the patrol on foot. Making our way towards the center of the market area a few blocks down, Big Joe grabbed some meat on a stick.

We snaked our way through the market, and I was pleased to see some normalcy slowly return to this area. The market was packed today with the locals lining up and down both sides of the street. But even with some calm, I always instructed my squad to always use extreme caution when interacting with the locals.

*Let your guard down for a moment and you'll have your head blown off,* I thought ominously.

So as we worked our way through the market, we held our weapons at our sides. Smells of the vast choices of local food were cooking: fresh vegetables and fruit from around the region. You could see the smoke from the cooking grills rise as it swirled and twisted throughout the market—it reminded me a lot of the local fairs back home in Wisconsin.

Chicken Street ran in a north-south direction for about a mile. On the south end, there was a roundabout to handle the heavy traffic flow from the east and west. The north end of the market curved to the left in a westerly direction for a mile or so, trailing off into a neighborhood displaying years of neglect.

At the north end of Chicken Street, there stood three storage buildings that served as a distribution point for the Americans. They were used primarily as a cache for supplies during lapses of deliveries when the fighting prevented supplies from coming in or going out.

We headed north in the direction of the three storage buildings off in the distance.

*Click!* Suddenly, the radio sounded. I began listening to the hand held radio on my belt clip.

"Tex, turn down that music, Goddammit!" I yelled, as I listened to the enfolding details on the radio.

"Alright! The batteries are going on me anyway," Tex replied. Big Joe chuckled.

"We've captured a car bomber," I heard on the other end of the radio. As I listened, it became clear that the car bomber had been parked outside a local restaurant where many of our soldiers spent their free time. The quick thinking of our troops in the capture temporarily stopped the bloodshed that would've soon followed.

The three of us huddled together, listening intently to the details of the capturing of the car bomber. Our adrenaline picked up as we scanned the crowd before us: A car bomber meant that insurgents were active, and anything might happen today.

I took a sip of water as we continued our way through the market, heading toward the three storage buildings off in the distance, trying to calm my nerves and prepare myself for whatever the day might bring. This stretch had been our patrol now for the last few months.

And while it made me feel good that I still had all my men in one piece—the other patrols had been hit hard with casualties—I knew everything could change in a matter of seconds.

# CHAPTER 3

# DASTGIR

Dastgir, Pakistani by birth, had lived most his years crossing back and forth through the treacherous mountains between Pakistan and Afghanistan. At 6'5" and lanky, Dastgir was always dressed in the traditional Pakistani clothing: kamiz shalwar and sindhi cap. While his hair was snowy white, a distinctive black stripe ran down the center of his white beard.

Dastgir enjoyed living in the shadows, always ready for any opportunity, always on the prowl for one particular traded good. He had made himself quite valuable to the Taliban warlords and the corrupt businessmen throughout the area. While most despised him, many relied on his services. Just a handful of locals knew of his corrupt ways: the exchange of money for their young innocent boys—the *bacha bazi boys.*

Adjusting his clothing from the strong breeze today, Dastgir was heading in the direction of the market. Looking up, he noticed off in the distance three American soldiers heading his way.

He was halfway between the market and three storage buildings that were always under constant supervision by the American Soldiers, so he turned and quickly headed back the way he came.

The storage buildings were Army built, corrugated metal attached to 14-inch cement supports. Several years ago, the three structures had been used by the Americans primarily as a cache for artillery in the proliferation and distribution during the Afghanistan War. Their purpose was successful then, but now they were primarily used for storing materials used in the rebuilding of roads and infrastructure. All three structures were 17 feet wide, 20 feet long, and 12 feet high, and they were in perfect line with each other—running end to end with only a five feet gap in-between.

The structures provided the perfect location for exchanges. Dastgir had used the three storage buildings over the years as a meeting place for his business dealings or for hiding if needed. Today, it would be used for hiding from the Americans heading his way. He worked his way through the crowd as fast as he could, trying not to bring attention to himself.

Dastgir had designed and built small stepping pegs running up the end of the middle building. The pegs were the size of a small finger, starting at waist height, continuing up the side of the building, and increasing in length the higher up you went. They were well hidden unless you happened to look up at the right angle.

Dastgir approached the center building, positioning himself on the first small peg. Looking over his shoulder toward the market, he could see the three soldiers heading his way. Over the last few months Dastgir's business had been quite good, but he continually worried that his activities would be discovered. These soldiers could be harmless, but it was better to be safe than sorry.

Dastgir peered around the side of the middle building. He adjusted his footing on the first peg while he reached for the next peg. The soldiers were nearing his location, and he could hear their muted voices conversing. When he reached the top peg, his trouser leg caught—making him lose his balance and causing him to roll over on his left side onto the corrugated metal roof.

The metal was burning hot from the intense heat of the sun. As he scrambled to avoid touching the metal with bare flesh, his right sandal slipped off as it fell to the hard packed dirt ground below, making a loud *slap!* as it landed.

"What do you say to a couple rounds of backgammon tonight, Mike?" Tex asked.

"Sure," I said. "But don't forget you owe me two months of your hard earned pay already. Big Joe has officially become my accountant. He gets 10% of my take to make sure you pay up."

"Aw, shit," was Tex's only reply, as Big Joe gave him a tough guy smirk while we approached the first storage building on the right.

*Slap!*

As we approached the first building, we heard a slap noise just ahead. We pointed our rifles in the direction of the center building. I signaled Big Joe to work the right side of the buildings, while I took the left. I motioned for Tex to cross over to the other side of the street and keep an eye out.

So far, I couldn't see anything. Big Joe and I slowly passed the first building, reaching the gap to the second building simultaneously. We glanced at each other as we continued to the second building.

Dastgir was lying on his stomach trying to keep out of sight. As he re-positioned himself, the metal roof strained from his weight, causing a metallic *pop*! He reached for the handgun he always carried strapped to his side under his shirt.

Knowing that he was no match for all three, he made the decision to run the length of the roof, if necessary, and jump the five-foot gap to the next building. He wanted to get to the crowd in the distance and blend in as quickly as possible.

Passing the second building, I glanced over to Big Joe—who was shaking his head. Nothing. I looked to Tex across the road to see if he noticed any movement. Tex also just shook his head. Still, we all felt the tension in the air.

*Pop!* A faint metallic ringing reached our ears.

Passing the third building, we heard Tex softly whistle to us, pointing back at the middle building. There was a head bobbing on the top. Big Joe and I worked our way back to the middle building, positioning ourselves up tight to the side. I motioned Tex to move in.

As I glanced up to the roof, I stepped on something: a sandal. Looking up the side of the building, I observed odd spike-like stubs attached to the building. From my angle, it looked like a makeshift stepping grid; the higher up they went, the pegs became longer and more substantial.

To the left of the pegs was a small door, so I shook the handle, finding the door secured. I raised my foot to the first peg and tried to get a foothold while trying to balance myself—but in full gear I had no chance.

Dastgir's heart raced as he strained to listen to the soldiers circling the building. Peering over the edge, he could only make out soft whispers below. But something in him told him to bolt.

At that moment, he quickly jumped to his feet and ran full speed across the top of the building. With a powerful jump, he pushed off and leaped the five-foot gap to the next building, landing perfectly. He sprinted to the end of the first building and jumped off the 12-foot drop to the ground, landing hard.

Dastgir took off running toward the market at full speed.

I flinched from the loud popping sound above me as I heard footsteps that ran the length of the building. Instinctively, I pointed my M16 toward the roof line and followed the movement above. I looked to Big Joe to see if he had a visual.

"Over here!" Tex yelled as he pointed. "He ran toward the market."

The three of us took off after the man who was sprinting toward the crowd. He stopped for a brief moment near the crowded market and looked back. That was when I got a full view of his face: a white beard with a black strip down the center. He stared right at me before disappearing into the crowd.

The three of us sprinted to where the man had disappeared into the crowd. We bent over, hands on knees, gasping for air before we continued through the market crowds.

"Did you see that son of a bitch run?" Tex screamed. "He just vanished!"

"What the hell! Why didn't you squeeze off a shot, Mike?" asked Big Joe.

"There were too many people for me to get a clear shot!" I said. "And besides, we don't even know who he is or why he was here."

"Hell, most of the locals already hate us and the rest want us dead." Big Joe said.

We just stood there looking at each other, sweat soaked and breathing hard. We walked back to the storage buildings, and I picked up the sandal—thinking that we might be able to get his scent with the assistance of our bomb sniffing dog, King.

Tex and Big Joe followed me, and Tex noticed a few blood droplets there on the ground. I pulled out of my front chest pocket a small vial used to collect any DNA out on patrols, then gently scraped the blood droplets into the container.

"What do you make of it, Mike?" Tex asked.

"Not sure," I said as I lit up a smoke, leaning against the building. "The guy's actions seemed out of place, with this area being a neutral zone for the last year. There've been minimal incidents. It's just weird. Why'd he run?" I asked this to no one in particular.

"Is it enough blood for a DNA match?" Tex asked.

"We can at least drop this off at the lab. I'm sure Brian can get something," I said. "Our new database has hundreds of terrorist names, photos, and pertinent information."

The two nodded.

"All right," I said. "Let's do another quick pass through the market. With some luck, maybe we can spot our runner."

We circled the market for about an hour. I had the strange man's face and facial hair burned into my brain. With no sign of him, we headed back to the base. After dropping off Big Joe and Tex, I headed over to the lab to drop off the blood sample with Brian.

*The man was clearly running from us. What did he have to hide?* I pondered. *If he had been with a terrorist group, there would've been a number of men. He didn't fire on us, but he is definitely someone of interest.*

I felt for sure that forensics would be able to help.

# CHAPTER 4
## FORENSICS

The forensics lab sat toward the back of the base. It was a small, nondescript-looking structure loaded with state-of-the-art equipment that was able to handle the smallest amount of body fluids or hair fibers. With the help of new technology, we'd been able to successfully connect the dots with the movements and relationships of the Taliban.

The lab was a secure building with cameras attached to the outside entrance that circled its perimeter. Standing outside of the lab door, I pushed the button to get buzzed in. The camera methodically panned the door with a low buzzing sound: left to right, right to left.

The door clicked. Entering the lab, the smell reminded me of a hospital. It was sterile, white, and packed with equipment. The room was only about 30 by 30 feet wide, and the windows on all four sides were small and close to the ceiling, allowing minimal light to penetrate.

"Hey, Brian," I said as I walked in.

"Mike! How goes the fight today?" Brian asked as he washed his hands. Brian was short and heavyset, with a scruffy red beard and large black framed glasses. He was balding with a few red wispy hairs that fell forward over his forehead. Brian dreamed of being a doctor someday, but loved the challenge of forensics, and he was the best in the business. He enjoyed anything he could do that helped in the capture of this ruthless regime.

"Two months without any casualties," I replied.

"Does Big Joe still have his insatiable appetite?" asked Brian.

"Of course. I heard the Army is considering discharging him, due to his meal tab—he eats twice the amount of any other soldier!"

Brian laughed and walked over, drying his hands on a crisp white towel. "So, what do you have for me?"

"Today on patrol near Chicken Street by the storage buildings we took pursuit of a male," I explained. "It appeared he was trying to hide from us. Odd thing was, he was on top of one of the old storage buildings alone and never fired a shot. Son of a bitch ran the rooftop, jumped off, then bolted for the market. That's where we lost him. I was able to find some blood—he must have cut himself on the metal roofing. The building had some weird climbing pegs up the side."

I handed the vial of blood to Brian. I felt guilty dragging in dirt to this clean environment.

"Some mystery you have there, Mike," Brian said as he took the sample and quickly placed it into the centrifuge, studying it under a bright light. "There might be enough here, but there sure is a lot of debris. I'll see what I can do. Give me a day on this and I'll call you."

As I was opening the door, Brian called me back.

"Hey Mike, I need to ask you something. Got a minute?"

"Sure," I said. "What is it"?

"Have you ever heard of a *bacha bazi boy*?"

"Bacha bazi boy? Nope," I said.

Brian went on to explain about a long-standing tradition of boy sex slaves, trained in the art of dance and dress, who performed for the corrupt businessmen and Taliban warlords. He told me these boys could range in age as young as seven to puberty. Their families typically were in a state of poverty, destitute, looking for extra money for their families. When the families surrender them, most of them don't realize they'll never see their boys again, or what they will be subject to.

"I've been trying to get the word out to the squad leaders to pass along to their men," Brian continued. "With the push back of the Taliban, we have a great opportunity to see if we can get some inside information as to the whereabouts of these kids. This practice is so well-hidden from outsiders, the organization is difficult to penetrate.

The humanitarian community has provided me with a whole lot of information, if you're interested."

"Where does this activity take place?" I asked.

"Typically in out-of-the-way places in Afghanistan and Pakistan; it's been a tradition among the men in this area for many, many years," Brian replied. "The mountain ranges offer hidden cave dens. They are supposedly tough to penetrate and well guarded, since Taliban are always present."

"Okay, I haven't heard of this before, but I'll take your information and talk it over with my Commander," I said. "I'm not sure how this will go over with him, but I know he wants to take out as many Taliban as possible before we head home, especially the higher ranking Taliban. But we'll be putting more lives on the line spreading our men thin if we get too involved with local traditions."

"Look at it this way, Mike," Brian continued. "This is a great opportunity for our troops to corral a few more of these Taliban warlords *and* rescue some abused kids. Find the boys, and you will find warlords."

# CHAPTER 5
# MIKE'S MEN

It was the morning after our mysterious encounter with the strange bearded man. My squad consisted of ten men—one of the smallest on base. We had three small housing units located near the center of the base that sat side-by-side facing north.

My personal unit on the left of the three sat next to a big shade tree. It consisted of a small kitchen area, bed, and bathroom. I had several pictures of my wife, nine-year-old son, and seven year old daughter pinned to the ceiling above my rack. They were the first and last thing I saw every day.

The larger middle unit housed the five highest ranking squad members and was our main hut used for cooking. There was a large room for the entire squad, an open sleeping area, bathroom, kitchen, and a TV lounge. The lowest ranking men slept in a smaller hut on the far right side.

Each day began with a squad meeting where we shared any intel we had obtained from the previous day's patrols. My morning ritual was always a solitary coffee while the men were shaking off their sleep.

While the squad was preparing for the day, I decided to visit the Commander on the other side of the base about yesterday's events. As I headed outside, I passed Big Joe leaning up against the door frame. He was always the first up, dressed and ready to go. He was munching on a plate of cold pizza from a couple days ago.

"Make sure these girls are ready when I get back," I instructed.

"Sure thing," he said as he shoved more pizza into his mouth, gazing off in the distance as two helos passed overhead.

Driving across base, I made a quick stop for a coffee refill at the food wagon. It was a warm morning already. This time of year the October weather would fluctuate from a cool start in the morning to the upper 70s in the afternoon.

The base stretched out in front of our living quarters for a mile or so. The perimeter fence of the entire base encompassed a two by four mile area. In the center of the camp sat the main chow hall. To the left of the chow hall was the officers' and enlisted men's clubs: nondescript white brick structures with the paint starting to peel from the weather and neglect. The officers' quarters stood out with the American, Afghan, and POW flag—and all three flags flapped in the warm morning wind.

I decided to stop by the Commander's office. I was amazed how lush and green the landscaping always was for this dry and parched countryside. The office was surrounded by a sea of verdant, thriving green grass with colorful flowers peppered in. I could smell the aromatic flowers, reminding me of home in the springtime.

The front door of my Commander's office was always open, and there was a small waiting room inside. The Commander's assistant Bob—or 'Door Knob Bob,' as we liked to call him—greated me.

"Good Morning, Staff Sergeant," Bob was a hard worker; the quintessential paper pusher with round glasses that sat on the tip of his nose. He reminded me of Radar on *Mash*.

"Good Morning, Bob! Is the Commander in?"

"He should be right back—morning coffee makes his movements like clockwork. You can set your watch to it!" Bob said with a smirk.

"I'll wait outside," I motioned.

I went outside and lit up a smoke, leaning against the humvee and observing the activity going on. There was always the noise of the machines of war, the smell of fuel hung in the air. I was here to discuss the events of yesterday and wanted to bring up the the bacha bazi boys. I wanted to get his take on the man we saw yesterday, even though the Commander was going to view any type of rescue as a possible boondoggle.

I was curious to see if it was true that this activity would lead us to the Taliban and corrupt businessmen providing money and intel to the

Taliban leaders. This would be a mission that, even with its possible insurmountable risk, could have a huge payoff. It could be a huge break in taking out the regime. I wasn't necessarily thinking that my squad would be involved in a rescue at this point, but was strictly thinking about a means to capture the upper echelon of the Taliban structure.

Rounding the hut, the Commander interrupted my thinking as he adjusted his pants and shirt—looking slightly red-faced from his obvious trip to make a bowel movement.

"Good morning, Staff Sergeant," he said gruffly.

"Good morning, Commander." I jumped right in, knowing time shouldn't be wasted. "Sir, I'm getting ready for our morning meeting and there are a couple of events that took place yesterday that I need to discuss."

"Sure, come on in," the Commander waived me into his office and motioned that I take a seat on the small sofa.

As he sat down in his squeaky army green chair, I dove into my story.

"Yesterday while on patrol with Tex and Big Joe, we took chase after one local man at the three storage buildings. He went as far to avoid us by climbing to the top of one of the buildings, then took off jumping the 12-foot drop. We lost him as he ran into the crowd at the market. I was able to get a blood sample when he cut himself on one of the buildings."

"Seems peculiar," the Commander commented.

"I stopped by the lab with the blood sample to be analyzed," I continued. "Brian brought up the subject of the bacha bazi boys—seemed he was pressing me a bit. I never heard of this activity. Out of respect for him and my curiosity, I wanted to ask your opinion of the boys and working along with some of the human activist groups to see what we can do."

The Commander sighed. "Brian has been very proactive about this for a long time," he said. "As a matter fact, he was the one who contacted the human rights groups. I guess he feels that our men could be best used right now in the pursuit of these matters, taking into consideration our prime location for this activity. I feel that our mission is to secure the area and assist these hard working people in establishing their freedoms, a democracy, and infrastructure. Let the people take back their city while we come up with an exit strategy and get the hell out."

I could understand his sentiments: But I knew I needed to stand my ground. "I do feel that this is worth exploring further, due to the fact that Taliban leaders are involved with purchasing these boys," I explained. "It could be a way in we've never thought of before."

The Commander paused as if thinking. "Did Brian hand off any info?" he finally asked.

"Yes, and I plan on looking at that," I said.

"I'll give you what I have so far," the Commander passed me a brown folder off the shelf behind his desk. "I'll have you know that with our drone intel, we have thousands of square miles to search—not to mention those caves. This could be, and I stress *could be*, a new avenue in the capture of the Taliban leaders, but it does come with a high risk factor. The bacha bazi business is so guarded and secret that you would have to get close to someone who could supply you with names and locations.

"Go ahead and gather what intel you can, but keep me informed of your progress. I want to know your every move on this. If I can get some coordinated efforts with the drones, along with any intel, maybe with some luck we can infiltrate the inner circle of the organizing of the solicitation of this activity. We do know that these boys are being purchased and passed around to some of the Taliban leaders, and it's been awhile since we've had a good hit."

I fingered the brown folder in my hands excitedly. "The man we pursued yesterday was a male in his 40s and looked like a local marketer. He slipped away into the crowd. Makes me concerned that someone is planning another attack. I'm not sure."

"Did you get a good look at him?" the Commander asked.

"Yeah, I definitely would recognize him again!" I replied. "We captured some blood droplets I took to the lab. I'm just waiting for the results—should have them tomorrow."

"Get some sketches made up and upload them to our intel server. Let the men know what to look for when patrolling that area. And see what we have on our database."

The meeting ended, and I left with the Commander anxious to give some new directive to my squad. The last several months had been becoming routine with not much for any targets, and this new task of finding the bacha bazi boys would spark some inspiration for our whole squad—if I could get a real lead on the subject first.

I was already running late for our morning squad meeting, but I wanted to make a quick pass through the market to see if I could spot Hakeem, my informant. My hunch was that he would know something about these mysterious boys. As I pulled through the crowd to park, I spotted Hakeem across the street: a frail looking man that looked older than his age of 30 with a graying full beard and small eye glasses.

Hakeem was born and raised in Afghanistan, familiar with these people and the traditions better than anyone. Over the last few months he has provided me with information about times and dates of some of the meetings with the Taliban. He knew he was putting his entire family at risk for doing so—but his information was invaluable, and I paid him what I could, which gave him extra money for his family.

Hakeem looked as if he was in the middle of negotiating with a fruit vendor, arguing over the prices. I just had to laugh. I approached Hakeem from behind, mocking a gun to his head as he dropped his bag of fruit.

"What the hell, you crazy son of a bitch asshole!" Hakeem said, noticing it was me. "What is it you want from me now?" he said as we both stared down at his fruit rolling around on the ground.

"Okay, okay, I'll get it," I said as I picked up the fruit, putting it back in the bag.

"What is it now?" he said looking around the market.

"Just checking to see if you have any new intel for me on targets, explosives, locations of the Taliban?" I impulsively threw in, "And the bacha bazi boys?"

"Please, can we step out of this area?" Hakeem replied. "I wish not for anyone to hear of our business. You Americans are very relentless on this information; now I must travel out of town to get information. What is it you mention of the bacha bazi boys?"

"I have information that this activity is occurring somewhere in this area," I pressed Hakeem. He was nervous, fidgeting and pacing. I had the feeling he knew more. He agreed to talk later that day seeming anxious. We both felt downtown somewhere would be best, away from intruding eyes and listening ears.

I was pleased and excited. If Hakeem did have information, this could be the one person on the inside leading us to the men we would be pursuing. He seemed anxious, almost as if he had wanted to share something, get it off his chest.

I headed back for my squads meeting as I pulled up to the 'yard,' as we called it. It was an area directly in front of our living quarters. The yard was a place we would get together to go over our day's mission and discuss collectively the intel of my squad. Our three huts sat at the top of a slight hill which sloped downward towards the the chow hall. One big solitary tree stood on the left side of my hut that offered shade throughout the day. We had a couple of picnic tables set up against the main hut, which we used for meetings and a place to hang out.

Pulling up, I saw my squad outside—some sitting at the picnic tables, a few lying on the flat dirt ground, arms behind their heads soaking up the sun with feet crossed.

The highest ranking men were Tex, age 30, who was naturally from Texas; Big Joe, age 31, who was from Miami and came from a family of military vets with three brothers and father who'd served our country; McDonough, age 26 had re-enlisted from Colorado; and Sal, age 23, the handler of the squad's bomb sniffing dog named King. Sal had joined the army just out of high school and had entered in the five-month dog handling training at Lackland Air Force base in Texas. Last but not least was Antonio, age 23, who was from Huntington Beach California. Antonio had been my rising star with the squad the last few months with his prior service, ambition, and readiness to learn. Tex and Big Joe were sergeants; McDonough, Sal, and Antonio were corporals.

The lowest ranking members of our squad were Jesus, age 20, from Albuquerque, that opted for the service over some time in jail for drug dealing. Little Joe, age 20, the house prankster from Minnesota. Gangster, age 19, had gained his nickname being from Chicago. And that left Bubba, age 19, from L.A.—who seemingly had regretted his enlistment. I was told Bubba had some family issues back home, and on a whim as a young man was out to prove a point to his father and enlisted just a few months ago. They were all privates.

Big Joe and Bubba were arm wrestling at one picnic-table, beads of sweat rolling down their foreheads. From my perspective, Big Joe looked to have a smirk on his face, getting ready to slam Bubba's arm to the table. The other men were cheering on their favorite.

Antonio, with his music blaring, was clapping to the excitement. As soon as I pulled up, most of the newbies jumped to attention, something that has gone to the wayside with the higher ranking men. I never expected it, but it was a pleasant surprise.

"All right!" I hollered, getting their attention. "First, I would like to commend Little Joe and Bubba for the apprehension of those explosives found on the west side yesterday. It's a small dent, but another hole punched in the proliferation of the explosives that we've been experiencing this last year."

As I spoke, I was thinking how badly I wanted to mention what I knew so far about the bacha bazi boys, that it would be a great opportunity for us. But felt I needed to gather more intel in order to determine a plan.

"Today, we are going to break into two teams. Big Joe, Little Joe, and Gangster—I want you to go back to the location where you found the explosives and talk to the locals. Nose around and see if you can come up with more intel. Jesus, Antonio, and Bubba—you'll go with me. I need to go over yesterday's person of interest with King. Any questions?"

"Yeah," Bubba said as he stood up. "When are we getting a mail call? It's been awhile?"

"I'll check into that," I responded, knowing all too well with the tightening up of our air strip incoming mail was always running late.

"Hell," said Gangster. "You ain't got no one interested in writing you anyway!"

Antonio jumped in, "Your Mama gave up months ago. I'll let you read my little sister's letter. That should keep your eyes dry tonight." The rest of the squad broke out in laughter. Bubba took the ribbing, but I could see he was missing home. Any contact whatsoever from home was a morale boost.

Each day before we broke out, I would have the guys join me in prayer. Some of the new men to the squad felt uncomfortable with the gesture, but the veterans of the squad knew that this could be the day they could lose one of their brothers or be taken out themselves. It gave us a sense of peace, knowing we had each other. Godly men or not, being spiritually prepared us for what the day had to bring and offered some peace of mind.

After that, I motioned Sal over with King, our squad's bomb sniffing dog. King was a five-year-old German Shepherd and Lab mix. He had the markings of a German Shepherd, tan and black—but unlike most pure breeds, King's ear tips flopped over slightly, adding character to his face. I didn't have the history of King's training or temperament, and I wanted to see what Sal had to say after handling King for several years.

"Hey, Sarge," Sal said as he walked over. King bounced at his right side, following Sal's every move. The two had been inseparable since coming to his squad, giving Sal a companion and helping him cope with the stress of being in the zone. Their bond was deep.

King had saved countless lives in his bomb sniffing efforts while putting his own life on the line. I'd seen many dogs get their heads blown off working around IED explosives and trip wires, and they had saved the handler's life and many of our soldiers. When these dogs were killed, it really took a toll on the handler. They got so attached to the dogs and developed such a strong bond, it was as real as losing a family member. I hoped Sal never had to face that loss.

"We might be pushing it here, Sal," I said as we sat down at the picnic table across from each other. "Will King track a person by scent?"

"King was trained in Mexico for the Red Cross as a search and rescue dog before his training for the military," Sal responded.

I looked down at the dog and saw his head tilt back and forth between us; it was like he could understand the conversation.

"Yesterday on Chicken Street, we took chase of a male who dropped this sandal," I explained as I pulled it out of my cargo pocket on my left hip handing it to Sal. "Do you think King would remember the scent and be able to follow the man's trail from yesterday?"

"I can't say," Sal answered. "He's not a bloodhound. *They'll* hunt a scent till they drop. But I guess we could give it a shot."

Sal took the sandal and set it down in the dirt next to King. The dog nosed it around, pushing it like a toy. He then flipped it over with his snout. We both watched the puffs of dust around his snout as he exhaled.

"What I would like you to do, Sal, is let him get familiar with the scent," I said.

"Sure, Mike, got it." Sal said, stroking King's ears. King sat alert at Sal's side, looking off at the rest of the men.

I called over the rest of the squad. "Today, we are headed into the market area. On yesterday's patrol we had some suspicious person I would like to follow up with."

"Yeah, we chased some dude off the storage buildings, but he got away," Tex jumped in.

"No shit," Jesus laughed. "You three managed to let him outrun 'America's finest'?"

"Quiet down," I said, regaining control. "We need to keep that market area secure as possible. You know how that market has come back to life. Wasn't that long ago we had suicide bombers almost everyday. I have some business with our informat, so we'll be heading into that quadrant again today. I'll take Bubba, Sal, Jesus and Antonio. Tex, you take McDonough and check around; talk with the people there see what intel you can get and keep an eye out for the illusive perpetrator from yesterday."

Antonio, Jesus, Sal with King, and Bubba loaded up in the humvee. As we drove the neighborhoods on the east side of Kabul passing Chicken Street, I was hoping to spot the zebra bearded man from yesterday. I just had a feeling about this guy, but couldn't put my finger on it.

Some of the neighborhoods had been rebuilding with some well-maintained new homes. The neighborhoods would go quickly from respectful homes to devastation in a blink of an eye. I knew the north side of Kabul was a hotbed for Taliban meetings. It was that area they we had a skirmish a while back, losing a few men. We had over time finally secured some of the gateway routes, at least for now. The concentrated efforts lately had been in the protection of the markets. I wanted a closer look here the next few weeks to see if we could spot any signs of the Taliban re-establishing this area for meetings.

As I slowed the humvee to a squeaking halt, I motioned for Antonio, Jesus, and Bubba to start the patrol.

"Okay, this is your heavy lifting for the day: patrol this six-block grid." I pointed to a map of the area. "Keep your radios on, eyes wide open. Here are the denoted areas we've had trouble in the past. Sal and I are headed to the storage buildings and see if we can pick up anything from yesterday. We'll be back at 1400."

The humvee pulled away in a plume of dust. I was in a hurry to run King around the sheds to see if he could spot anything from yesterday. Pulling away, I glanced in the side mirror—noticing Antonio being assertive in getting Bubba and Jesus to keep an eye out while he looked over the map on the ground.

Sal and King were in the back seat as we headed off in the direction of the three storage buildings. King looked as if he had taken advantage of the ride as he laid his head on Sal's lap to rest. As soon as the humvee slowed down, King was up and alert. Sal gave him a pat on the head and toyed with his floppy ears subconsciously as we pulled up to the storage buildings. Sal tugged on the leash and guided King out of the back seat. Once outside, King immediately looked around as if getting his bearings.

"Sal, this is the spot where we found the sandal, if you look here." I pointed at the ground below the pinky sized pegs. "He must of scaled up here to the top of the building, then ran the entire length of this building jumping here."

"Here, hold onto this," I said as I handed my M16 over to Sal. I continued to remove my gear, stripping down to just pants, t-shirt, and stocking feet. I walked over to the humvee and removed a pair of tennis shoes and slipped them on. Taking a deep breath as I wipe the sweat from my hands, I studied how small the pegs looked.

"Are you serious?" Sal commented. "Good luck."

I made a couple attempts to balance myself, but kept getting small cramps in my feet. I then decided to back up the humvee as close to the building as possible and start the climb off the top of the humvee.

"This should work." I started the climb and noticed the pegs at the top were larger. *Very smart,* I thought.

"Sal, run the dog around the building. I'm good here," I ordered.

"Sure thing."

King sprang to step with Sal as they circled the three structures. I continued the climb to the top of the hot tin roof, looking around for something to grab on to. I managed to grab hold of the corrugated edge of the roof as I pulled myself up. Once on top, I stood looking over the entire three buildings. I noticed a piece of material on the next building over.

As I headed over getting closer, it looked as if it was soaked with blood. Backing up, I sprinted the rooftop and jumped the five feet to the next building. The piece of material was blood soaked. I was happy to get a better clean DNA sample for Brian. Working my way back down, I steadied myself and noticed how much easier it was on the climb down. At the bottom cocking his head side to side was King looking up at me.

"Didn't find anything he hit on, sir," Sal stated.

"Okay, well, let him get a nose full of this." I removed the day-old bloody material from my pant pocket.

"Yeah, no kidding. Here, King," Sal lowered the material.

King took a big sniff, then sneezed. Sal let the material fall to the ground as King really took in the scent. He then nudged Sal's hand directing him to the first building were zebra beard made the jump. King sniffed the ground at that spot, wagged his tail, and made a sharp bark looking up at Sal panting, as he sat down. King was pleased with his efforts. The dog wanted its reward.

"Yep, I think we got her." Sal tossed a treat to King. Sal looked over and watched as I suited up.

"Let's go," I said, starting up the humvee.

Both Sal and King leaped into the humvee just as it pulled away.

# CHAPTER 6
# FARRIN & RACHEL

Farrin Khan was a Pakistani by birth, recognized by his peers as a gifted surgeon—a tall, dark, slender man that exerted confidence with every word or act. He'd attended college in Britain at the University of London for his undergraduate studies in medicine in the late 80s, but when his Father's health started deteriorating, he moved back to Pakistan to be with his mother and father. His father passed away just a few months after he returned to Pakistan. Farrin's mother was a strong woman, but with the loss of her husband she began to deteriorate and was soon put in to a care facility, where she still lives.

After his father's death, Farrin moved to Kabul to continue his education at Kabul Health Sciences Institute. Farrin's passion was being a physician to help and give back to his people, the people he loved.

All that changed when the fighting in the region intensified. With six years invested in being a fine surgeon, Farrin was forced to fix and mend the Taliban soldiers brought in to the hospital over the poor destitute people in need that lined the hospital halls—at times with a gun to his head. Farrin, with hate in his heart and held against his will, would perform surgeries to fix the very Taliban soldiers that performed heartless acts of butchering of the locals he loved. It wasn't long after when the American's liberated Kabul that Farrin was able to resume his passion.

Farrin's meeting with Rachel in 1991 was purely by chance, but it changed everything. It happened when Farrin's vehicle got a flat tire right outside Kabul's airport terminal. Farrin was kneeling in the dirt road changing the flat tire when he heard a woman's soft voice directly behind him. She had noticed him in his efforts to change the tire alone.

"Do you need any help?"

Glancing up, he noticed this beautiful American woman standing just behind him shielding the sun from her eyes with her right hand while looking down at him.

"I would appreciate another set of hands," he said with the well-spoken English he'd learned during his college years in Britain.

"My name is Rachel," Rachel smiled and extended her hand.

Farrin stood and shook her hand. After changing the tire, they had coffee together in the airport diner. Rachel was beautiful, with auburn hair, clear white complexion, and stunning green eyes. She was slender with a toned athletic body. She was a volunteer for the Red Cross, and Rachel's group had been held over in Kabul on their way to Kuwait.

They shared some stories of each other's families and how their lives had some similarities with the loss of a parent. Rachel went on to explain of her parents dying tragically in an auto accident. Driving around a curve one night, they were hit head on by a drunk driver. Shortly after that, Rachel quit nursing school, signing up with the Red Cross. With only one sister living in Minnesota, she felt her calling was to help others and get her mind off the loss of her parents in the process. She volunteered for the Red Cross and headed to Afghanistan in 1991. With outbreaks of fighting in the Kabul area, travel around the area was difficult, if not impossible, and the Red Cross group she was with were stranded at the Kabul airport for several days.

The connection was immediate. Farrin was taken by her, and Rachel was just as taken with him. It was at that moment during coffee that Rachel decided to stay on in Kabul. They fell in love and married that same year. Farrin, at the age of 36, was older than Rachel by eight years. Farrin was raised Islamic, and Rachel was Christian. Despite their seeming differences, they knew their love was one to last.

They decided not to have the traditional three-day Islamic marriage. Since their living parents were both un-able to attend, they decided to keep the wedding simple and private. They had a local elder perform the ceremony, it lasted five minutes, with only a few friends from the Red Cross and a few staff members from the hospital Farrin worked at. But no matter how small of a ceremony, it was perfect to them. They were now the Khans, united together as one family.

Farrin and Rachel Khan spent their honeymoon at the Hotel Safi in downtown Kabul. Farrin and Rachel existed in their own bubble, far removed from the existence of the pain and suffering of humanity out their hotel window and beyond. They glowed in each other's love.

It was 1991 when they married. Two years passed until Rachel found out she was pregnant. When Farrin heard she was with child, he grabbed her around her waist out of excitement lifting her up as they both spun around their small kitchen in happiness and love. This child would be named Jamil, meaning the 'Golden Child.' This would be the first of two boys they'd have together.

Farrin and Rachel lived in Farrin's home the first year of their marriage in a modest neighborhood. It was a smaller two-room home with a small yard in back. When Rachel moved in with Farrin after their marriage, the local neighbors expressed their distaste of the marriage, but they soon realized that both Farrin and Rachel were compassionate and generous—helping the locals in anyway they could.

While the neighborhoods were mostly lower class residents near poverty, there were lavish homes peppered in around Kabul, twisting up out of the slums; homes of the corrupt businessmen and politicians who had the money to build prestigious homes.

One year after they were married, Farrin heard of a beautiful gated home for sale. The stately home was owned by a relative of a physician with whom Farrin worked. The physician's uncle was a politician with ties to the Taliban. But the uncle had been executed in the streets by the locals. With no need for the home and expense, the fellow physician offered it to Farrin and Rachel at a reasonable price.

Rachel and Farrin fell in love with the house immediately. Built for a politician meant that it was well constructed with security in mind. The two-story home was constructed of cement for strength and protection, using shaved rock from the surrounding mountains for the exterior for beauty and strength. It had bulletproof windows and a security system with cameras scanning the yard. The house had a generator when power was out, sometimes for days. It was truly a fortress of a home, with a safe room and a secret escape corridor under the foundation.

Inside the home, it was luxurious with imported wood and tiling from around the world. It had a large kitchen with detailed tiling, appliances, and large cabinets. There were six bedrooms, five bathrooms, a kitchen, a large dining room, a meeting room, a library, and two sunrooms. The house faced south with plenty of windows, offering plentiful sunlight to help warm the home over the cold winters, and the yard was landscaped with a irrigation system pulling water from a cistern-holding well.

Constructed luxurious homes in the Kabul area were designed with a safe room. The entrance was in the library connected to a secret passageway, built for quick escape during attacks. The passageway ran from the library in the middle of the home under the entire house with the exit in the garage that sat 100 feet in the back of the home. There, an exit was in the garage floor with a hatch door built into the the cement floor. The hatch was well hidden and locked from the inside. Farrin and Rachel never showed Jamil, concerned about his curiosity to explore. The secret hiding room and tunnel were discussed only between Farrin and Rachel.

Rachel was pleased for the added security that the home provided. They moved in to the stately house after the papers were signed and enjoyed a full life inside their home.

Two years passed since the birth of their first son Jamil, and Rachel became pregnant again and had another child in January of 1995. This son would be given the name Asa, meaning 'Gifted One.' Asa was small at birth, but he showed signs of being a precocious child.

Farrin favored Asa over Jamil. Rachel loved and treated both boys equally. Jamil was a momma's boy, sticking at her side. With only a few women to socialize with, she devoted her time to her boys.

With only a few run down schools in the area, Farrin and Rachel decided to hire a tutor for the boys to school them at home for the first years of their education. Rachel was a stay-at-home mom for now, while Farrin continued with long shifts, only home for hours to sleep before he headed back to the hospital. With the tensions rising of anti-Americanism, they were both constantly worried for Rachel's safety and the safety of their children. Asa grew into a smart child; he exceeded most the children his age, solving complex math tests and puzzles. He also quickly learned the two native languages, Pashto and Dari, from his studies. At six years of age, Asa began surpassing Jamil in math, science, and history without much effort. Still, Asa loved Jamil and looked up to him as his older brother, trying to help and encourage him as much as possible.

As the boys grew older, when Jamil was eight and Asa was six, Farrin and Rachel knew that they needed to make friends and socialize. Jasper, the boy's tutor, provided names of families nearby that they could trust to make friends with the boys—especially for Jamil, who was nearing the age where he must be learning to engage with the outside world.

But as Jamil entered the outside world, the friends Jamil met had introduced him to a lifestyle his parents did not approve of. His association with the new friends had changed Jamil for the worst. He constantly disobeyed his parents, he was argumentative, and he ignored the simplest house rules. Jamil frequently would come home with money, giving a portion to Asa. Asa never did ask how Jamil made the money, but he made sure to stash it in a old oil can he found in the garage, hiding it on the top shelve in his closet.

While Jamil constantly got into fights with his parents, Jamil and Asa were always close and loved each other; they would lay awake many nights talking in their beds. Jamil spoke little of life outside the home to Asa and his new friends he made against their parents demands.

When Asa turned seven in 2002, a common age Pakistani boys become circumcised with a surgical procedure called *khitan*. This was considered a passage into manhood. Asa was allowed to have friends over and celebrate the event prior to the surgery. In most cases, the surgery was a semi-public event—but not for Asa. Farrin took Asa to the hospital and performed the surgery himself.

But, Asa would never forget that day, because it was the same day Jamil went missing.

His parents at first wrote it off as just Jamil being stubborn and careless. But as hours passed with no word of Jamil, the celebration for Asa turned from celebration into a small search party combing the streets in search of Jamil.

Days passed after Jamil went missing. Farrin and Rachel contacted authorities, posting flyers at the local markets in hopes of finding their son. Deep depression set in as Rachel managed Asa and his schooling. She spent listless days inside her home that had seemed so safe and secure from the outside world.

Months passed with no news of Jamil. Asa lay awake almost every night, sobbing, missing his brother, his best friend. To keep his thoughts off Jamil, Asa threw himself into books, often reading up to four a week.

Rachel began feeling isolated, but still kept to the house, only going out on occasions to the market and visiting Farrin at the hospital. To get her mind off Jamil and the loneliness, she took up oil painting. She perfected her technique through countless paintings, becoming gifted with the art of brush and canvas.

At times in the middle of his surgeries, Farrin would be consumed with his missing son, handing over some of his surgical calendar to a few other staff doctors. But he tried hard to keep himself together and remain the strong man he knew Rachel needed.

Two years passed as the memory of their son Jamil started to dim. Asa often had dreams, dreams of his brother. Dreams of Jamil in pain, images of him floating in the air. Asa had hope that someday he would see his brother again.

Rachel, Farrin, and Asa lived in a strange, numb cocoon, hoping tragedy would never touch their family again. The Khans had been touched by a mysterious, unspeakable tragedy that now haunted their lives.

But at least in their home, their fortress would keep them safe.

# CHAPTER 7
# HAKEEM'S STORY

After dropping the others off back on base, I headed over to our intelligence building hoping to recognize some photos of the terrorists spotted in the area lately. I wanted to see if I could get a hit on the zebra bearded man from the other day.

The intelligence building was a well-guarded area. The information was esoteric in nature, only for the higher ranking men and squad leaders. I had hopes there would be something on record, some photo resembling the man I was looking for. After spending a good hour pouring over photos going back from 9/11 to current time, I went through photos of all of the upper echelon of the Taliban,—noticing most were either in Guantanamo or dead.

It was 2000 hours, and my meeting with Hakeem, my informant was another hour and a half away. I gave up on the endless amount of photos and decided to have our military sketch artist work up the drawing. The photo would immediately be on our intel system to view. This tool was helpful to get these images in the hands of the men out on patrol. All digitized photos gathered could be posted for all levels of the military to view within seconds of input.

Sitting down with the artist, I realized how Afghanistan and Pakistan men had similarities in their facial features and dress styles—making it difficult to distinguish one from the other. It really came down to the beards and beard colors and clothing choice that offered a quick ID.

After an hour, we had generated a decent photo that was quickly uploaded on our photo ID system. I had a few printed for posting back in the main hut for my squad.

And now, it was time for my meeting with Hakeem.

The Safi Hotel was located downtown Kabul: a 3.5-star luxury hotel that was considered one the best in the area with excellent security. It housed ten floors in total, two restaurants, an inside bar, and a large patio attached to the hotel that faced west.

Our meeting was to take place at the patio that extended out from the hotel from the main lobby. The patio offered a 180 degree view of the city overlooking the busy streets just out front. The entire patio deck sat four feet off street level, with steps on the left and right that lead to the street below. We decided on a small table on the patio against the building facing the street. Above us hung a decorative bright yellow canvas piece covering the entire patio. Anchored to the hotel wall it sloped down, creating an umbrella effect overhead. The covering was for protection from the sun and rain. For me, it offered a sense of security from prying eyes above.

Tonight on one side of the patio was a chef offering the guests the night's special dinner that included hand carved prime beef that permeated the air with an intoxicating smell as the fat from the beef rose up smoky into the night. Looking out beyond the patio, there was a brick walkway that lead to a garden court 30 feet away from the patio. In the middle of the courtyard stood a tall decorative two tier water fountain; the sound of trickling water could be heard cascading down to a small pond below. The walkway from the patio to the fountain was landscaped beautifully with trimmed hedges and colorful exotic flowers.

Hakeem's recommendation to meet here was well-chosen: it was a lit up area of downtown with hotels and restaurants. Tourists from all around the world gravitated to this area for safety purposes, and the tables were full of customers tonight. We'd blend in pretty well here. Still, I had Big Joe stand watch on the left side of the patio, while Tex stood on the right, just in case anything happened.

Approaching, Hakeem seemed even more nervous than usual as I stood to greet him at our table.

"Hello, my friend!" he said as he started shaking my hand.

"Hello, my friend," I shook his hand back eagerly.

"I apologize for this minor inconvenience of meeting at night," Hakeem said with a slight bow.

"It's fine," I said as I waved over the waiter, ordering tea for the both of us as we sat. I kept an eye on the crowd, scanning the faces. I made sure Big Joe and Tex were within sight. I wasn't sure what Hakeem had to share, but I wanted no interruptions. The tea arrived and we both starting sipping. I didn't want to rush Hakeem because he seemed very anxious, so I let him pace the conversation.

"I have some information for you," began Hakeem. He nervously took another sip of his tea.

"Okay," I said, leaning back in the cushioned wicker chair and trying to seem as patient and calm as possible.

"I want you to know that what I'm going to share with you could, if the wrong people found out, bring harm to my family," Hakeem went on. "I must trust you to never say this came from Hakeem!"

"Hakeem, you've been a trusted friend that has gone to great extremes to help the Americans for some time now," I reassured him. "We are friends that can trust each other."

He nodded, took another sip of tea, and then seemed to finally feel ready to divulge his story.

"A few years back, my oldest brother moved to Kabul with his family of five. I have four siblings, including two other brothers and a sister. My oldest brother and I were the only ones to come to Kabul. The fighting back home were we grew up was so intense, the area called the Korengal Valley. Have you heard of this area?" Hakeem asked.

"Yes," I said. "A Taliban stronghold: unforgiving area, very rough terrain."

"Yes, you know it, then," Hakeem said. "My oldest brother left for fear for his family's safety with so much fighting there. He was threatened by the Taliban that if he in any way offered help to the Americans that they would cut his head off, slaughter his family. My brother was nothing more than a simple man, a goat herder." Hakeem paused.

"Go on," I urged.

"That is when he moved his family here with me approximately a year ago. But just after the move, my brother's oldest son of eight years at that time suddenly disappeared for a few days. We all could only imagine the worst, thinking he had got caught up in some outbreak of fighting or had wandered into an area of land mines.

"It wasn't till the third day after he went missing that he returned home with a strange man. This strange man wanted to talk in private with my brother. After a short conversation with the strange man, my brother returned with a troubled look to his face, holding his son's hand tightly."

"What did he say they discussed?" I leaned in, listening intently.

"You see, with life very difficult here and having his five children, we are very poor without much opportunity, many mouths to feed. The strange man that returned his son was offering my brother an exchange...an exchange of money for his son," Hakeem explained.

"For his son, you mean to purchase?" I questioned.

"This man is the man who supplies the dancing boys to the Taliban and businessman, the bacha batzi boys." Hakeem spoke with hatred about him as he continued. "This is a very dangerous man with many connections."

"Why not go to the local police here?"

Hakeem laughed painfully. "You don't understand. You see, the police are corrupt. They are part of the protection and help in the promoting of this activity. They protect this man who offers the boys, the money is good for these men."

The waiter returned, leaning into my ear. "That rather large soldier over there would like to add a cheeseburger to your tab, sir." The waiter gestured towards Big Joe.

I glanced over at Big Joe on the street just where the steps came down the patio to the street. He was rubbing his belly in a circular motion with a wide grin.

"Yes, go ahead," I answered, shaking my head. "And get that other soldier over there whatever he wants." I waved a hand at Tex. I wanted to get all I could from this conversation, even if it meant a couple burgers at my expense.

"What did your brother do?" I asked, continuing the serious conversation.

"He denied the man. But the next day his son vanished," Hakeem look down, wiping the corner of his eye. It was the first time he had shown real emotion in front of me like this. "This is why I come to you, Mike, my friend. For my brother and in hopes that his son is still alive, I offer what I know at the risk of them finding me out. We are desperate, and if this is a mission I can help you in anyway well, I will take that risk."

"Do you have any names or locations?"

"The man who sells the boys—his name is Dastgir," Hakeem said. "I've heard he has many places of hiding. I have seen this man only briefly in town. He seems to be very elusive, moving at night and in the shadows during daylight. We have heard from a few sources that he has the boys trained in the art of dance and dress."

"What does he look like?" I asked.

"He's tall, thin, with a beard with a strange black stripe down the middle," described Hakeem.

*Ah!* I thought. *Now we're getting somewhere, could it be the man that eluded us?* "I ran into someone that may fit that description recently," I said. "Where do they take the boys?"

"The information is that they end up in the mountains separating Afghanistan and Pakistan. There, they use the caves for entertaining for these Taliban and corrupt businessman. This place is very, very treacherous, almost impossible to find."

"What area?" I prodded.

"On the north east side of the Kunar Province near the Hindu Kush mountain ranges. There with any luck you would find the caves," Hakeem added.

"That's got to be over 100 miles away!" I exclaimed as I leaned back in my chair. I felt a little overwhelmed.

"Yes, I will offer myself as a guide for most of the journey," Hakeem said. Hakeem was starting to get nervous again. I could see talking of this was getting him more and more antsy and upset. My head was racing with all the possibilities of this information, the possibility that this could be the break I was looking for to get intel on this man who sold the boys. If we could just find him, we would be able to possibly track him, find where the boys were being held—leading to the Taliban, our targets.

I glanced over to Big Joe and Tex, who were licking their fingers while trying to keep an eye on the crowd around them. I pulled out a hundred dollar bill from my cargo pocket and slid it into Hakeem's hand.

"I will be in touch with you, Hakeem. I admire your bravery for coming to me with this. This will give me what I need to hopefully put together a plan and team so we can get clearance for a mission. We'll see what the Base Commander has to say. I will do what I can to help your family in any way. I think what we need to do is not meet for a while. Let me work on this, come up with a plan, talk with my Commander."

My thoughts were running overtime. It truly could go very bad for us in that part of Afghanistan, and the reality of the seriousness of this undertaking began taking root in my mind. I now understood my Commander's own hesitation to get involved, but I also knew how important this could be.

Hakeem nodded his thanks; his words had left him. We sat in silence, gazing out at the people passing by while finishing our tea.

# CHAPTER 8
## AFTER THE MEETING

It was nearly midnight with all the lights off in my hut save for the bathroom light as I washed my face, staring into the bathroom mirror. My mind was running wild with possibilities of infiltrating the corrupt circle of the organized group that exploited the boys.

*What part of the squad will be best suited for a extremely dangerous mission through the snowy Hindu Kush mountain ranges? How much intel will I be able to gather, and what loss of life will there be? Will this mission, if approved, be worth losing any of my men if we come up empty handed?* The questions were endless.

What concerned me the most was the safety of my men. But the thought of these poor boys held captive to perform despicable acts against their will made me think of my family and how much I missed them. I glanced over to the right bottom corner of the steamed bathroom mirror where I stuck a family photo in the band edging. As I stared at the picture, a cold shiver ran through me.

*What if it was my son taken to perform for these men?* The very thought of it filled me with hate for those men involved in this disgusting activity. The thought of Hakeem's brother living each day never knowing what hell his son was going through made me want this more than ever.

I dried my face and tossed the towel to the side. I stretched out on my bed in just my boxers, staring at the spinning ceiling fan. Filtered lighting from the yard was coming in through the window a few feet above my head.

Hakeems' intel was critical in convincing the base Commander of a mission. I knew if cleared for such a mission I would be taking full responsibility for my team and the boys we could possibly encounter. I started to drift off, envisioning images of snowy mountain peaks....

...In the silence of my room, the radio suddenly blared on.

"Sergeant, you there?"

Suddenly wide awake, I grabbed the radio. "Yeah, who is it?"

"Brian, at the lab. Did I wake you?"

"Nope! Just counting the revolutions of the ceiling fan. What have you got?"

"I have the results in. Something...interesting here. Can you stop by now?"

"On my way." *Does this guy ever sleep?* I was thinking while getting dressed.

Pulling up to the lab, I observed how illuminated the building was at night with yellow fluorescent lights that ran around the roofline on all sides; the lighting offered a glowing look to the lab in the darkness. I gave a tap on the door and saw the security camera scanning above me as Brian buzzed me in.

"Hello, Staff Sergeant," Brian said.

"Good evening," I said, looking around at the equipment.

"Sorry to bother you this late," Brian said, not seeming very sorry at all. "But I think you will find the results of the blood sample interesting."

My heart rate picked up.

"I had mixed results the first time I ran the tests," continued Brian. "It was negative on the first test, so I ran a second different type of test. The first time the tests were not as extensive—simple testing to establish a cross match from anything on our database. The second test, called a polymerase chain reaction for DNA, pulled up a match on one of the top five terrorists in our databases."

I slowly sat down, listening intently, thinking how close we were yesterday in a possible capture of a higher ranking Taliban soldier.

"What the test results show is that he is not on our terrorist list, but possibly a direct relative: a father, son, or sibling," Brian explained. "The structure of the DNA rules out any second prior generation beyond that; the only way to confirm is by obtaining a DNA sample from the actual target person himself to be 100% accurate."

"All right, is the information on the database now?" I asked, ignoring the explanation of the scientific jargon.

"That's why I have you here. I need your signature and the usual stack of paperwork to upload. What level of security should I enter it at?" Brian asked.

"Let's keep it hidden for now. I need to talk with my Commander about what we are going to do with it. I will get back to you tomorrow."

"Did you look over any of the bacha bazi boy information yet?" Brian asked.

"No, I'll have time for that tomorrow. I have some additional information I've collected since we've talked a few days ago that I want to discuss with you. But first, I have to clear this good news through my Commander before I can say anything. Good ol' chain of command."

After leaving the lab, I was wide awake. It was only 0100 hours, but I knew the officers' and enlisted men's clubs were still open for two more hours. I could use a good stiff drink and a smoke about now.

I radioed Tex back at the hut, who was ready to do just about anything at this point. It was a quiet on base with the exception of a distant rumble of jets: a low flying helicopter exercising a maintenance flight. I could smell the jet fuel most of the time, and I certainly could tonight.

The enlisted men's club comprised of two large rooms separated by a bar that ran full-length straight down the middle. On the right side as you walked in was the dining area with tables neatly in rows and booths along the outer right wall. The bar lounge area on the other side also had tables that were randomly strewn about. A dance floor could be found in the far back left corner, and two pool tables took up the opposite corner.

The entire dining room and bar offered low overhead lighting with little red candles at each table. Tonight was karaoke: I could hear someone butchering an AC-DC song. We chose the dining room side with a booth in the far back corner that overlooked the entire restaurant and bar.

Just as we sat down, a waitress was quick to take our order. I ordered a jack-coke for the both of us as I scanned the room.

"I can always tell when you have something to talk about," Tex said. "Tonight you seem more apprehensive than normal."

I didn't reply right away. I just silently watched him. Tex and I were more than just squad brothers; I trusted his opinions. The both of us had served in the Navy together from 1986 to 2000. We went on two tours of duty together attached to the U.S.S. *Kitty Hawk* aircraft carrier. When at sea, our work schedule aboard the carrier had been a grueling 12 hours a day, seven days a week. During those cruises, we talked of home and played countless games of backgammon to pass the arduous eight months. There had been times we wouldn't make landfall for up to 80 days, pushing our angst to its limits.

Tex had been engaged to a girl back home during our first cruise. She wrote to him frequently, but then one day he received a Dear John letter from her. I remember him mentioning she was cheating on him and had fallen in love with another. At sea is the worst place to be when you have a cheating woman back home, so naturally helplessness sets in. I helped him navigate the heartbreak that occured.

Eight years into our Navy careers, we discussed re-enlisting after a close fellow Navy friend of ours named Armando died mysteriously when we ported in Perth, Australia. And we did—re-enlisting in the Army.

Remembering these things, I lit up a cigarette and gazed off into the distance. I could see the bar side through three large square openings in the wall that separated the two rooms; the center opening had a fish aquarium in the center that showed neglect. A group of soldiers were joining in on a song by John Cougar Mellencamp called "Ain't that America" as the waitress brought the drinks.

Tex took a long sip of his drink with most of it dripping from his bushy mustache. Tex liked keeping his mustache as long as possible—unlike the younger men who preferred clean shaven, high-tight haircuts.

"How did the talk go with Hakeem?" Tex asked.

"Some of his story was just heart wrenching."

"How so?" Tex asked, leaning in with his arms crossed on the small table.

I started talking in detail about the course of events over the last few days. I explained about the connection of the man they chased off the storage buildings—how he was related somehow to one of the terrorists.

"I believe that with Hakeem's intel, I can honestly say that we could have a good chance to get clearance for a mission," I said as I lit up another smoke. "According to Hakeem, he has some intel on not only the whereabouts, but the names of a few men who are part of this sex slavery organization."

I shared my thoughts in detail with Tex about pursuing the mission with the Commander. The one part of the information that was bothering me the most was the location in that sector: a very dangerous area.

"My biggest concern about the area is almost certainty that some of my men might not make it," I said.

Tex paused for a moment as the waitress brought over two more jack-cokes. "You know, ever since the humvee accident you had a year ago, you haven't been the same," he said. "Your decision making has been hampered at times from that experience."

I remembered the day vividly. The blood, the dust, the mangled bodies. "I take any loss of life in my squad personally," I said. "I loved those men like brothers."

"Remember back in 1994 in the Philippines?" Tex asked me.

"Philippines?" I said.

"Yeah," Tex went on. "The day a group of us headed off into the jungle in that jeepney cab heading to Manila? That was a 25 mile ride through the jungle, and we realized the driver was in on it, taking us to an area to have us beaten and robbed."

"Yeah. What about it?" I wasn't sure where Tex was going with this.

"The driver stopped at a point where the jeepney could hardly proceed any further," Tex went on. "It was after dark, and we had no idea where we were, but a group of thugs started surrounding the jeepney. You noticed what was happening and immediately ordered the group of sailors to 'Move quickly! Get out! Start moving!' " Tex imitated my barking command.

"I remember," I said. "We all made that walk back to the main road. It took over an hour through the jungle. We could hear the thugs on our tails most the way back. We were split up from the rest of the group, and those two drunken sailors had no Idea what was happening."

"And instead of hightailing it out of there, you were adamant in helping the other two sailors get to safety, making us back track. We didn't need to do that, but you insisted that we help them," Tex said, as if he was reliving that night. "We heard their screams off in the distance as we backtracked in the complete darkness. The two sailors were surrounded by four Filipinos. One of the sailors was stabbed in his stomach, and the other one was going to get hurt soon.

"You saved those guys!" Tex continued. "You took control of our guys. You gave us the plan of attack on those four using the darkness as cover and forcing them to run off. If they only knew it was just the two of us. We ended up all getting back to base. If I remember right, we later found out one of the two drunks was a chief petty officer, looking as if he pissed himself!"

I laughed. "The son of a bitch was stabbed and so drunk he probably didn't remember a thing; but he did need about a thousand stitches."

"What I'm saying is that you have a sixth sense about you," Tex went on. "You have the instinct and awareness with a great sense of direction that kicks in when there is danger present that I haven't experienced with anyone else. I've known you long enough, and I would without any hesitation be on board with your decision for any mission. You can train a man with scenarios all day long—but when you're put into a life or death real world situation where you have asses on the line, that's when you have the ability to think with clarity under pressure. I've seen it, Mike."

I didn't say much after that. It was three in the morning as we headed back to the huts. I dropped Tex off, noticing all the lights out.

"See you in few hours," Tex said as he walked away.

"Tex."

"Yeah?"

"Thanks."

Thinking about Tex's words, I went to call my wife. I needed to hear her voice, too, as I mulled over the next day and what it would hold. Tomorrow, I would talk with my Commander, decide if this mission was even a possibility. But I felt more determined, more sure of myself, than I had before meeting with Tex.

Maybe, just maybe, we could pull this off.

# CHAPTER 9
# WAR ROOM

As I waited outside of the Base Commander's office, also known as the War Room, it seemed an eternity passed as the Commander and Officers discussed the details and risk of a possible mission in private. The command post wasn't much more than a glorified construction hut that has been continually added on over the last few years. The base had taken a lot of hits after 9/11 that forced the army to rebuild several structures, this one included.

My mind was spinning. What ground and air support would be required? The trek would take us late into October into the Hindu Kush mountain range during the winter months. The Hindu Kush mountain range was treacherous anytime, not to mention this time of year. The thought of the extreme conditions we would be facing concerned me.

More importantly, the mission would probably require only a small group of men to move quickly being undetected. We would have to trek beyond the Korengal Valley through the Kunar Valley up the mountains, faced with the snowy cold conditions. The enemy was well adapted for this environment, and we would be on their turf, exposed and vulnerable. I had to decide on what men I could trust to get this mission done.

As I was consumed in my thoughts, I heard my name called out from down the hallway. It was my Commander wearing his multicam camos as he headed my way. I took a long sip from the drinking fountain, my mouth dry with anticipation.

"Before we go in, Mike, I want you to know I went to bat for you on this," said the Commander, debriefing me quicky about the environment

I'd walk in on. "Not sure if they are totally convinced. We have the Base Commander, Officer Anderson of Operations, and our Intel Warrant Officer Tucker, all in there. The Base Commander is old school; he's the hard sale. My impression is that the other two are chomping at the bit for this. But we need to go in there and flat out convince the old man that we have this great opportunity to either capture or take out a few of the upper echelon of the Taliban we have been chasing for months."

I nodded, agreeing silently.

"With Saddam Hussein captured now, we have with most certainty proof that it's Osama Bin Laden we are after," continued my Commander. "Intel says he was behind 9/11—and he's supposedly in that area. How well do you trust this information your informant has provided you?"

"One hundred percent, sir."

"It's your show, then. Let's head in." The Commander gestured towards the door.

Entering into the War Room was stressful. My superiors were standing near their respective chairs, I offered a salute and snapped to attention. The room was small—20 feet by 30 feet at most—and bundles of wires ran through the open ceiling tiles that kept the digital flow of data moving at high rates of speed. A large long table was set dead center in the room with enough chairs to seat eight. There were maps on the walls with notes and scribbles like a big kid's coloring book, and photos also lined the right wall as I walked in. These displayed the top 5 upper-echelon of Al-Qaeda and Taliban targets, those captured or taken out in the American attacks.

The Base Commander was dressed in his desert digital camos. He was a tall, thin, gaunt looking man with thinning gray hair as he pointed to a chair on the opposite side of the table from him. My Commander sat next to me on the right.

The inquiry began.

"Good afternoon, Staff Sergeant," said the Base Commander while looking down at a file in his right hand. He hardly even looked at me, jumping into the issues right away as he pulled a file in front of him. "I have looked over your request and have some concerns about this. I have Officer Anderson here, who you know from your day-to-day operations. I don't believe you have met our Intel Officer, Tucker. We have several questions we'll be inquiring about. I need direct and honest answers. No bullshit. Understand, Staff Sergeant?"

"Yes, sir," I replied.

"First, I'm interested in your relationship with your informant. Let's see here..." the Base Commander put on his reading glasses, leaning forward and holding the file close to his face. "Hakeem. What exactly is your relationship?"

"Hakeem has been a trusted informant now for the last 12 months," I replied. "We have been successful with the information he has provided on various Taliban meetings in Kabul that led to the opportunity in taking out the third-in-command, Nek Mohammed, connected to the Osama Bin Laden cell. Hakeem has been putting himself and his family at risk working with us." I glanced at a picture of Nek Mohammed over the Colonel's shoulder on the wall.

"Has the information been consistently accurate?" asked the Commander.

"Yes. One hundred percent."

The Base Commander hardly blinked as he changed the subject, flipping through the file. "I see here that you have a well respected time of service within both the Army and Navy, I see here you had an unfortunate loss of the three soldiers when your vehicle hit that mine a few years back. When was it? 2003?"

I nodded in the affirmative.

"Do you have full strength of your leg?" the Base Commander asked.

"Yes, sir. It's as good as new."

A long pause commenced as the Base Commander scanned my file. Finally, he spoke again.

"Officer Anderson has been in charge of our day-to-day patrols working in conjunction with Officer Tucker. We have gathered intel from the drones patrolling that area and all agree that the area offers a hotbed of terrorist activity that we have not been able to penetrate. They're very elusive. These caves mentioned are extremely difficult to find. The hideouts throughout the area your informant has mentioned, if true, will be invaluable. From our intel collected the last few years we understand the boys are taken into the caves and passed around with the warlords. God bless those boys."

"It's hard to imagine this activity going on," I said.

"Look at these photos of what looks to be a boy party in some hidden area," the Base Commander slid over the photos to me. I looked at the men sitting in a large circle on the ground as the boys—dressed in women's clothing—danced while the men clapped, lustful desires on their faces. The faces of the boys were filled with sadness and fear. It made me sick.

Standing up, the Base Commander walked over to a map pointing to the area Hakeem had mentioned: the Kunar Province. "One of my concerns is the operation running through the Kunar Valley. This type of mission would be more successful with a few men, under the radar so to speak. We would need you to move surreptitiously, under drone surveillance. In doing so, you will lose the strength of numbers. We will only be able to monitor you with drone patrol."

"Drones are limited," Intel Officer Tucker jumped in. Up until this point, he had been silent. "We have had an increase in demand as we expand our theater zone, and we would be able to commit only one drone to the mission. The MQ-1, the Predator, has a range of 400 nautical miles average, and a flight time of approximately 14 hours. Depending on the weather conditions, we could have problems with icing. Not to mention there will be a blackout period of time when we need to retrieve the drone for refueling." As Tucker leaned back, his chair squeaked from the strain and weight, tapping a pencil on a notepad in front of him. He was thinking hard, I saw. "We would need to establish your route into the mountainous area and tweak the drones for the higher altitudes and weather conditions."

"We would have to carefully consider your selection of men," the Base Commander said. "We can only offer your team a small window of time for you to get in and out. I don't see here that any of your men have special forces experience, so we would have to assign a sharpshooter from Delta Force. These guys are consistently accurate from distances of a mile in perfect weather conditions. One of your men would have to be his spotter. These men are trained extensively with a spotter for precise targeting."

"The weather will not be in your favor either, Staff Sergeant," my own Commander added. "You have only a couple mountain passes that would allow you to access the area you'll be going into. The fact you are from Wisconsin and are familiar with the cold winters could be helpful here." This earned a light chuckle from the others in the room.

"I understand," I said as the reality of this mission was taking on a real sense of its weight. All this news had been like rapid fire in my mind, and absorbing it all was overwhelming. But even in the midst of this information overload, I was thinking just how badly I wanted this more than anything. A great sense of determination was setting in.

"Officer Anderson, what would be the best route into the mountains?" the Base Commander asked.

"The most direct route is on the northeast side of the Korangal Valley—what we refer to as the 'Valley of Death'—that runs into the foothills on up into the higher elevations of the mountain range called the Hindu Kush."

"The locals called the Shura throughout the valley refuse to cooperate with the military," said the Base Commander. "Most are related to the Taliban...very difficult stretch. The elders will expose you if you're not careful. Your own Commander tells me that Hakeem is willing to guide your team through the villages. Is that correct, Staff Sergeant?"

"Yes sir, but only to a certain point. He will then arrange for another guide for us—a rendezvous would be arranged at the snow line through the mountains to the location where the cave is located."

The officers looked at each other. I had the feeling they were thinking my trust in Hakeem might be over-zealous. The Base Commander glanced at an oversized clock on the wall and shifted in his chair.

"Let's take a time out. We've been at this for an hour. Staff Sergeant, why don't you step out for 15. I would like to discuss this in private with the officers."

"Yes, sir." I stood and saluted. As I walked out of the room, I was thinking that the Base Commander's tone was somewhat skeptical. I headed outside for a quick smoke. Here I was, waiting again. The time seemed to pass even more slowly now.

Suddenly, my Commander opened the door and waved me in again. I entered the War Room with a salute, sitting back down.

"Well, Staff Sergeant, after kicking this around, I see this as a great opportunity to find these elusive cells we have been chasing our tails over," said the Base Commander. "What makes this more of a challenge are three things. You will have but only a few men, leaving yourselves vulnerable. Weather conditions could be adverse, and the biggest concern is a possible population of bacha bazi boys. It would be one thing to move in on the terrorists, target their location, and hammer the shit out of them—but with the possibility of boys in there it could be very dicey." The Commander played with the edge of the file sitting in front of him on the table.

"But, if we can GPS a fixed starting point, we would be able to target that and use the drone throughout the mission," Intel Officer Tucker explained, sipping on what looked like very cold coffee. "With laser technology, we could target a missile strike via satellite if needed. The wild card are the caves themselves; our technology would not be able to penetrate the rocky structure of the caves. It would take radio contact once a location was determined by GPS coordinance radioed in and relayed to the command center. But the risk of the radios could be monitored by the terrorists."

"It is the element of surprise that will be in our favor." The Commander flicked again at the edge of the file sitting in front of him on the table. "You have to understand that moving silently with minimal radio contact is crucial here."

I nodded. "That is understood, sir."

"I'm going to put this into a planning phase— Program Objective Memorandum," said the Base Commander. "From this point forward, we will call this mission 'Snow Leopard.' Everyone here in this room will not mention this to anyone unless through me. Is that understood?"

The Commander looked around the room at the men, and we all said a strong, "Yes, sir!"

"Staff Sergeant," the Base Commander said, standing so I followed his lead. "What I suggest you do is think long and hard about who your selection of men will be. Each man will carry huge responsibility, and you need a solid team, understand?"

"Yes, sir," I replied with a sharp salute. The room was charged with electricity and excitement. I could tell that everything was now falling into place, and my heart raced.

The mission was really happening.

# CHAPTER 10
# ASA

"**A**sa, you need to be more active! You need to let the other boys know that you are not just a bookworm. You must make more friends." Sounding like his father, Jasper, Asa's tutor, was hounding him about his antisocial behavior.

Asa sighed, tuning out the old man, watching as Jasper loaded his worn out briefcase with books from today's studies. It was time to get out and away for the day!

Ever since his brother went missing, his parents had been pushing for Asa to become more extroverted to get his mind off of Jamil. At the age of nine, Asa was well educated, a handsome boy with the dark features of his father and emerald green eyes, bright smile, and dimples from his mother's side. But he was also small for his age and was constantly picked on by the other boys.

There was a reason he did not like to play with the other boys much. Coming from a interracial marriage, Asa was ridiculed relentlessly. Most of the adult locals that knew of Farrin and Rachel had no problems with that fact; they both were highly respected for their contributions to the region. But Asa didn't fare so well with the younger children, who laughed at him constantly. It also didn't help that his brother had mysteriously disappeared, because many treated him as if he were cursed or were somehow responsible for his brother's disappearance. It was easier to escape into books than face laughter and judgment every single day.

*I wish my parents would understand,* he thought sadly.

But Asa did have one other love besides books, and that was soccer.

And his soccer companions were the only friends he felt like he did have. After his schooling today, Asa was going to meet up with a few boys for a game of soccer. Leaving home in hurried excitement, he forgot once again to change his clothes. He was wearing the traditional knee length trouser and embroidered hat called a *sindhi cap* that was hand stitched by his mother. He had promised his mother that he would be careful not to wear these clothes out to play, but he always forgot until it was too late.

The walk to the lot where boys often would play took him through the dirty alleyways winding through run down homes with cracked exteriors, missing doors and windows, and ripped material for curtains. The crying of an infant could be heard. His route also took him through his favorite area of Kabul: Chicken Street, a bustling marketplace that made him feel a bit less sad every time he watched the people scurrying about their days and bartering with the sellers.

The boys played in an open dirt lot once used for parking in front of the Darlamane Palace built in the 1920s by King Khan in honor of regional peace. After decades of neglect and damage, the building was still majestic, but it now sat empty. The rocky dirt lot was surrounded by small scrub brush on three sides. The one long side of the lot had steps that lead up to the vacant palace.

As Asa made his way to the soccer field, he saw a few of his friends waiting on the steps near the vacant lot. His favorite was Esmat, a tall, gangly boy who was always the consummate prankster. Esmat was from Pakistan; his entire family had been killed in a bomb attack a few years ago. He stayed with his uncle in a run-down one-room apartment. Esmat did not show any outward pain of losing his family. His sense of humour was the medicine for all the suffering he had been through.

Asa's other friend, Zaahir, was a chubby boy who was big for his age with a quick temper. Asa and the others had a nickname for Zaahir: Jellybean. Zaahir always had jelly beans in his pocket during the hot summer months, and most of the time they would melt together in to a big lump in his dirty pockets. Zaahir always had to win, even if it meant getting into a occasional fight. Still, the kids on his team would put up with Zaahir's temper, because his size alone meant they would have a good chance to beat the other team at soccer.

The scrimmage would pit Asa, Esmat, and Zaahir against four other boys. With Zaahir's size and Asa's speed and agility, they never had problems winning when outnumbered. Asa was fast. His quick thinking made him better than the others. The time he spent playing soccer with his friends gave him confidence, taking his mind off the loneliness he felt at home.

"Zaahir, you flip the toss," one of the boys shouted, "I will call it."

Zaahir dug deep into his pocket and found his prized American 50 cent piece he was given by an American soldier sometime ago. The coin was sticky from the jellybeans, sticky dirt coated the coin. Zaahir tossed it.

"HEADS!" the other child yelled, and won.

They played for hours as the sun sank lower in the sky. They used stones and sticks for the goals. Arguments over whether it was a goal or not were common. During the final play of the game, the other team was up by one point. Asa was going in to score the match point when he was intentionally tripped by one of the boys. Asa went down, hitting the ground hard. One of the other opposing boys came in at full speed, kicking hard at the ball as Asa lay on the ground curled up around it. The boy's foot missed the ball and hit Asa in the face.

Asa momentarily blacked out...When he came to, his ears were ringing, blood running down his face. Sprawled out on the ground, he rolled his head to the left and noticed Zaahir sitting on the instigator, hitting him in the face till he started to bleed from his nose. Cries could be heard.

It took both Asa and Esmat to extricate the two still going at it on the ground. Two of the other boys took off running, while another boy helped his beaten friend to his feet. As the two groups walked away from each other, the shouting and cursing and threats could be heard echoing off the walls of the palace.

"Your beautiful face looks like a puffy fish," Esmat said, laughing at Asa's swollen eye and cheek as the boys walked up the steps to the palace, then towards home off in the distance.

"My mother is going to kill me!" Asa screamed as he glanced down at his clothes, which were covered in dirt and blood. Getting closer to the edge of the market, they stopped for water from a vendor with no teeth and a goat tied to a pole as his pet. Asa always paid for the other two, since they usually had nothing—except for Zaahir's precious 50 cent piece. Asa was good to his friends.

"I should've killed that kid," Zaahir said, agitatedly kicking a rock at a passing dog.

As they rounded the next corner, they bumped into a tall man. The startled boys stopped, taking one step back away from the odd man. The man just stood still, looking down at Asa; Asa noticed he had a white beard with a zebra-like black stripe down the middle. Moments passed, and then the man turned and walked the other direction into the crowd ahead.

The boys looked at each other, shrugging it off.

"Old man!" Zaahir shouted. "Watch where you walk!"

"You spoke too softly, big man, I don't think he heard you," Esmat said to Zaahir, smiling.

"If I see him again I will tell him he smells of a donkey and eats its shit!" Zaahir shot back. They all laughed.

The boys said their goodbyes as they neared home. Asa had the furthest to go: a route that would take him back through Chicken Street, then on through the neighborhoods to the west.

Even though Asa enjoyed Chicken Street, his mind drifted today as he walked with random thoughts of Jamil.

*Is he alive? Is he all right?* He wondered. Some days, he wished he wasn't alive. Home was lonely without Jamil. His father worked long days and his mother did her best to preoccupy him, but there were times Asa just wanted to run away and look for Jamil on his own.

As he walked, he wasn't focused at the faces passing by until he noticed that strange man again they had almost ran into. *Could it be him, the one that stared at me?* Asa thought to himself. *That was a ways back, how could he be here so quickly?*

Asa was nearing home and kept looking back for the strange man. He saw his home in the distance as the sun was setting. He instantly felt worried, once again, for the state of his clothes. He remembered that his mother would be furious.

At the security gate he punched in a code. He waited as the gate slowly creaked open. He slid through it quickly hurrying to get in and turned to push the slow groaning gate shut. In an open lot under a tree across the street, that same man from the marketplace was watching him.

Both stood looking at one another. Asa rubbed his eyes and watched as the man turned and disappeared. All he could remember was the snowy white beard with a black stripe, and those cold, piercing eyes.

# CHAPTER 11
# THE TUNNEL

**"D**amn it! God, I'm looking old today!" Rachel laughed wryly, leaning into a wall mirror in the library of their home and observing herself intently. The three-by-six-foot mirror hung directly centered within the main bookshelf in the library were Farrin kept his medical books perfectly alphabetized by year and anatomy. The mirror was framed in beautiful hand crafted decorative jewels, sparkling with brilliant colors as sunlight gently bounced off the jewels and reflected on the ceiling above her in a rainbow of colors.

With her face inches from the mirror, Rachel was scrutinizing the few small wrinkles around her green eyes. *Who knew a 35-year-old could look so sad, so tired, so worn?* she thought wearily. The past few years had truly aged her in more ways than one.

She turned from the mirror and observed her surroundings. Centered upstairs near the bedrooms just at the top of the stairs, the library was decorated in deep rich maroon and brown tones with gold trim on the wallpaper and carpeting. Decorative oak carved book-shelves ran along the entire length of the wall from floor to ceiling. Expensive leather chairs with perfectly placed floor lamps next to each chair.

Now, though, it was another story. Rachel walked to a canvas that was set up in the library. Over the past few years, painting had become Rachel's obsession as the library slowly became her studio and escape. Starting with simple landscapes from home back in Minnesota, she moved on with detailed works of the local buildings, and the slums with children with big sad eyes soon took over. As she perfected her technique, her subjects became more detailed, complex. She painted Jamil the way she remembered his face, his soft brown eyes.

At first, Farrin had resisted the idea of redesigning the room from a library to an art studio, but due to her persistence, he surrendered more and more of the room over to her in time. But he had asked Rachel to leave one section of the room near his desk open, and she had honored that request.

Stacked atop all of the beautiful tables and furniture, and perched along the walls were art supplies: framed blank canvases in various sizes waiting to be given life, brushes that were washed and unwashed, and oil paints of all colors. The library had become her refuge over the last few years since Jamil went missing. Her painting was her solace.

Rachel turned again to the mirror.

Rachel loved the home, and as an added security there was the safe room. The safe room was hidden behind the wall where Rachel now gazed into the mirror. The trigger to open the secret passageway into the safe room was a small turquoise jewel about the size of a penny on the bottom right corner of the mirror. The mirror designed as a two-way mirror, allowing those in the safe room to view into the library. Once the trigger was set, the bookshelf slightly pivoted to the left, allowing entrance into the safe room on the right.

The safe room wasn't much larger than an large closet. Inside, there was a cache of enough provisions to last a month. Shelved along the four walls were water bottles, dried fruits, and vegetables. Cans of evaporated milk, various vacuumed packed meats, nuts, and candy filled the gaps. It was fitted with indirect red lighting along the ceiling for a low-lit environment so that intruders in the house would not be able to see lighting through the mirror.

Once inside, steps from the interior of the safe room went down 50 feet below the house and connected to a tunnel. The entire tunnel was constructed by the best masons the area had to offer. It was five feet wide by six feet tall and was made of a smooth troweled cement surface. The tunnel ran 100 feet towards the backyard and then out to an exit in the garage floor hatch. The exit hatch in the garage was so perfectly made it was invisible to the eye, blending in with the cement floor.

Halfway through the tunnel, a small one-room area sat to the left that added some comfort if locked in for days. It was a small-sized bedroom that offered a table, two small beds, and a small pot used as a toilet.

Rachel sighed. She had thought such a stronghold would've protected her family. But it hadn't. The outside had been too strong, taking Jamil from them outside the home. *It's no good dwelling on it,* Rachel told herself for the millionth time.

Desperately pouring a glass of wine for herself, she walked around the library—looking for the perfect color for the final few strokes of a piece she had been working on for several months for the hospital's lobby where Farrin worked.

The piece was an eclectic, bright, splashy painting where fragmented faces and history of the area were frozen in time on the canvas. This painting, the size of a living room rug, was her best accomplishment yet. She was anxious to finish it. The next night, there would be a ceremony at the hospital with local media where she would present the painting to the hospital, and local dignitaries and staff would be present with a reception afterwards.

Rachel drank the wine, thinking about what would make the finished piece truly done.

*Slam!*

Out of the silence, she was startled by a door slamming as she heard Asa return home. Startled, she dropped her glass of wine, spilling it all over a table of open paint trays. The wine mixed with the paint in an oily collage of colors.

"Shit." Rachel quickly mopped up the mess with her painter's smock. There was something about the door slam that made her wonder if something was wrong with Asa. Out of the corner of her eye, she saw Asa storm past the library, hurriedly heading for his room.

*Slam!* Another loud noise reverberated through the space as Asa slammed his bedroom door.

*Something is really wrong, then.* Rachel followed him and stood at his closed bedroom door. "Asa, sweetheart, why is the door locked? Please open the door, honey." Rachel jiggled the door knob.

Silence. The clock tick-tocked in the hallway. Rachel leaned into

Asa's bedroom door, pressing her ear slightly against it. She could hear water running in his bedroom's bathroom.

"Sweetheart please unlock the door. Is everything okay?" she continued.

"I'm okay, Mom, I'll be right out. Just give me a minute," he called through the door.

After a few minutes, the door slowly opened. Asa peered at her through the slightly cracked door as if to see if Rachel was still there... she was.

Asa, peeking through the cracked door, saw his mother looking down at him with her arms crossed over her chest as he turned his head to conceal his "puffy fish face," as Esmat had called it. The whole left side of his face was swollen and bruised, and he finally broke into tears. But the tears were not for the puffy bruised face, but for the clothes...the clothes his mother had made.

"What happened! Did some boys do this to you?" His mother knelt down, analyzing the swollen cheek.

Asa looked down, staring at the marble trim along the threshold to the bedroom as he mumbled a short version of the soccer game and the kick to the face. "I'm sorry, Mom, I didn't mean to do it," he whispered as he sobbed. Rachel took Asa by the hand and walked him to his bed as they both sat on the edge.

His mother held Asa close as he cried. Asa noticed through his tears that she was staring over at the other empty bed by the wall... Jamil's bed. He was so happy that she was here with him. Since he went missing, his mother usually avoided entering the bedroom. Most the cleaning of the room was done by the housemaid, who swept and cleaned Jamil's area. Jamil's clothes still hung in the closet. Moving her eyes around the room, she noticed Asa's dirty clothes on the floor in the bathroom doorway.

"I'm sorry, Mom. I forgot to change before soccer. I promise I won't do it again...I...promise."

His mother pulled Asa away from her, looking into his eyes.

"Where did you play soccer today?" she asked sternly.

Asa looked down. If she wasn't upset already, she would be shortly, since the game was on the other side of town. Since Jamil went missing, she had become more protective and concerned when Asa was out of the house.

"By the Palace," he said. "It was the other boys deciding where to play. I couldn't say no, they would've given me a hard time."

"You know how I feel about that," his mother definitely sounded frustrated, and she shook her head. "I mean, since your brother, Asa"... She welled up with tears and trailed off for a moment. "I just couldn't stand losing you. It would tear me apart. Promise me, please, that you won't do it again. That's just too much of a risk, okay?"

She kissed his forehead and grabbed him by the hand.

"So let's go downstairs and ice that beautiful swollen face. Maybe some of your favorite ice cream? What do you say?" Asa wiped his eyes as he exhaled deeply. He loved his mother.

They ate ice cream and then cuddled in his bed for hours, talking of Jamil, days passed, how Asa had become a young man. Asa felt comforted—although he would've never admitted it. At around bedtime his mother tucked Asa in for the night. He watched his mother bending over to adjust his pillow, and her being so close—so close to Jamil's bed, to his clothes—made him wonder.

"Mom, is Jamil alright?" he asked. "Will we ever see him again?"

With a smile and a kiss, she said, "I hope so soon. Someday, we will see his goofy smiling face coming through the door."

They both giggled. But Asa knew she was not really saying what she really felt.

"Good night, sweetheart," she quietly left the room as Asa began to burrow himself into his blankets.

"Good night, Mom. I love you," he said as she switched off the light. Rachel's heart ached when Asa mentioned Jamil. Her heart was heavy as she left his bedroom and closed the door.

Farrin usually got home between 9-10pm at night, and he rarely called letting her know he was on his way. The hospital was just a short drive through town.

Rachel slipped on her short pink bathrobe and headed to the bathroom to clean up the remaining dried paint on her face and hands. Suddenly, she remembered that she'd forgotten to turn off the library lights. Still drying her face with a towel, she headed back into the library. Taking a quick last glance at her painting, she pondered once more how to finalize the painting that upcoming morning.

*Thud!*

It was a faint thud, but it was enough to make Rachel jump. She did not like noises at night. She quickly dimmed the lights in the library and walked to the window, looking out into the yard below. She flicked on the outside security lights. The neighborhood below was quiet and dark. Leaning into the window, she looked right, then left. Everything looked normal.

*Thud!*

Again Rachel heard the noise. Grabbing the flashlight she searched the entire house...nothing.

*Weird!* She thought to herself. *But I'll have Farrin look around the house and tunnel when he gets home.*

# CHAPTER 12
# THE ABDUCTION

Tuesdays were Farrin's day off. The sun was shining brightly through the five large European-style windows in the kitchen, and Rachel was being fastidious in the kitchen working on a particular Pakistani breakfast which was Farrin's favorite. Asa sat at the breakfast counter near her, sipping down the milk left over from his cereal and tipping the bowl back with a hearty gulp.

Rachel was preparing eggs for a breakfast dish called *Khagina*, which consisted of scrambled eggs with red and green peppers, red chili powder, and pepper. It was served with puri, a whole wheat bread fried in oil with a side of fruit in a honey juice.

Even though it was only the morning, Rachel was getting excited for tonight. The dedication of the painting she had been working on for several months was finally here. But she was still concerned by the noise she'd heard last night. As she was cooking the eggs that steamed in the pan, she just couldn't shake the feeling.

Last night after Farrin had gotten home, she'd asked that he look into the tunnel before the art ceremony. Farrin had agreed, although he'd laughed a little at her concern. "Our tunnel is solid, secure!" he'd assured her. "But I'll have the hospital handyman, Rameez take a good look."

*Solid, secure.* Rachel echoed the words in her mind as she tossed the scrambled eggs around in the cooking pan.

"Mom, who's watching me tonight while you're gone?" Asa asked.

"Samina," Rachel answered, distracted by her own cooking and lost in her own thoughts.

"Our cleaning lady?" Asa seemed interested. "Why her?"

"I'm having her clean at the same time. We will only be gone a few hours, so I've instructed her to give your room special attention," she said as she scuffed the back of Asa's head. "Now run up stairs and get your father. His breakfast is ready."

She watched Asa take two steps at a time as he ran up to their master bedroom.

"Daddy, breakfast is ready!"

"I'll be down in just a minute! Thanks, son," Farrin responded, out of breath. The master bedroom had a treadmill and an elliptical set up along the bedroom windows next to the bed. Farrin had always had a disciplined workout routine since college. He had even participated in a few marathons over the years. It helped keep his head clear and stamina up. The demands at the hospital would keep him most days over 14 hours.

Throwing a towel around his neck and downing a quick glass of water, he headed out of the room as the treadmill groaned to a stop. Farrin ran down the steps and entered the kitchen. Walking up from behind Rachel, he wrapped his arms around her waist—making her nearly drop his full plate of breakfast.

"Honey," she giggled, "Sit your butt down!"

"So when do I see the pièce de résistance? You haven't allowed me near the painting since you started."

Farrin knew that Rachel was excited and nervous at the same time. Farrin was not a critical man, but she was feeling a little insecure as to what his first response would be. She shrugged off his comment, sitting the plate of food in front of him.

"After you pick up Rameez at the hospital, would you stop at the market and pick up Asa's favorite pizza? I have allowed him to stay up and watch a movie tonight," she said.

"Will do, sweetheart," Farrin replied with his mouth full of fruit. "I know our handyman from the hospital is as good as they get. Rameez is going to help this morning clearing out the lobby of all the donations for tonight's dedication, and then I'll see if he'll come help me look over the tunnel." Farrin stood with empty plate in hand.

After a quick shower, Farrin dressed and grabbed the car keys to head to the hospital. Lightly knocking on the open door to the library while leaning on the door frame, he watched Rachel with admiration as she put the finishing touches on the painting. The painting sat on a easel with its back facing him as she peered over the top.

"See you in a bit," he said as he blew her a kiss.

"Love you," she said, more focused on the painting than her husband.

Farrin headed to the hospital. It was around 11am, and he wanted to make sure all was in place for tonight. Along with some of the staff, friends of Rachel's from the Red Cross, and some local media, he also had a special surprise for Rachel. Farhad Moshiri, a well-known Iranian artist, would be at the event. Farrin had contacted Farhad at his current home in Tehran and promised Farhad all expenses paid to attend. Farhad agreed with honor.

After spending an hour clearing out the lobby, Farrin and Rameez put a few finishing touches in the lobby, setting up a few tables and chairs. Rameez had been staffed with the hospital now for over 15 years. Now in his 70s, he'd quickly become family with the staff, and his work was excellent. Farrin mentioned about looking around the tunnel, and Rameez agreed wholeheartedly.

Rameez sat in the front seat of the MG as Farrin headed for home. Rameez held a bag of tools on his lap and sat quietly watching the people in the streets as they drove by. He wasn't the most talkative of people, Farrin had observed. Pulling up to the front of the house, Farrin helped Rameez with his tools.

Rameez suddenly made a little gasp. "My father had helped build this house," he said with tears in his eyes. "It has been sometime now since I have been to this area."

Farrin wondered if his father was part of the team that helped in the construction of the tunnel as they made their way upstairs after a brief hello to Rachel.

Entering the tunnel, the low red lights barely exposed any issues of integrity of the craftsmanship. Farrin handed a flashlight to Rameez while Farrin switched his on. With flashlights in hand, they entered the safe room. As they continued deeper into the tunnel, Rameez explained the history of the home as best he could remember.

"Construction took a year to complete," he said. "And times were more violent and many workers died during that year." He went on to tell Farrin that there was a missile that had a direct hit to the yard many years ago, just missing the house. The bomb landed in the back-yard, making a hole to the left side.

Farrin watched as Rameez was tapping and feeling the wall structure as they walked, inspecting the structure like a dentist looking deep into someone's mouth in search for a cavity as he shone his light into the darkness.

As they rounded the last bend that lead out to the garage access, Rameez pointed his flashlight to the floor, then up the wall. "There is discoloration of the wall at that point," he said. Tapping that area, Farrin could hear the old man's small hammer hit a hollow sound. Looking close, he tapped again. The area increased in size, looking to be the size of a small opening.

"What is it, Rameez?" Farrin questioned.

"This must be the entrance to the old tunnel," said Rameez while looking over his left shoulder at Farrin standing over him. Rameez knelt down, looking along the floor. Reaching into his tool bag at his right, he grabbed a mason's hammer with a sharp edge, tapping it gently into a small crack along the floor and wall. It was nearly invisible. As he did, the lower half moved. He gently pulled at the bottom as it slid outward. He continued working at the sides next.

"This must be the old exit," he said. "After the bombing, they re-designed the tunnel exit." Rameez had the entire door removed, exposing the old tunnel. The back of the hatch was made of a curved wood structure with a light coating of cement.

On the backside of the hatch door, two handles were attached for quick placement from inside the tunnel. The hatch was fairly light in weight, enough for one man to handle. On the bottom and top there were makeshift guides to help assist in placement. The masons had taken such care in concealing the opening that it took a trained eye to spot it.

"Did you know about this?" Farrin questioned Rameez.

"No, sir. I only knew of the bombing to this yard area. I've heard of a rebuild, but no one knew for sure...until now."

"Hmmm," Farrin said. He wondered if Rachel had heard a portion of the old tunnel collapsing or something the night before. Maybe it was unstable now. "I would be more at ease if we could make sure this area is stable," Farrin said as they both pointed the flashlights into the dark cavernous hole.

"Yes, I can do this for you," Rameez replied. "But I'll have to go get the tools needed for this. It could take a few days. "I will have this entire old tunnel collapsed and filled with dirt soon as possible." Farrin said looking into the darkness.

It was now only a few hours before they had to get ready for tonight's dedication. Farrin stepping back from the opening of the old tunnel kicked some loose dirt directly in front of the hatch. Thinking nothing of it they headed back through the tunnel. Rameez measured and took notes.

As they exited the safe room, Farrin noticed Rachel was wrapping the painting in brown kraft paper for the ceremony. She stopped what she was doing noticing by Farrins look that something wasn't right.

"Honey," she said in a tone he was familiar with.

Farrin handed Rameez the keys from his desk drawer for the pickup truck in back.

"I will return soon," Rameez said as he headed down stairs to the garage.

Rachel walked over with arms crossed, waiting for Farrin to explain what happened.

"We found another older section of tunnel."

"Older?" she said. "What do you mean older?"

Farrin went on to explain while Rachel sat down on the edge of the library table, staring down at the decorative carpeting. "Rameez will be back later to secure the hatch," he concluded. "I will get someone to collapse and fill in the hole; that's the best we can do. Look at the time. We need to start getting ready soon."

"I'm not going," Rachel said softly.

"Not going? This is a special night."

"I just have a feeling that old tunnel has some connection to the noise I heard. I'm worried," she said looking towards the safe room opening.

Farrin walked over and pulled her up from the table. "Maybe the sound you heard was part of that old tunnel collapsing in on itself. It's been there for years just rotting. We can fill it up, and everything will be fine. Rameez will take care of it."

Reluctantly, she agreed. Samina would be there shortly.

Heading upstairs with her, Farrin slipped on his Anderson Sheppard suit. Only on rare occasions did he wear it. It was black with black embossed detail, a crisp white shirt with a raspberry color tie with small black dot patterns. He put on his fine gold jewelry. Rachel wore a sequined Malene Birger evening dress that fit snug to her shapely body, splashing on her favorite perfume, Clive Christian. With her shoes by Manolo Blahnik, she looked exquisite.

Both stood in front of the large bedroom mirror making adjustments when they heard the chime at the front door.

"Samini is here, Mom." Asa yelled from downstairs.

"Tell her I'll be down in a minute," Rachel said as she adjusted the top of her dress.

Farrin stood behind Rachel with his hands on her shoulders in front of the mirror, kissing her cheek as they looked at their reflections. Farrin felt her tension. He couldn't decide if she was annoyed about the tunnel or anxious about the evening or both.

"You're so beautiful," Farrin said. "Everything will be fine."

"You're no chopped liver," Rachel said, trying to lighten the mood and turning to face Farrin while wrapping her arms around him. "I'm so nervous about tonight."

"You will be fantastic. The way you look, you wouldn't have to say a word, and you would still wow the crowd."

Farrin loaded the painting into the Toyota Land Cruiser, carefully sliding the painting in to the tight space in back.

Rachel was going over the bedtime rules with Samini for Asa. Farrin knew that Rachel had come along way since Jamil went missing, and this painting was a statement of her regaining her healthy state of mind. The ceremony absolutely had to go off without a hitch.

*Tonight, everything will be perfect,* he thought, jaw clenched with determination. *It has to be.*

They sped off and headed to the event.

Asa broke out *Risk*, a game that he used to play with Jamil. Samini had never heard of such a game. Asa was being diligent in going over the rules. It took almost an hour before Samini understood. Rachel was going to allow Asa up late till they got home or 10:30—whichever came first.

Getting bored of the game after winning all three rounds, Asa wanted to watch a movie.

"*Die Hard*!" he said with a smile. "Please?"

They made popcorn and headed to the living room, plopping down on the overstuffed sofa.

Halfway through the movie, Asa heard Samina slightly snore as he looked over and noticed her eyes were closed. Looking back to the TV screen, then back to Samina, he got up quietly.

He knew what he wanted to do tonight. He wanted an adventure. Asa rarely was allowed in the library because of his mother's painting habit. He wanted to take advantage of being alone to go explore the very room in which he never got to go into, and Asa knew he had to make it quick.

Walking around the library, he took in all the painting supplies scattered throughout the room. Sitting on a table by a stack of canvasses was a small bowl of mixed paint colors. Asa grabbed a small brush, dabbed it into the paint, and made a few strokes onto a broken canvas nearby.

Bored, he continued to the bookshelf and scanned the covers of his father's medical books. Then he saw the huge mirror, staring up at it. He'd always been fascinated by the bright colorful jewels. Wanting to get a better look, he pulled a chair closer directly in front of the mirror.

"Wow," he murmured. Leaning forward, he stared at his reflection with both hands on the mirror's edge as he leaned forward. It was then he heard a click, and the wall started to move.

Looking back to the hallway, his excitement grew, and he slid through the opening in to the safe room. He looked around at the supplies on the walls. With the red lighting on, it took a few minutes for his eyes to adjust.

"Cool!" he said out loud. "Cool!" He spotted the steep steps going down to the bottom. He went back to the opening in the library to see if he could hear anyone...silence. Half hesitating, he decided to go down the steep steps into the tunnel. At the bottom of the steps, he looked back up, and it seemed so far away. He looked down the tunnel as it disappeared into the semi-darkness.

Moving quickly, Asa glanced at the sitting room—noticing the table and beds. Not knowing how much further the tunnel went, he was nervous, but his excitement made him continue further in the direction of the garage. His eyes adjusted now as he saw the last bend coming up. An old hatch door was leaning against the tunnel wall. Half stepping into the opening of the old tunnel, Asa noticed no lighting; it was pitch black. Confused which tunnel was which, he grew scared.

Suddenly out of the darkness he heard something or someone walking towards him. The footsteps on the rocks cascaded into a slight echo. It was so dark his eyes couldn't make it out, but a shadowy figure darker than the dark space itself came towards him.

Asa, frozen in fear, just stood there as time slowed to a crawl. A shadowy man took shape out of the darkness. And then a flashlight shone full on Asa's face, making him squint. The snowy white bearded man stood before him. All Asa could see, as if a spell was put on him, were the cold eyes he remembered from the walk after his soccer game. Even in the darkness behind the flashlight, his eyes glowed in a most sinister way.

Their eyes locked as the man towered over him. Asa tried to scream with no real sound behind it. He saw a flash of movement as he blacked out.

The hospital was packed with staff and friends of the Khans. The dedication was winding down with hor-d'oeuvres and champagne. The painting was placed in the lobby's central main wall above the small food stands—a perfect place for all to see.

Farrin was pleased. As he stood talking to another doctor, he noticed Rachel across the room with a Farhad. Farhad was in deep conversation with hands moving, probably discussing the art of the brush and canvas. Rachel looked highly interested. Rachel's beauty reminded Farrin of his love for his wife. He thought about later that night when they would be alone. As he glanced at his watch, he saw that it was going on 11pm.

"Doctor Khan, please go to the nurse's station." Farrin heard a hospital page for him as he walked towards the nurses station. Rachel followed him. The head nurse handed over the phone and punched a button.

"Hello," Farrin answered. On the other end, he heard Samina speaking in her native language. It was hard to understand her because she was hysterical. After calming her down, it finally came out.

"Asa is gone!" she said crying.

"What are you saying?" Farrin practically yelled into the phone. He could feel his stomach hitting the floor. She explained the movie one minute and *he was gone* the next.

"I think into the tunnel," she said. "I was afraid to look for him, but the mirror in the library was open that lead in to a large, black room I knew nothing about."

Farrin stood staring at the head nurse as if he was looking through her.

"What is it?" the head nurse asked.

"Asa is gone."

"Gone?" she asked, confused.

Farrin turned in Rachel's direction as he dropped the phone. She was watching him, her face white. He knew she'd heard. At that moment, Rachel collapsed to her knees. She started wailing out loud. "No! Not again!"

The room went silent.

# CHAPTER 13
# T-MINUS 4 HOURS

It was the 20<sup>th</sup> of October, the Base Commander along with Officer Tucker arranged the mission, covering every detail. A week has passed with our deployment for the mission closing in. Looking at the digital clock on my desk, it blinked 0700 hours and glowed red in my dark bedroom. I was laying in bed staring at the ceiling as I exhaled a lungful of smoke from my cigarette, blowing a perfect trio of smoke rings towards the ceiling fan and watching as they were sucked into the vortex of the spinning fan. I stared at my family photos on the ceiling. I missed them all so much it hurt.

I'd had one last conversation with my wife last night that had left me missing home. She did most the talking, largely about the kids school reports and new neighbors that had moved in with kids. We talked of my return home in less than four months, plans she had for us, how nice it will be to sleep together again—those were the sorts of things that kept us going.

I mentioned we would be headed into the mountain ranges for a few weeks with reports of a Taliban stronghold and that she might not hear from me for a while. Her voice sounded stressed, knowing all too well the dangers. I didn't want to add to her already sleepless nights, so I left out the mission we were preparing for and the extra dangers we would be faced with. She already knew.

My decision of what men I was taking on this mission had been a no-brainer. In total five men: Tex, Big Joe, Antonio, Sal with King our bomb sniffer, and Ben, a sharp shooter who came to us per the Snow Leopard memorandum from Delta Force. Ben had been working with

Antonio for the last two weeks. Antonio, with some prior spotting training and good at it, made him the perfect match for Ben.

My Commander and I discussed in detail about taking King. The dog was trained for sniffing out planted mines and bombs and had prior extensive training as a cadaver dog in search and rescue. The Base Commander was against it at first, thinking that King would jeopardize or location. My instincts told me the caves would be when I needed him the most, so the Commander relented.

All of these men, along with our trusty canine, were brave, dedicated, and had hearts of lions. We were ready for whatever might lie ahead.

We had a briefing with my Commander in the morning at 1000 hours. We needed to discuss if we had the go ahead for the long trek. Already, my head was buzzing with all of the information and planning we'd done over the last few weeks.

Our drop off point was to be pinpointed with GPS as instructed by Hakeem. It was just outside the Korengal Valley: the Kunar Province north of the Korengal Valley. To the south ran the Khyber Pass for 28 miles at lower elevations and connected Pakistan to Afghanistan. By train it had 34 tunnels and 92 bridges. Considered one of the oldest trade routes in the region, it had been embroiled in conflict over the years as a strategic military stronghold of the Taliban. American forces used this as a supply route.

After the drop, Hakeem would guide us through the hilly terrain outside the Korengal Valley on up to the rendezvous point. We would follow the goat trails through lower elevations for a full two days. Then we would meet with Hakeem's family member, who would then take us on up to the higher elevations to the caves.

Mission control was pulling together weather predictions. Temperatures could range from an average of just above freezing to sub-zero on up to the higher elevations this time of year. It had been a snowy cold stretch in the higher elevations already.

The missing part of the equation was the guide Hakeem had selected. What route would they recommend? We had topographic maps with detailed terrain information and notes of possible Taliban strongholds and movements in detail for about a 200-mile radius from our drop off point.

Jumping out of bed, I flicked on the coffee maker as I headed for the bathroom for my last Hollywood shower for a few weeks. As I waited for the water to heat up, I stood at the sink edge, staring at my kids and wife, wondering what they were doing at the moment. I kissed my fingertips and pressed them to the photos.

After rounding up the men, we headed over to our Commander's office. Ben, a highly decorated Navy Seal that stood tall at 6'2 and focused. He was the sharp shooter assigned to our team for the mission. He stood there, exuding an inner strength of a man that took his job seriously.

The briefing was with my Commander at his office surrounded by that lush green verdant landscaping. The small office was almost 15 feet by 15 feet in size with the Commander's desk centered against the back wall facing out. On the left and right side of the small office sat two sofas up against the wall. They were army green vinyl and covered with random cracks where the stuffing poked through. The cushions sagged from years of use.

Following the Commander into his office, Ben, Antonio, and Tex took a seat on the left side sofa. Sal with King and I sat on the right side. Big Joe stayed standing next to me as we faced the Commander at his desk. Sitting back in his squeaky chair with a clean set of camos, he looked around at the men's faces. King sat at Sal's feet began panting in the stuffy office.

"I just got word from Ops that it's a go. We have men loading your gear as we speak. Staff Sergeant has hand selected you men, and I agree with Mike's choice. Each of you brings something to the fight. We have your physical results back, and you all are as healthy as a horse. No incoming health issues that would prevent you going on this mission."

Standing up from his squeaky chair, the Commander walked over to the map on the wall to the right of his desk. Grabbing his pointer from the aluminum tray, he pointed to the drop off point, tapping on the heavy plastic map as he went over the new route we would be taking.

"We have drone confirmation of intense fighting today near the first selected landing point here," the Commander said as he pointed to the map. "So unfortunately, we had to move your drop off point to here," he pointed again, tapping firmly on the thick plastic map with a loud tap-tap noise. "Fifty miles to the northeast. Hakeem is with our people now going over that area. This should not interfere with our timeline. Hakeem reassures us that he knows this area well."

We all nodded.

"And one last thing before we head over to the departure point," said the Commander. "This mission is different from any other you have been part of. Communications will be at minimum for this one. In order for this to be a success, we cannot expose your location. You as a team must work in unison, moving quietly, unnoticed. This is an area with Taliban all over these mountain trails and caves. The drone will pass twice a day. That will allow us the eyes to check your progress. Staff Sergeant and I have gone over a exit strategy plan if needed, and that call will be Staff Sergeant's alone.

"If this is a success, it could be a big feather in our caps finding the hole this Taliban cell has been hiding in. It's uncertain if the caves hold the bacha bazi boys or not. We will deal with that when we have confirmation. I wish you a safe journey, and Godspeed."

We all stood in unison as the Commander snapped a salute.

Door Knob Bob was preparing all maps and documentation we would be packing with the rest of our gear. Part of our success would be traveling light as possible.

It would be the weaponry that would be scaled back. The weapons of choice for this mission were the M4 carbine guns with a range of 500 yards, 9MM Beretta pistols, and KA-bar knives. Our sharpshooter Ben would have his M82A1, which was extremely accurate with a range in perfect weather conditions of an half mile, or more.

Our crew had two terrains to deal with: lower elevations with vegetation and shale rock, and the higher elevations with the snow and cold. The mission in most part would be taking place in the higher elevations. The Taliban always had their eyes and ears on, so the snow gear was white and designed for the extreme cold conditions. In order to conceal King, we had a white camouflage velcro vest for him when we headed into the mountains.

Our day-to-day gear would be the MTV-plated kevlar vest, ISO mats, gloves for warmth and cold conditions, ponchos, and tools for digging in. Two helmets with tactical headsets built in and two pair of boots for the elevation change also weighed us down. Only one sleeping bag called the Bivvy Bag fit in our pouches due to its design ease of carrying and easy access with gloves and boots on. All white in color, it could be fully zipped in a matter of seconds.

We would also have a military-issue snow sled for hauling our gear and snowshoes, MRE food packs, binoculars for day and night, and other vital tools. We tried to pack for anything and everything.

As we geared up, we estimated a timeline of nearly two weeks if we were lucky. But who knew what dangers we would face on the trek to and inside the caves? We headed outside where two Humvees were waiting. As we walked towards the Humvees, King took the opportunity to relieve himself on the flowers along the sidewalk. The Humvees pulled away in a cloud of dust as we headed towards the launch area. The Commander followed us to the helipad in his vehicle with Door Knob Bob holding the maps with one hand and his hat with the other.

It was a somber ride for the short few minutes as we headed to the tarmac. I was looking around at the men's faces as we drove; most seemed in deep thought, even Big Joe with his insatiable appetite was quiet, no food visible.

I looked off into the distance at the direction we would be heading, seeing nothing but a bright blue sky. The drop off spot was over 60 miles northeast of Kabul. Our ride to the drop off point would be the HH-60 *Pave Hawk* helicopter derived from the older version *Black Hawk*, with a cruising speed of nearly 200 mile per hour. It would put us at our destination in about an hour. We would need a flat area for a quick drop before our position was revealed.

Pulling up to the helicopter, we could see a flurry of activity. The ground crew was meticulously loading the chopper. I spotted the Base Commander with Tucker the Ops Officer in deep conversation, hands moving quickly as they talked.

Standing alone near the helo was Hakeem, waiting for some direction as the men loaded the gear. Hakeem looked out of place in his traditional clothing. He was wearing a salwar kameez—a one-piece outfit of white cotton—a colorful shirt called a kurta, a brown leather vest called a waskat, and a turban. That was Hakeem's trademark: a colorful clean turban, white with subtle red and green decorations. He had thrown a small backpack over his shoulder.

The Base Commander spotted our crew pull up and waved me over, pulling me aside as my crew stood in a semi-circle facing each other, adjusting their MTV vests. Some took sips of water from their day bags. The Base Commander put his arm around my shoulder as the turbine-whining noise of the chopper grew louder, the blades cutting through the air in a *thump-thump* noise above us.

"Staff Sergeant, we have cleared the LZ," the Base Commander yelled over the noise. "It will be a hot landing. We have GPS coordinates that will place you a few clicks beyond the Korengal Valley near a small town called Arab Khel.

"The area you're headed into to at this time is a hotbed of activity, so watch yourselves. We have the first pass of the drone in two days. After that it will pass twice a day. The first at just after sunrise, the second at sundown. After your guide establishes your access into the mountains, you will radio in those coordinates. From that point forward, it will be the drone passes that monitor your day-to-day progress."

"Yes, sir," I acknowledged.

"Now, go get those bastards!" the Base Commander yelled with a slap to my helmet.

I saluted as I spun around, ducking from the wind and debris and heading back to my men. Walking up behind Big Joe, I grabbed his shoulder. The rest of the men made a circle around us. I knelt down, pulling on Big Joe to kneel with me, and the rest of the men followed our lead and all knelt down. Each one laid a hand on the shoulder of the man next to him.

"Lord, we pray that you watch over each man here, and that when the shadows of darkness come before us, we pray that you give us the strength and perseverance to succeed our mission and get back safe," I prayed. "Protect us and guide us. Amen."

"Amen," all said.

King sat in the middle of the group, intently listening and looking around at the faces, turning his head from side to side. He then gave a quick sharp bark.

All men jumped in the chopper as we took our places in the cargo area. King laid next to Sal with his head across his lap closing his eyes. Hakeem was the last to get in as I leaned over and pulled him in by his arm, with the loose tails of his turban being pulled straight up by the swirling wind of the chopper's vortex directly above.

Both side doors were left open on the chopper as we lifted off. The chopper slowly raised off the ground 30 feet as it slowly turned right. Looking down, I watched the ground crew and Base Commander collectively head back to the tasks of the day.

The flight would give me time to focus on the days ahead. The terrain ahead at the drop off reminded me of back home in Wisconsin with tall pine trees, green sloping hills, and green rich vegetation looking like it's going to go on forever. The noisy cargo area kept most of the men's thoughts to themselves.

After 20 minutes, the pilot spoke over the speakers alerting of the Korengal Valley coming up on the right side of the chopper. The Korengal Valley was a treacherous area, so the helicopter climbed to a safe altitude.

Looking out the side doors, we could see the fighting taking place below with the bright flashes and smoke from the mortars landing on their targeted positions. Smoke billowed up towards the sky like puffy white clouds, caught by drafts through the valley and pulled in all directions. We could see the flash of rocket launchers aimed at us as we clipped along at 120 knots. The pilot took care not to climb too high so that it wouldn't affect the stability of the chopper as we pressed on. We could hear the chatter over the speakers in the cargo area the pilot left on.

I saw Hakeem clutch his backpack tightly with dilated pupils, as he gripped the side of his seat as we banked hard right up over some ridges. The cool air circulating through the cargo area was a relief as I leaned back and loosened my vest. I watched Big Joe shove a stick of beef jerky into his mouth.

As I closed my eyes, I pictured my wife and kids faces. *How much have they changed since I saw them several months ago? Have they grown much? Did my daughter get her way to have her hair grow out against her mother's wishes? What are they doing now?* My thoughts started to blur and meld together with what lay ahead the next few weeks.

Just then, the pilot announced our landing spot in 10 minutes. The chopper shook as we hit turbulence.

Looking to the east off in the distance, I saw the range of the Hindu Kush mountains: perfect white jagged diamonds set in a sapphire blue setting. So benign looking, so innocent, so beautiful from up here.

I suddenly had a sick feeling come over me as we set down. Jumping out, the men quickly unloaded the gear. As they did, Hakeem and I stood together looking at the terrain ahead of us, discussing our direction. Hakeem pointed in a few directions, for the day's journey into the higher elevations.

With a swooping *thud*, the chopper lifted off as we stood watching it disappear in to the vast sky. Silence fell over the group.

Our mission had really begun.

# PART TWO
## THE MOUNTAINS

# CHAPTER 1
## THE GOOD VILLAGE

At this elevation, there was nothing but dry hard dirt, shale rock, scrub brush, and pine trees all around. Goat trails led off in all directions. The foothills were peppered with boulders of all sizes. The Korengal Valley was at our backs, and the steep hilly terrain was ahead of us. After patrolling the Kabul area for the last few years, the countryside was intoxicating. We still could hear the mortar rounds and fly bys of the choppers down in the valley we left behind.

We gathered our gear. Big Joe and Tex loaded the gear onto the sled. We walked the trails inline: Hakeem was our point, Sal walked with King in stride, Big Joe and Tex carried the sled with our gear in the center of the group, Antonio and Ben followed, and I was in the rear.

"We have a two-day journey to the rendezvous spot," Hakeem said. "That is where the snow line starts just beyond the last village. Our guide will be waiting there. This guide is familiar with the higher elevations and the location to the caves."

"How will we know who this guide is?" I inquired.

"The guide will find us, and I will stay with you till then," Hakeem said, smiling. "This will be good; it is a family member I have not seen in some time."

As we walked, Hakeem told us of his family, and how they had been considered by the local villagers in the area as hard working, simple farmers—always willing to help anyone in any way. But as the area became more embroiled in war in this part of the Kunar Valley, their village had taken on more artillery hits. One day, an air strike took out most of the village while they worked their crops.

With the increased fighting growing closer to the village and more Taliban passing through, Hakeem's parents pleaded with two of his three brothers to please take Hakeem and Zaleah his only sister to Pakistan for their safety. Young girls and boys were subject to rape, even death.

Hakeem, at 30 years old now, continued with the story of the days on the farm while we started traversing the hilly wooded countryside.

"Have you seen your brothers since?" Tex asked Hakeem.

"Two brothers have distanced themselves from the rest of the family at an early age. I would not even know them if I saw them. It is only the oldest brother that I have left in Kabul." He had a deep sadness and regret in his voice.

It was getting late in the day as the sun was sinking below the peaks ahead of us. We could see the sun glimmering through the tall pines. I hadn't smelled the countryside in some time. Inhaling the fresh air and strong pine smell reminded me of the days I went deer hunting with my father and brothers in Wisconsin. The terrain grew steep quickly as the trail started a zigzag pattern through the shale rock, progressing through a small valley along the hillside.

"Let's take five!" I yelled when we reach the top of the ridge. I looked through the binoculars, scanning the landscape of the valley below. Reaching the crest of the ridge we saw a village off in the distance we would be passing through. Curious, I handed the binoculars to Hakeem, concerned what we might be walking into. The others joined in, looking through their binoculars at the village.

"How many villages are we going to pass through?" Big Joe asked looking over to Hakeem.

"We have two, including this village, which I remember as a child living near here with my family," Hakeem explained. "The other village is just before we reach the higher elevation."

"How well do you know these people?" I asked, lighting up a smoke, kneeling down on my right knee.

"My Father knew most of the farmers in this province. It has been some time since I have talked with any of them—that is, if any are still alive," Hakeem commented, looking down at the valley.

"Looks quiet, just farmers," Tex said, standing near me in the middle of the group.

We all had the same concern knowing that many of the villagers are related to the Taliban. I glanced back the way we'd come. King was staring off into the woods in the other direction, alert. I was pleased with deciding to have him with us. King did offer the added edge with his keen sense of smell and hearing.

I scanned the small village through the trees, judging the trek to be a hour or so. From here I counted approximately ten huts. I could see villagers working in the field. Children were running about playing. There was a stiff breeze from the valley thermals that put us down wind from the village, and I could smell the village's cooking fires.

The village below consisted of only meager huts built from what they could find available in the area. The wooded mountainous terrain offered most resources they needed to create some comfort without depending on outside help. Unfortunately, some of the farmers in the area took up growing opium to provide for their families, but most stayed with tradition—raising goats and growing vegetables to sell at the surrounding markets.

As we approached the village after a long walk, we saw a group of five men hoeing the fields. One of them saw us and stopped his work.

"As-salamu alaykum!" this man said, stepping forward to great Hakeem.

"As-salamu alaykum!" Hakeem responded as they gave a customary hug.

"I am Rashid," the man said, he looked much older for his age enduring the hard life he had lived. Brown and tanned, his weathered face displayed deep lines. His beard almost all gray now was long and straggly.

I stood back with the men while Hakeem discussed our intrusion with Rashid. The villagers kept looking at Hakeem, then to our group of soldiers as Hakeem reassured the village men our intentions were peaceful. The day was fading as the sun began to fall behind the mountain range.

Finally, Hakeem looked back at us, smiling and showing his brown-stained teeth as he walked up to our group.

"I know of this Rashid," Hakeem said, "These are my people. My father farmed with some of these men. They wish for us to stay the night and share in a meal. They will provide us with whatever we need."

As Rashid spoke through Hakeem's translation, we learned that he was a father of four and was one of the elder's of the village, having lived here his entire life. Right now, the villagers were harvesting potatoes, cauliflower, tomatoes, and onions to sell at the market. The people of the village were like family, working together for the success of the crops.

"We keep a constant eye on the trails from the outside world," said Rashid through Hakeem. "We are peaceful, simple people caught in the middle of many years of war. Now it is the Americans and the Taliban." Still, Rashid assured us they meant no harm and would welcome us.

Big Joe gave Tex a slap on the back, nearly knocking him over. "Looks like no digging in tonight, my friends," Big Joe said with a wide grin.

I watched as all the men collectively exhaled with relief to spend their first night in comfort. We all knew the next few weeks would be harsh and would test our strength and will.

We began to walk into the village. Most villagers spoke Dari and Pashto, a few some broken English. The village was located in an open valley along a river in an open grassy stretch between two wooded ridges on each side of the open grassy strip that led in the direction of the slopes to the west. The river that ran along the village offered water from the snow melt from higher elevations. This provided a lifeline for the people and their crops. The soil was rich with nutrients, fertile and full of possibility. There were ten huts in total, five on each side facing each other.

Rashid led our team to one of the huts, with a slight bow he gestured for us to go in. Our hut was on the end facing out over the open field. The huts sat to the east side next to the river that ran along the edge of the tree line, and our one room area was about 30 square feet in size. Though rudimentary in design, it was clean with handwoven rugs covering the entire floor. The window on the front side faced the walkway between the two rows of huts, another window positioned on the side had a view looking out over the valley.

As the men entered the hut, they immediately removed their gear. Tex and Big Joe hoisted in the sled full of gear. The men settled in, watching as Big Joe readjusted the gear on the sled. The mood of the men was that of appreciation and relief as they looked forward to the first night with good company and warm food from the villagers. Except Antonio.

"Shit! I wanted to keep going, put some distance in!" Antonio yelled to the group as they unloaded the gear.

"There will be time for that," Tex shot back. "Enjoy tonight. It will be a while before we have a roof over our heads."

"Keep your voices down!" I ordered. "These people have offered their village to us. They will present us with food tonight, so show respect."

It was at that moment I heard Hakeem calling to me from outside.

"Hello, my friend! Let's take walk to the field. I have some information to tell you," Hakeem seemed anxious as he stood a few feet from the door.

"Big Joe, Tex, come with me," I said as we stepped outside.

"What is it, Hakeem?" I said, glancing out at the open field.

"Rashid has warned me of the next village we will be passing." Hakeem said while walking towards the field.

"What is it?" I ask Hakeem. "I thought these villages are people you had ties with."

"Yes, this is true, but it has been some time now, and the Taliban have taken over some of the villages. Rashid has heard of beheadings the next village over, the very village we must pass through."

"Is there a route option that will take us around?" I asked.

"Maybe so. It has been some time since I have traveled that area. From here to the next village, the elevation will dramatically steepen with rocky terrain. The trails become more difficult. Perhaps to travel at night is the only choice to make."

"If this is true, they will have several Taliban scouts in place. Any intruders at night will be viewed as a threat," Big Joe interjected while holding a freshly picked potato.

"Tex, what do you think?" I asked.

Tex looked at Big Joe, then back to me. "Hands down, daytime," he said. "If we have Hakeem ahead of us, I think he would be able to disarm any scouts, maybe draw them out, see what we are dealing with."

We stopped near the vegetable garden. I looked down at a hand-woven basket full of potatoes and onions for tonight's feast.

"I agree," Big Joe commented. "We have Ben, who is able to shoot the balls off a fly from over a mile. I like the daylight option."

"It's extremely important that we keep to our established time-line," I said. "The Base Commander is expecting a GPS coordinates radioed in the day after tomorrow to establish drone surveillance. So let's move during daytime for now."

The others nodded as we reached this agreement. "Let's head back," I said.

Walking back to the huts, Hakeem embellished on the old days in the area. I could see it was a homecoming of sorts for him—but I only had tomorrow on my mind as I slapped a bug on my cheek. The night's weather here was much cooler than Kabul. The cool weather here reminded me of the harvest time back home with football and family. I was looking forward to tonight's home cooked meal.

As we entered the village again, I observed Sal sitting on the ground with King next to him. The village dogs were laying directly in front of Sal's feet keeping their distance from King. King looked regal, sitting proud over the village dogs only feet away. Sal grinned wide when he noticed us coming his way.

"Where are Antonio and Ben?" I asked Sal.

"They mentioned they were sighting in his rife in the new terrain," Sal pointed to his left over the ridge

I nodded. Over the last couple weeks, the two had perfected their teamwork on coordinating the accuracy and precision of Ben's technique. They would be indispensable in the days to come.

That evening as the darkness fell over the village, we sat as friends with the villagers, gorging ourselves on an Afghan dish called Kabuli Pulao. It was a delicious dish made of steamed rice, vegetables, and goat. For dessert, it was Sher Berini: rice pudding with almonds and pistachios.

We then all sat around a fire listening to the stories from the villagers. Even King was taking in the pit fire as everyone encircled it, the occasional flash-pop of the fires light that reflected of the faces.

While the stories of their village were fascinating, I couldn't fully engage. I started thinking of tomorrow, becoming consumed with the journey's potential dangers. I had respect and love for my men, and I was determined to get them all home alive. Bearing this leadership was a huge responsibility, and nothing could shake the heaviness I felt no matter how peaceful and beautiful this quaint village was.

Later that night, all my men settled in as complete darkness fell over the the village. The slow crackle of the campfire with its dim flames slowly fought its last gasp of air. Silence fell over the village as we drifted off to sleep.

The last noise I heard was Big Joe farting—a comforting, comical sound in the midst of all this new terrain and heavy thoughts.

"God, Big Joe! Keep it to yourself," Antonio moaned.

"Good night, girls," Big Joe said, mumbling in his sleep.

"Get some rest," I said, rolling my eyes. "Up at six bells."

# CHAPTER 2

# THE BAD VILLAGE

I was under water swimming towards the surface but never reaching it. *The water was a bright beautiful turquoise blue, and the sunlight above sparkled off the surface. My lungs burned as if they were about to burst from the lack of oxygen.*

*No matter how hard I kicked to reach the surface, it was always just out of reach. With my eyes wide open underwater, I kept looking towards the surface. There, I saw a dark figure standing above at the surface watching me struggle...*

...I went from a deep dreamy sleep state to wide awake. Sweating, I sat up and realized where I as. I could hear voices in one of the huts offering prayers in unison to Allah. Looking to my left, I saw Big Joe and Tex still asleep. I could smell the fresh aroma of tea and bread.

*I'm here in Afghanistan*, I thought, almost in relief to be rid of the drowning sensation in my dream. It was 0530 hours in the morning.

Outside our hut near the campfire, a few of the villagers had gathered. Hakeem was speaking in Pashto to the men, talking of the old days. I stood up and kicked the boots of Big Joe and Tex; their "good morning" sounded more like a groan.

"Damn, I'm starving," Big Joe mumbled, standing as he began to scratch his ass with his right hand.

Stepping out of the hut, I noticed Sal had King's leash off. King was actually playing with the other three village dogs. Being on base with a regiment the past few years with no other dogs around brought another side I haven't witnessed in King.

Rashid spotted me and greeted me with a simple bow. He informed me that the men of the village wished to have a sit down discussion prior to our leaving. Hakeem translating looked to me waiting for my response.

"Agreed," I offered a slight bow in return. With my towel over my shoulder, wearing only my camo pants and t-shirt, I headed for a wooden water bowl that was attached to a uneven tree stump next to the huts for washing up.

The sun rose higher in the early morning sky and shone brightly on the mountain range to the east—in the direction we would be heading in just a few hours. With one more village between us and the snow line not far off, we should start gaining elevation relatively early in our trek. Even at this distance with a few days journey in, I could see the snowy peaks off in the distance looking much closer now.

I ordered Tex to round up Ben and Antonio for the sit down with the villagers in the main hut after they ate. They were out working on elevation shooting.

Rashid's hut was the largest in the village. Able to hold 30 people or so, it provided ample room for my men and the villagers. Just inside the hut, Rashid stood waiting for us with the other village men, some already seated in a semicircle on the floor with their legs crossed. We sat on decorative, hand-woven rugs placed perfectly throughout the hut.

Rashid started the meeting, his hands constantly in motion while he talked looking around the room at the faces of the men. The men's voices were very intense, expressing strong emotion with years of pain and suffering from years of war. A few of the elders just needed to vent their frustrations. The Taliban had been using the villages for hiding, blending in, using them as gateways to the caves. Taliban soldiers threatened beheadings if any of these village people helped the Americans. The villagers were worried about their own safety.

We assured Rashid that we would inform our commanders that this was a friendly village, and we would do what we could to provide a watchful eye for his people's safety. The villagers prayed for our safe journey.

The meeting with the elders lasted about an hour. They had prepared food bundles for our trek filled with goat meat and vegetables, enough for the day's journey, including a specially large one for Big Joe. The village women giggled as they handed the food bag to him.

"Thank you, ladies," Big Joe said with a big grin.

We shook hands, and a few of the villagers embraced us. We parted ways as friends and allies.

We headed out of the village in a northeast direction, picking up a well traveled trail that headed toward the next village, a good day's journey. Leading the group, Hakeem mentioned it would be near sundown before we would make it. Thinking of what Rashid said about the next village had us on edge. Whether this village was friendly or not, we needed to be prepared. One concern I had was the Taliban soldiers and where they might be posted. I wanted to make up for lost time and get to the village before darkness fell.

Hours passed with minimal conversation between the men. Other than an occasional stop for water, all were keeping alert. Even King seemed undistracted by an occasional tree squirrel or bird fluttering past. The terrain quickly turned to shale rock, and the goat trails disappeared. Steep ridges started making the trek more difficult.

"Keep your eyes along those ridges," I ordered while navigating the uneven, loose shale terrain.

It was 1500 hours, and I was hoping to get to the foothills just beyond the next village tonight. We had another day to be in position for taking the GPS coordinates that needed to be radioed into base. Our rendezvous with Hakeem's guide was to take place in two nights.

We found a spot to rest under a large old pine tree near a rocky shale wall protecting us from any enemy eyes above. We sat on some random small boulders.

"Hakeem, do you remember what the surrounding terrain is around this village?" I asked while sitting down, reaching for my water.

"No. It has been many years and this was a direction we rarely traveled. I was only a young boy then," Hakeem said.

"Then this is what I think we'll do," I started explaining. "We'll scout the village, assess if this is still a simple farming village, and we should be able to make a determination just by what the villagers are doing. If we are lucky and it's just a farming village, we'll have Hakeem walk into the village alone, making him as visible as possible. Let whoever is there see he is unarmed and alone. We'll stake out our spots in a semi-circle around the village and stay well hidden."

"Are you sure this is a good plan?" Hakeem said looking at me with a concerned look to him.

"It will be fine. We'll have Ben in position, and if we see any threats we will take action. No harm will come to you," I reassured Hakeem, knowing of his extreme nervousness.

The others agreed, and we continued on our trek. The next few hours offered unrelenting terrain, making us work around steep shale hills and large boulders. Off in the distance, we spotted smoke twisting up out of the tree tops. The village was close. As we got closer, there was one more shale ridge before the village that gradually rose up fifteen feet, blocking our view. It appeared the village was just over that ridge.

"Tex and Big Joe, climb up that wall and get a look-see," I ordered.

We all watched as Tex and Big Joe scaled the shale wall, nearly losing their footing a few times. We took advantage of the time, looking for a out of site spot for our gear.

"Here," Antonio said in a soft voice, pointing towards a small crack just deep enough to stash the gear near the base of the shale ridge. It was a small cave-like recess with enough room for our gear.

We worked quickly, keeping an eye towards the top of the wall that was directly above us. Huddled together in the darkness that fell, we started getting apprehensive while waiting for Tex and Big Joe to return.

Complete darkness fell over us as we waited, a solid hour or so had passed when we finally heard them scaling back down a few feet from where they went up.

"Not good!" Tex reported. "No welcome wagon this time."

"We are going to have our hands full," Big Joe said. "It appears to be a Taliban training camp. From what we could tell, there are five Taliban soldiers, about eight or so new recruits. The recruits are getting ready to retire for the night."

"Perfect place for a training camp, I would say," Tex commented.

"This complicates matters!" I said, looking up towards the ridge, half expecting the Taliban soldiers to open fire on us any moment. "We will position ourselves near the huts where the recruits will be bedding down. Ben and Antonio will find the best vantage point for clean shots of the guards."

"Hooah!" Big Joe whispered to Tex.

"I would prefer waiting until daylight and working around the village," Hakeem interjected.

"No way," Big Joe said. "That will add too much to our timeline and delay us for the GPS reading tomorrow. This is a great opportunity to level this training camp. If we don't blow these assholes to shit, we will have them on our asses into the mountains."

"Sal, Hakeem, you hang back," I ordered, looking directly at Sal.

"No way! I want to be part of this," said Sal.

"Listen, Sal, you stay put, watch our gear and Hakeem. Plenty mileage on this mission. You'll get your chance." I reached under my jacket and handed Hakeem my 9MM pistol. Hakeem just looked down, staring at it as I shoved it into his hand.

"Keep this close, Hakeem, you might need it. You know how to use it?" I asked. "If not, Sal will show you."

We cautiously scaled up the shale wall, pausing for a moment when we reached the top. We could see the village was 80-90 meters straight ahead. We all put on our night vision binoculars as we knelt next to each other. The terrain between us and the village was level. There were three huts to the left and two on the right. Directly in the middle, a campfire was burning bright, flames lit up the darkness directly in front of the huts. We observed five Taliban guards gathered around the campfire, the recruits started filing into the small three huts on the left.

Ben nudged me. "Just behind the two huts, there's a small rise of shale about twenty feet above. That'll put me within forty meters with a full view of the campfire and the middle of the village."

"Let's wait, give them time to settle in for the evening," I said. "I'm sure we could expect two, maybe three of the guards to keep watch."

We waited for thirty minutes, finally convinced the recruits were all in for the evening.

"Tex, Big Joe, we will work our way around behind the three huts to the left where the recruits are," I said. "Tex, you position yourself behind the farthest hut, I will take the center one, and Big Joe will take the one on this end. Once Ben and Antonio are are in position and we see soldiers drop like bags of shit, move in and take out anything that moves. When we are satisfied the guards are dead, we'll move in on the soldier's huts. I want to make damn sure we take out those recruits. Chances are, they sleep with their weapons. If Ben takes out these five soldiers from his position, this should be like shooting assholes in a barrel. Everyone will move in on the remaining two huts. Ben and Antonio, hold your positions at that location until the job is done. Watch our backs, be our overseers. Understood?"

Everyone nodded. They were ready for action.

"Ben, are you able to take out those guards from that perspective? I see a few tree branches standing in your way," I said.

"Long as I have most of the target in my sites, should be no problem. Before they can blink, they'll be a grease spot," Ben said while looking through his high powered rifle scope at the five guards near the campfire.

"We'll give you time to get into place." I was looking at my watch. "I'll give you until 2200 hours, about 40 minutes. That should give everyone the time needed to get into position. At 2200, it's your show, Ben. Let's make sure our helmet mics are working properly, keep down the chatter. Now let's move," I ordered.

I took the lead while Tex and Big Joe stayed close behind. I glanced up to see that the moon was getting high enough to offer some filtered light. This made it much easier to navigate the rocky terrain and vegetation. We swung wide of the three huts, finding our spots just behind the structures. I peered around the right corner of the hut, spotting three of the five soldiers casually just standing in front of the fire with a smoke and some laughter. I estimated they were fifteen meters directly in front of me.

We waited for what seemed like hours. Looking over to Tex and Big Joe, I made eye contact, pointing to my watch I held up both hands. *10 minutes!*

Big Joe and Tex acknowledged with a tilt of their heads. They were ready.

I put my ear up against the side of the hut. It was quiet. I noticed where I stood there was a small crack opening in the side of the hut a few feet away. It looked like some rotted wood was missing, leaving a gap big enough to see inside. The bright light from the campfire came through the open front door and offered a low glow on the inside. I spotted little movement inside. The recruits' bodies lay in two perfect rows on each side of the hut. One of the recruits sleepily turned to his side.

I held up one hand to Tex and Big Joe. *Five minutes!*

Big Joe repositioned his weight and stepped on a small branch.

*Crack!* He froze. I held my breath, slowly looking around the corner of the hut towards the campfire...nothing.

Big Joe gestured with his hand, *A-OK.*

There was one minute left as we steadied ourselves, our adrenaline racing.

*Pop! Pop! Pop!*

Three pop noises in fast rapid succession could be heard from Ben's rifle. I saw one guard fall forward into the fire, his cigarette still in his hand. The other two guards had their heads blown off, dropping like a bag of rocks. A red mist filled the air over the campfire. The first guard's clothing caught on fire.

I was amazed at Ben's speed and accuracy. It startled me in the quiet of the night. The three soldiers were taken out clean and fast. *But where are the other two?* I wondered. I wasted no time signaling Tex and Big Joe with a quick wave of my arm. Both knew there was no need to knock on the front door. The huts were old and rotting, just a strong wind alone would be enough for them to fall over on their own.

The three of us walked meticulously along the side of the huts, firing with precision. The placement of the rounds ripped through the side of the frail old wood siding, bullets finding the warm flesh inside. Splinters of wood and bone flew in every direction. The recruits never had a chance. The loud gun noise echoed through the woods, eventually lost in the vegetation.

Complete silence was all that was heard as the hazy smoke from the rounds hung in the air.

I quickly looked back to the two huts across from us and saw one Taliban guard running full speed towards us with his rifle extended out in front of him, firing off rounds in our direction.

*POP!* could be heard from Ben's rifle with a clean shot to the head as the guard fell forward just outside the front door a few feet from me, blood shooting from his neck.

I was looking around for the fifth guard. I spotted Big Joe and Tex walking out of the two other huts. Empty. Two of the three dead Taliban soldiers were sprawled out near the fire. The third was engulfed in flames.

"Holy shit!" Big Joe said staring as the fire that engulfed the one Taliban soldier. "For once, I can honestly say that I have no appetite at the moment."

I lit up a smoke, motioning for Ben and Antonio to come down. But there was still the issue of the other guard we'd seen earlier, and I knew we were not safe yet.

Sal and Hakeem heard the gunfire off in the distance. Hakeem knew that Sal was feeling agitated and anxious. "Hakeem, you stay here!" he yelled at Hakeem. "I'm going to the top of the ridge, take a look-see."

"But Mike said to stay put!" Hakeem pleaded, feeling uneasy.

"Here." Sal seemed to ignore the tone in Hakeem's voice. "Hold onto King and keep him here with you. I'll be back before you know it."

Hakeem stood frozen, looking around in the darkness near the small opening of the shale rock. Moments passed in silent agony. He held onto King's leash, but suddenly the big dog leaped and pulled away from Hakeem's grip.

"King!" Hakeem whispered. But the dog was gone. Hakeem huddled in silence, listening intently to the night. He thought he heard distant pops coming from the village, but he wasn't sure.

Sal scaled the fifteen foot shale rise to the top. He spotted the glow of the campfire in the village off in the distance. Pulling out his night vision binoculars, he scanned through the trees. Too much obstruction. *Damn*, he thought to himself. He had his rifle slung over his right shoulder and walked slowly in the complete darkness, listening for some sign from the men.

Out of nowhere, he heard a snap of a twig to his right. Sal swung around, dropping his night vision binoculars to the ground, fumbling for his rifle, but it was too late. There in front of him was the fifth Taliban guard standing just a few feet away. He saw a bright flash from the rifle.

Sal lost his balance, stumbling backwards as he grabbed at his hip, feeling the burn of the shot. With his adrenaline high, it was as if there was no pain—just the warmth of his blood running down his right leg.

Out of the darkness, a dark silhouette appeared in Sal's peripheral on his right. It was King! Out of nowhere, Sal saw King airborne, baring his teeth as he attacked the shadow of the man that shot him.

*Bang!*

Another shot rang out loud from the Taliban guard missing its target. A loud agonizing scream could be heard from the Taliban guard as King with full biting force tore into his left forearm. Sal lay on the ground fumbling around looking for his rifle in the rocks and weeds like a blind man...no luck. Sal crawling away from where he was shot was disoriented using all his strength he dragged himself by his elbows crawling away from the Taliban guard as he tumbled down a steep 20 foot ravine.

*Bang!* Another shot fired, and a loud howl of anguish could be heard.

King was hit! Feeling light-headed from the loss of blood, Sal re-positioned himself looking out from the bottom of the dark hole, all that could be heard was King in the black of the night yelping as he ran into the woods. Sal lay there motionless, not knowing if the Taliban soldier was still alive. Listening to the deafness of the night, he could hear movement; it was the Taliban soldier down below in the direction of Hakeem. Sal lay in pain in the deep ravine looking up through the treetops at the brilliant bright stars above before passing out.

Now Hakeem knew he'd heard gunshots. Trying to make himself as small as possible, he squeezed sideways into the recess of the shale wall next to the equipment. Breathing heavily, he heard movement just a few feet away. Then silence. Some shuffling of footsteps. Then silence.

His heart was racing. Hakeem was afraid that his pounding heart could be heard from feet away. Suddenly, he heard loose rocks as if someone was walking. Standing there in the darkness not more than an arm's reach in front of him, he saw the dark silhouette of a man: a Taliban soldier.

*I'm sure he will see me!* Hakeem thought, heart pounding.

Suddenly, he remembered the pistol Mike had given him. Trying not to be noticed, he found the pistol in his waistband. Would he be able to remove the pistol and get the drop on him? Hakeem froze.

The guard vanished before Hakeem had time to react, and he remained motionless. With all the shots heard, a fear set in. Was he alone?

All that was heard in the quiet darkness of the night was the yelping of King in a high pitched yelp-bark, sounding as if he was miles away.

# CHAPTER 3
# THE PRIVATE INVESTIGATOR

A few weeks had passed since Asa's disappearance. It was now October 14th. Words couldn't truly describe how awful it had been for both Rachel and Farrin. Farrin watched with love and concern as Rachel began diving into more deep depression than ever before. Since Jamil went missing several years ago, Rachel had just started to come out of her depression by taking up painting. Now with Asa's abduction, her world had been turned upside down...again.

Farrin watched her deteriorate, trying hard not to cave into the darkness himself. He knew he must be strong for Rachel's sake. At least for now. Farrin had suggested a trip back to Minnesota. Maybe a family visit would do her good. After days of coaxing her to go, she finally relented. Her older sister lived just outside Minneapolis with her husband and three children.

Rachel had agreed with little resistance.

On the day of her departure, the sun shone brightly through the kitchen windows. Farrin was preparing breakfast. Rachel was upstairs getting ready for the trip. For a moment it seemed like such a normal morning if it hadn't been for the nightmare of losing two children.

"Rachel, breakfast is ready," Farrin called out, trying hard to sound fine. No reply, Farrin grabbed the plates full of food and headed upstairs. Maybe it would be better to just eat there anyway while Rachel finished packing.

He headed upstairs, passing the library on the left with all her painting materials. The window shades in the library were pulled down, blocking out the bright sunlight. Rachel had stacked several blank framed canvases of all sizes directly in front of the secret passageway where Asa was abducted. Farrin had scheduled the tunnel to be collapsed once and for all. It seemed all in vain with both the boys missing. The house seemed cold and dark to the both of them.

The door to the their bedroom was slightly open. Farrin tapped gently before entering the room. He noticed Rachel's clothes stacked on the bed; her suitcase sat on the floor, still empty.

It was then Farrin heard sobbing coming from the master bathroom. Pushing open the bathroom door, he saw Rachel sitting on the edge of the jacuzzi bathtub, leaning forward with her head in her hands. She was wearing just her black bra and underwear.

"Rachel, we need to get moving," Farrin said. He sat the plates on the bathroom vanity. It took all he had to stay strong, to keep as positive as possible. Rachel being gone in Minnesota would leave him alone, but he dismissed that thought. Farrin mustered his strength and looked at his watch.

"I feel so incapacitated. It's just not like me," Rachel mumbled as she picked up the suitcase and slowly set it on the bed. "I can't even decide on what to wear. I mean, what the hell is the weather in Minnesota in October anyway? It's been so long."

Farrin held Rachel, the emptiness they both felt was excruciating. Looking at the stack of jeans, sweaters, and shoes Farrin couldn't imagine all that fitting in her suitcase.

"I have something to tell you," Farrin paused. "I don't want to give you any false hope, but I have an appointment later today with a private investigator. I'm meeting with him to discuss what we can do to find our boys."

Rachel began sobbing again. "I really hope this time we can get some news. *Any* news would be a blessing. First Jamil, now Asa..." Her voice trailed off, and she sat down and started picking at her eggs and fruit. *At least she is eating something*, Farrin thought with relief.

Together they packed the last of her clothes, Farrin loaded her suitcase into the backseat of the MG, waited as she dressed. With the top down they headed for the Kabul airport. Rachel was wearing her dark sunglasses with a floppy brimmed sun hat. She'd become even more paranoid than ever about her safety as an American since Asa's disappearance.

They didn't talk much on the drive. Farrin's mind was consumed with thoughts of their boys, wondering what the odds of finding them were. He was curious and anxious to talk with the private investigator after the airport. *Are my boys still alive?* his heart sank.

With Rachel in Minnesota for a few weeks, Farrin would have the time to focus on the search for the boys, taking some time off from the hospital. The private investigator was from Peshawar, Pakistan, he came highly recommended by a fellow physician who had commented that he was the best around at finding missing persons. After Jamil went missing, they were naive—blaming their loss on the hazards of having children so nearby the fighting outbreaks.

*But something deeper must be going on,* Farrin thought. *Why would two of our children go missing? It doesn't add up.*

The Kabul airport over the last year had picked up in business with civilian and military travelers, and more flights were coming in to the airport. Pulling up to the curb near her airline departure gate, Farrin parked the car. The airport was a one-level structure with most windows boarded or bricked shut, with the exception on the tarmac side. Farrin was the most concerned for Rachel's safety at the take off, because the Taliban took random shots from the surrounding foothills at commercial flights almost daily.

Farrin observed the faces as they passed through the checkpoints. Most the guards they passed were involved in conversation as they methodically scanned the suitcases, checking passports. Farrin looked at his watch; they had minutes to make it to the gate.

The plane sat on the tarmac with the engines already turning in a high pitch. Reaching the door of the airport that lead outside to the plane, they held each other tight.

"God, I hate to leave you. You're my strength!" she said. "Bad enough the boys are missing, but now leaving you?" Rachel looked down, fighting back her emotions.

Rachel gave Farrin one last kiss, quickly grabbed the handle of the roller suitcase, and headed for the plane.

"I love you," she said weakly, looking back at him with an almost childlike kind of sadness. It again made Farrin feel sick, because the woman he had married had been strong and capable of enduring so much. Reaching out Farrin grabbed Rachel by the hand, pulling her back in to him as he held her tight one more time. He didn't want to let her go. Ever. But he knew he had to.

"I love you. Please call me when you touchdown. I won't sleep until I know you have touched down safely," Farrin instructed. "I will do all I can to find our boys."

Farrin watched as Rachel walked the remaining 50 feet to the rolling steps of the planes entrance. He stood there watching, his heart aching for her, for the two of them.

As Rachel boarded the plane, he noticed how beautiful she was, standing in the sun outside the plane as her floppy sun hat was jostled in the slight breeze. She was wearing a pair of tight jeans, a burnt orange turtleneck sweater, and a black leather jacket. She gave a final wave as she disappeared into the plane.

That image of her would stay in Farrin's memory until he saw her again. Since meeting Rachel years ago, they have never been apart much longer than a day.

*I will find our boys*, he promised her silently. *If it's the last thing I do, I will find them. And everything will be okay. We will make our love last, we will fight for our family no matter what.*

The meeting with the private investigator was set up ahead of time at a Pakistani coffee shop near the hospital. His name was Abdul Rehman, and his fees were steep, but the money was of no concern to Farrin. He wanted his boys back home where they belonged. At this point, all Farrin knew was the investigator came highly recommended, and he was desperate for someone to help with the search.

Farrin parked the car just outside the small coffee shop and sat down at a table on the patio. The coffee shop was without glass in the window openings due to years of bombings, and the inside was small and cramped—but it was a haven to the locals who enjoyed the intimate relationship with the brown beaten coffee, called soft coffee, that Pakistanis created as an art form.

Grabbing *The New York Times*, Farrin wanted to get caught up on politics and his investments he'd made over the years. From where he sat, the smell of various foods cooked along the street mingled in with aroma of the rich, dark Pakistani coffee.

Farrin thought about the odds that both his boys had gone missing. *When Jamil had disappeared years ago, we could only conclude it was the war. We tried to accept that loss. Now that Asa went missing, it just seems odd, too coincidental.*

Looking over the top of his paper, Farrin spotted a heavy set man headed his way. It must be the investigator. Abdul was a short, portly man who looked as if he was stuffed into a suit two sizes too small. He wore dark sunglasses. Farrin stood to greet Abdul, who offered Farrin a customary handshake with a meaty right hand.

As they stood shaking hands, Farrin noticed sweat beading up on his face and bald head. Before sitting down, Abdul pulled out a wadded handkerchief and mopped his face and head, shoving the handkerchief back into the inside left pocket of his suit.

"Hello, sir. So good to have made your acquaintance," Abdul expressed with a wide grin, a stogie dangling from his lip as he spoke.

"Yes," Farrin responded curtly, pointing to the chair across from him at the table while ordering water with mint for the both of them. The man's sloppy appearance made him a little worried. Abdul adjusted the wooden chair back a few feet to squeeze in behind the table; his girth alone tested the buttons on his shirt looking as if they were ready to pop at any moment.

"I see we are both Pakistani by birth? What neighborhood do you call home?" Abdul asked. The waiter returned with the cold glasses of water, the mint clinging to the ice cubes.

"The neighborhood I am from in Peshawar is called Faqeerabad," Farrin said while taking a sip of his drink. "It used to be a beautiful neighborhood, but with the influx of many displaced Afghans it has, well, you could say, it's a bit like the old Peshawar community."

"Our mutual friend, Dr. Murzed, mentioned you still have family in Pakistan. Is that true?" Abdul asked inquisitively.

"That is true," Farrin nodded. "My mother and father raised our family there most our lives. I went off to medical school in Britain and returned when my father's health started to deteriorate. I relocated here to finish my schooling in Kabul, and I was eventually hired on at the Kabul hospital, where I am now chief of staff. I met my wife Rachel here purely by chance. She was a volunteer for the Red Cross. I do return home on occasion to visit my mother. Another family member is taking care of her."

Abdul went silent for a few moments, and Farrin let him remain quiet. He himself was too tired to drive the conversation. After a few moments, Abdul cut straight to the point. "You say you have two sons that have gone missing?"

"Yes, Jamil and Asa," Farrin felt like a man living in a movie, describing something that could never happen in real life. "Jamil was taken almost three years ago, and now our youngest son, nine years of age, went missing just a few weeks ago."

"This is such a painful time as a parent." Abdul reached in his pocket pulling out a small notepad and pen. "May I take some notes?" he asked.

Farrin agreed as he started telling Abdul in detail of when and how the boys went missing. Farrin explained after Jamil how they contacted the local police, putting up as many posters around Kabul as possible, and many volunteers had helped for months. They had assumed that Jamil must've been injured or went missing in some way due to the war or scuffles that were constant.

Abdul kept taking notes, taking a moment to pause and sip the water. At first impression, Farrin had been concerned this was a man who was sloppy and unorganized, but now he seemed very detailed.

It wasn't until after a good half hour of Farrin talking that Abdul asked a question. "Have you heard of a bacha bazi boy?" he asked, looking directly into the eyes of Farrin while tapping his pen on the table.

"Bacha bazi boy?" Farrin responded. "Well, no." Abdul seemed somewhat surprised, but went on to explain of the tradition, especially how common but hidden this activity had been since ancient times. "That being said, it is considered a crime if men involved were caught participating," he concluded.

"Surely this isn't true?" Farrin sat in shock. A surreal feeling washed over Farrin, and he suddenly felt nauseated. "Wouldn't the authorities shut it down? The police?"

"Unfortunately, the police in many areas are part of the activity protecting those involved. The boys," Abdul continued, "are intended for sexual pleasure supplied to powerful rich men."

Farrin sat speechless.

"Sir, are you okay?" Abdul questioned. "I'm sorry you have to hear this from me this way. But, I think I may be of assistance. I have a few associates that have connections with those close to this activity. As a matter of fact, most of the young boys that go missing are subject to this unfortunate tradition. Have you ever been approached by any strange man discussing your children?"

Farrin was trying to get his head around what he just heard before answering. "No," he said in disgust. How would Rachel handle this news? He would have to keep it from her, at least for now.

"Have you ever had any dealings with the Taliban?" Abdul asked.

"Yes," Farrin nodded. "For some years, I was forced to perform life-saving surgeries for the Taliban at the hospital in Kabul. Until the Americans came to rid them of their power, allowing me back to my duties at the hospital."

Abdul looked at him, and Farrin could see him pondering. "I would say this Farrin, because of your status and money, truth be told, whoever took your sons probably did so because they knew they came from comfort and affluence. Most the locals here have reluctantly surrendered their children purely as a way to feed the rest of the family. It's like cutting off a hand to save the limb.

"How much?" Farrin asked. He couldn't stand anymore horrible news. "How much money do you need? I would like to retain you, and I want my boys found."

"Usually," Abdul started, "I ask for $400 American per hour. But since you've been recommended by a friend and since you are in the plight you're currently in, I'll only charge you $300 an hour, plus mileage and expenses. And, if it's easier for you, I also accept the same amount in other currencies as well."

Farrin nodded, relieved. "The cost doesn't matter. Whatever you need, whatever is necessary."

Abdul suddenly leaned forward, grabbed Farrin by the left arm and seemed to stare right through him. "My son was taken from me the same way, sir. It is not as uncommon as you'd think here in this miserable area. I searched many long years, and I found him. I want you to know this and understand I will do all in my power to get your boys back. These sick animals have to be stopped. If I had my way, I would line them up and behead the lot of them. My experience and contacts are far reaching. Go home tonight, sir, and know I will not rest till we have your boys home."

With his head spinning, Farrin somehow managed to shake Abdul's hand and instructed him to stop by tomorrow for his retainer funds. He watched as this frumpy man disappeared into the crowd.

Farrin sat back down. Dark thoughts swirled through his head, and he had a sudden overwhelming sense of urgency, a sickening feeling in his stomach. *What if? What if my boys are being used in such intolerable ways?* Rachel could not know what was going on, at least not now. It would destroy her fragile mental state, he knew.

It might very well even destroy him.

# CHAPTER 4
# ART OF DANCE

Asa struggled to sit up, rubbing his eyes he started to regain some blurred vision. Distorted images danced in front of his eyes, voices echoed in his ears. Moving his head around, he tried to recognize his surroundings. *Where am I?* He felt confused, more confused than ever before.

The images in front of him appeared watery in appearance as he tried to shake off the drug. Two men's faces started taking shape just outside the cage in front of him. Both were staring down at him. The smell of sweet incense in the room made Asa feel nauseous.

*Could it be?* Asa squinted while looking at the faces. The one man's face Asa did recognize; it was the zebra bearded man he saw in the tunnel. The other man's face was kind in appearance with a gentle smile that was in contrast to Zebra Beard, as Asa now named him in his mind. The other man spoke in a soft, melodic voice in Pashto to Zebra Beard. His voice soothed Asa.

Reaching up, Asa felt a large bump on the top his head. Looking around he realized he was in a cage: a steel box with several circle-shaped openings large enough for a hand to fit through. The cramped box allowed Asa only enough room to kneel. Above the cage was a small dirty window offering a sliver of light that illuminated the twisting spirals of incense smoke.

Asa could see he was naked except for a colorful pair of crocheted shorts in red, yellow, and green patterns. While his head began to clear, the fear set in. He struggled with his thoughts, trying to remember what events took place leading up to being a captive, being caged like a dog;

he couldn't remember a thing. Looking out across the room beyond the cage he could see that the room was narrow in width. The cage was on one end of a long room, and the other side trailed off into darkness.

"You! Wake up!" Zebra Beard ordered. He hit the side of the metal cage with a piece of wood.

Startled, Asa jumped from a loud deafening metallic noise that made his ears ring in pain. Asa recognized the bamboo stick held in his right hand as a rattan used for punishment. Pushing tight up against the back of the cage, Asa tried to put as much distance between himself and Zebra Beard as possible. Zebra Beard stood towering over the cage with menacing eyes.

Zebra Beard reached down, unlocking the latch to get Asa out. Pressing back tight against the steel cage, Asa tried to avoid his reach. With the rattan in his right hand, the man hit Asa's feet hard with a loud *snap!*, striking the soft skin on the bottom of Asa's feet. Shooting pain ran through his legs. Asa screamed out loud, trying to fight back the tears.

Both men reached in, grabbing Asa by his feet and started tugging on him. Asa grabbed onto the holes in the back of the cage with both hands, kicking and fighting the two men. The strength of the men caused Asa to be suspended in the air momentarily, but he lost his grip as the men quickly dragged him out onto the dirty floor.

*Snap!* Another strike of the rattan bore into his left side, nearly making him pass out. It took everything inside of him to maintain defiant. Curled up outside the cage, shivering, his side burning from the rattan strike, he heard the kind-faced man scolding Zebra Beard while standing between them.

Speaking in Pashto to Zebra Beard, the other man was pointing to the door. "Leave, leave now!"

Reluctantly, Zebra Beard turned away and stormed towards the door, stopping as he pointed to the kind faced man with his left arm extended, rattan in hand.

"You better train this one to perfection!" he yelled. "This is the one boy I'm counting on to bring in a high bid with my customers." He walked away into the darkness, as he left the building. Asa could no longer see where he'd gone.

The kind-faced man then turned towards Asa with a slight smile, helping him on to a overstuffed gold colored floor cushion next to the cage handing Asa a small cup of water. The man kneeled in front of Asa, putting his right hand on his shoulder. He watched as Asa gulped down the water.

"What is your name?" he asked.

Asa just stared at him, still feeling the burning pain of the rattan on his body. His head was groggy.

"My name is Iffy," the man said, asking again. "What is your name?"

Still, Asa remained silent. He was finally getting a good look at this stranger. Iffy was clean shaven with short black hair parted to one side, neatly dressed with gold rings on all fingers. He wore a embroidered white silk shirt with navy pants and old worn out dress shoes. He reminded Asa of the entertainers you see on TV.

"Do you not have a name?" Iffy asked again with a smile.

Asa finally mustered the energy to speak. "My name is Asa," he said in a whisper, barely getting it out.

"Well, hello, Asa. You are a very bright boy. Dastgir has mentioned your special talents to me."

"Dastgir? You mean the man that brought me here?"

"Yes, that is correct."

"Why did he? I need to go home. My mother and father will be upset and worried.

Where am I?"

"You are far from home. Now, you will be my student."

"Student?" Asa asked, confused.

"Yes. I am so sorry, but you will not be going home. Not for a very long time."

Asa felt a sudden pain in his heart. This pain he felt in his heart was stronger then the welts on his feet, the burning of his side. Asa wanted to go home. Asa stared at the floor, his tears dropped to the floor, mixing in with the dirt.

Iffy begin to pat his head. "You will be fine. I will watch over you. Dastgir is a very angry man, and you must not agitate him."

"What is it I will be schooled in?" Asa asked as Iffy started to pace back and forth in front of him.

"You have been brought here for training to perform for successful men. If you listen to me and remember what I say, you will be treated very well. Maybe you will see home someday."

"But how long will this take? What is expected of me to make it home?" Asa asked, rubbing his side.

"The schooling will last weeks. We must have you ready as soon as possible. You are a beautiful boy and will be admired very much. This will be your home for awhile."

It was then Iffy took Asa by the hand, lifting him off the cushion. Asa winced in pain while getting up.

"Come with me. I must show you something."

Still holding his hand, Iffy walked the distance of the room to the other side—75 feet or so. The floor where they stood was uneven, rough cement that gave way to a smooth shiny marble surface.

Iffy switched on a light. High above them was a beautiful chandelier that illuminated brightly. The marble floor felt cool on Asa's feet, taking away some of the burning. The marble floor area was as wide as the room: about 30 feet. The side of the room where the caged box sat was stark white, plain with peeling paint. A few threadbare rugs covered the dirty cement. This side, in contrast, was decorated with velvet burgundy curtains on the side walls that draped from ceiling to floor. The marble floor was clean and shiny. A piano sat in the left corner against the back wall. On each side of the room against the walls were colorful floor pillows and cushioned benches. Scattered in between the seating were small tables with unlit candles.

"This is where you will be trained to perform," Iffy said. "I will teach you here."

At that moment, Asa noticed the curtain move behind the piano. A gap in the curtain allowed for him to see someone peeking through from a back room. Then the mysterious person disappeared into the folds.

"I'm sorry, but you will have to sleep in the cage for a few nights until we know you can be trusted," Iffy was saying. "You behave and you will get privileges. Understand?"

Asa did all he could to muster a nod, feeling like he had just entered hell. Later that night Asa lay awake in the small cramped box

122

most of the night in pain. Iffy had provided him with a blanket and pillow. His side swelled up from the strike of the rattan, leaving a large bruise.

The night seemed it would never end. The room was stuffy, and Asa was nauseated from the sickly incense smell that hung in the air. The cage was locked, leaving him no option but to relieve himself in the cage—so he ended up laying in his own urine.

Asa prayed to God that this nightmare would soon be over. He wept. He knew he was so far from his family and friends, but he also knew he must be strong, otherwise he would never make it home. Hours went by until Asa noticed the pale light of early morning coming through the small window.

*I will work hard,* he promised himself. *I will try to be good and learn what I need to learn very quickly, because maybe I will see home again.*

Iffy was in early that morning to get started. Although he was exhausted, Asa was relieved to get out and stretch his legs.

"We must bathe you," said Iffy. "Come with me. After your bath, you will eat, and then we must begin working on your dance."

Iffy wore a traditional white thobe—a shirt and robe outfit with a black vest and sandals. Taking Asa by the hand, they walked to the other side of the room. Behind the piano there was a curtain, Iffy pushed the curtain aside so that it revealed a small room about 10 feet deep and 20 feet wide.

There was a small kitchen table against the wall in the center. Shelving above the cooking stove held various food items, and a small ice box sat under the sink against the right wall of the room. There was a small window above the kitchen sink that allowed some filtered light through the greasy glass panes, and one flickering light bulb dangled by two wires from the ceiling in the center of the room. The other end of the back room had some clothing and instruments hanging from bent nails.

Asa noticed two boys laying on the floor about his age with only a few blankets for comfort. Iffy barked an order as the two boys quickly began setting up a washbasin. By looking at them, Asa could see that their bodies were covered in bruises and welts. The smaller boy was without his right eye and had a large scar that ran from his right eye to his ear. The other boy had a twisted back and was hunched over, walking with a limp. Both avoided eye contact with Asa.

"This is Rachim," Iffy pointed to the boy with no right eye. "The other is Zaahid. You are not to talk to them. They work here with me and are only to speak when spoken to."

Asa stood watching the boys scurrying about. Rachim filled the water basin that was set up in the middle of the room. Zaahid was preparing a big bowl of rice and fruit for breakfast.

A variety of musical instruments hung along the wall of the small room: a dutar—an Afghan two stringed musical instrument—tambourines, bells of all sizes and a wazh, an ancient harp. The walls were painted halfway up in a bright yellow that feathered in with a old pea green color on the upper half to the ceiling. Hooks ran along the other wall, holding shiny colorful outfits and scarves. A small bench underneath the outfits gave the impression of a backstage changing room.

As Asa stepped into the water basin, the frigid cold water made Asa wrap his arms around his chest for warmth. Rachim used an old rag and washed Asa quickly and efficiently as if he had done this a thousand times before. He was careful and gentle around the bruises on Asa. Zaahid wrapped a towel around Asa as he stepped out of the water handing him a new set of clothes: a light brown tunic with matching trousers. They were completely silent as they worked.

For breakfast, they all ate the prepared food with no words spoken. With each mouthful of food, Asa could feel his strength return. Asa avoided looking at Rachim and Zaahid. He didn't want the two boys to get uncomfortable with his presence. The clothes they wore were dirty with small holes visible, and Asa wondered how long they had been held here. Asa thought of the homeless boys he'd often seen on the streets near home in Kabul, and he wondered if this was a better life than that on the streets.

"Come with me," Iffy stood, pushing away from the table and grabbing a dutar as they headed to sit near the piano. Stepping through the curtain, Asa made eye contact with Zaahid—and Zaahid displayed a crooked smile before Asa slipped through the curtain.

Iffy pointed for Asa to sit on a floor pillow next to the piano. He switched on the chandelier as he sat facing Asa, their knees almost touching.

"Have you danced or sang before?" Iffy asked while tuning his dutar.

"No," Asa responded. "My brother and I have sang to the radio. American music."

"Do you not know of the music heritage where you are from?"

Asa paused. "Our father plays Pakistani music in his car often."

"This is good," Iffy said, smiling. "I hear your father is a gifted doctor in Kabul. Is this true?" Iffy stopped, tuning the dutar to wait for Asa to answer.

Asa went quiet for a moment. With grief and homesickness in his heart, Asa managed a soft, "Yes."

The dutar was made from beautiful dark wood along the neck and body. White pearl shell was inlaid along the center of the fret area, and gold patterns could be seen in the dark wood that sparkled in the pale light. Iffy began to play, and the sound was spellbinding. He then set the dutar in a stand next to the piano. Standing up, he started to dance.

"Now watch, Asa," he instructed as he floated around the room with arms and legs moving in synchronized rhythm. It was as if he was dancing on air across the room.

"Now, here, you try. I will show you." Standing in front of Asa, Iffy begin to adjust his feet and arms to position. Iffy moved, holding Asa's hands and going through some dance steps.

"Leg up, leg down, this arm up, while this one extends. Now spin!" he instructed. "Repeat the sequence."

Asa did as he was instructed. It felt natural to him. He'd always been smart, and when he set his mind to something, he always succeeded.

Iffy sat and began playing the dutar, watching as Asa kept repeating the steps. "Excellent, excellent. Now keep to the rhythm of the music."

They spent the whole day working on dance moves. Iffy seemed pleased and provided Asa with extra fruit, which made Asa happy; even basic necessities seemed the most rewarding at this moment.

Asa worked on establishing trust with Iffy. If all Asa needed to do is simply perform for businessmen in order to get home, as Iffy said, he was ready to do so.

It was late in the day while they went over the dancing routines until Asa danced with perfection. Iffy, playing the piano, watched as Asa danced around the marble floor. His playing stopped when he heard the door open. Looking towards the other end of the long room, Asa spotted Zebra Beard—or Dastgir, as Iffy had called him.

Asa stopped dancing, feeling afraid. Dastgir stormed in and called out to Iffy to come to him in English. Iffy followed him to the opposite side of the large room. Asa could overhear their muffled voices, but he could not hear the exact words. At times Dastgir sounded angry.

Then both Iffy and Dastgir walked over to Asa and stood in front of him for what seemed several minutes. Asa looked at the marble floor pattern and used the sleeve of his tunic to wipe the sweat from his eyes. Iffy knelt down in front of Asa and barked an order to dance.

"Dastgir wants to see the progress," he said.

With his body sore and feeling the fatigued, Asa knew he had to please Dastgir. Getting home was his motivation. Asa would never expose his weakness. He must stay strong. Iffy commanded Zaahid and Rachim to sit, and Iffy began playing the dutar. Asa stumbled while getting up, took his position, then started in dancing.

Asa commanded his weak body with all he could to dance flawlessly. Dastgir, who now sat on a pillow against the opposite wall, began to clap to the music. That was the first time Asa saw what appeared to be a smile crawl across his face. Asa avoided eye contact, focusing on the moves. This went on for nearly 15 minutes.

Finally, Dastgir told Asa to stop. Asa stood there, breathing heavily. Dastgir ordered Rachim to bring water and fruit for for the both of them, and then he pulled out a small flask made of expensive ornate silver. He took a long sip, watching Asa.

"Come over here Asa, let us talk," he said. Asa hesitated. "Come now, don't be afraid." He patted the cushion in front of him.

Asa sat down on the cushion facing Dastgir, but he felt petrified. Dastgir leaned forward, wiping the sweat from Asa's face with his hand. He ran his hand through his sweaty hair, making Asa feel uneasy.

"I want to tell that I wish not to hurt you anymore. You are a beautiful boy, and you have done well today. I see that you will do excellently as one of my boys. You promise me that you will listen to Iffy, learn quickly, and I will take care of you." He paused, looking at Asa as he took another sip from the flask. "Maybe you will make it home someday if you do as your told. But, if you do not cooperate, I will have to punish you. You remember that pain don't you?"

"Yes," Asa responded with a lump in his throat. He knew he meant it. "I will be good and do my best to learn to dance. I will be ready."

"Now go, be a good boy, and work hard for Iffy." Dastgir stroked his hand over Asa's cheek as he got up. Dastgir motioned for Iffy to follow him out while putting his arm around Iffy's shoulder, smiling and walking towards the door.

Days passed while Iffy pressed Asa from morning till evening. The training was intense. He went so far as to set up small board steps at various heights to have Asa jump and kick to gain height over the hurdles.

Asa grew in strength and confidence. At the end of the day one evening, Iffy had Zaahid, Rachim, and Asa sit in front of the piano as he performed beautifully. Asa looked over and noticed Iffy seemed more relaxed tonight with Dastgir away on business. Tonight he was drinking, seemingly merry and at ease. But the other two boys seemed nervous with his drinking.

Asa sat between the other boys. He wanted to get to know the story of Rachim and Zaheed. *Do they have families? How long have they been here? Maybe they have some answers of how long the boys are held here and when they get to go home.* His thoughts took him back home missing his mother and father, wondering if they were looking for him.

Asa noticed Rachim falling asleep out of the corner of his eye. Suddenly, Iffy spotted Rachim nodding off, and in a fit of rage came around the piano and slapped Rachim hard, causing a nosebleed. Iffy grabbed both the boys by their arms and dragged them to the back room as they screamed out.

Asa sat in horror, not knowing what to do.

"Please stop!" Rachim and Zaahid cried. Asa could hear the snap of the rattan against their bodies. Asa cringed with each strike. He decided to go to the cage, closing the small metal door behind him, covering his ears. Finally, all went quiet as Asa fell asleep from exhaustion.

It was the middle of the night when Asa heard a voice, a boy's voice. Asa, thinking he was dreaming, woke to see Rachim sitting outside the cage. Nervously looking around the room, Asa was worried Iffy would catch them, punishing them both.

"He is gone," Rachim said, staring at Asa with his fingers poking through the small opening of the cage. Asa sat up, suddenly wide awake and curious to what was happening. His mind started racing with the opportunity of talking with Rachim and getting some answers.

"Where am I?" Asa whispered.

"You are in Jalalabad to be exact," he said in Pashto.

"Have you been here long?" Asa asked Rachim.

"Zaahid and I have been in this room for a very long time. We are locked in, captives. I have not felt the warm sun or cool rain on my face in over a year. Many boys have come and gone with their training. We have hoped that one of them would help in aiding in our escape." Rachim spoke with hopelessness in his voice.

Listening to Rachim, all Asa could do was think of his own plight. "Have you tried to leave, find a way to escape?" Asa asked, leaning against the back of the cage.

"There is a small window above the sink area. With our physical challenges and height, only one of us would be able to pass through the window to freedom. This would leave the other behind to face severe punishment or death. With a third helper to assist us, we could have our freedom together. I only ask that you consider this," Rachim pleaded.

Before Asa could respond, Rachim disappeared into the darkness of the room. Asa's mind was racing. He wanted to help, but what would be the risk for him? He had to be good, and if he was good, then maybe he would see home again. Struggling with knowing what to do, Asa drifted off to sleep.

He dreamed of home.

# CHAPTER 5
# THE ART OF ENTERTAINMENT

The name *Hindu Kush* means "Kills the Hindu," a stark reminder of the days when Indian slaves from the Indian subcontinent died in the harsh weather typical of the Afghan mountains while being transported to Central Asia. The mountain range runs approximately 370 miles of a the 500-mile stretch, the rest consisting of smaller mountain ranges. The range diminishes in height as it heads westward near Kabul, from a height of 19,700 feet to 14,800 feet.

The naturally-formed caves took thousands of years to develop, and they gave the locals organic, carved out living spaces in the rock openings. During the Soviet-Afghan War in the late 1970s and 80s, the displaced locals flocked to the caves for shelter. But it wasn't until after the September 11th attacks in 2001 that the American war in Afghanistan pushed back Al-Qaeda and the Taliban to retreat to the mountains.

It was then that the Taliban took over the caves, forcing out the displaced citizens. With many comforts added, the caves became a refuge and a strategic defensive location for the Taliban and Al-Qaeda. The caves offered protection from the American bunker-buster bombs that fell from above with deadly frequency.

This stretch of mountains was where Dastgir brought the boys for entertainment, far from the city. This secluded, elaborate cave system was his favorite, a most important piece of his lucrative business.

The entire length of the cave system where Dastgir ran his business ran east to west, approximately 400 yards long by 200 yards in width. On the east end of the cave, the ceiling tapered down to the floor with a small opening in the center, offering an access point into the cave only big enough to crawl through. This entrance was snow covered during the winter for months.

The main entrance was on the north facing side of the mountain, offering a narrow opening six feet in height by four feet in width, well hidden from the outside. The ceiling from the east end's lowest point slowly gained height, towering up to the highest point of 50 feet on forward to the far west end.

Once inside the main entrance, there was a rock ledge walkway to the right, jagged and uneven the walkway was approximately five feet wide that followed the entire right side of the cave. The rock ledge walkway rounded at its edge, sloping down gradually twenty feet to a clear turquoise blue lake that filled the entire lower center portion of the cave. The cave lake fed by the mountain snow melt, would vary in depth from ten feet during summer months to just a few feet over the winter. Generators hummed off in the distance across the lake for lighting and heat.

The rock ledge walkway ran 300 yards with random openings to the dens. There were eleven dens in total, varying in size and purpose. The main big den was next to the main entrance where the boys would entertain, and three smaller dens followed—used by the men with the boys. The remaining seven smaller dens ran along the walkway sporadically towards the west end is where the boys and guests would sleep.

The entire cave structure, able to hold a small army of men, was used only by the top Taliban and Al-Qaeda leaders and their armies. Most of the powerful businessmen and corrupt police from the area visited regularly.

The Taliban leaders, corrupt businessmen, and police had use of two helicopters when transportation was unavailable—specifically Russian Mi-24 attack units with room for eight passengers that only took thirty minutes to arrive from Jalalabad. Just outside the cave a landing zone sat 40 feet from the entrance to the cave. Climbing up the mountains to the caves by foot could take days, depending on the time of year and weather conditions. It was now late October, so winter storms could be intense above 14,000 feet.

These rich, powerful men were Dastgir's best customers; men always looking to be entertained and seduced by the boys. This was their pastime, and they are always willing to offer much money for his product.

That was why Dastgir was consumed with excitement for Asa—anxious to see what offer he would soon receive for him. It took months from the time he spotted Asa to the abduction. Because his parents had been well off, he knew he couldn't just buy the boy from them, unlike the rest of the families he had dealings with. So he devised the abduction. He knew of the secret passage to the house, having visited one of the prior owners. Dastgir knew it would be just a matter of time until he was able to capture the boy.

Now, finally, the time had come for Asa to be brought to the cave. Dastgir was pleased tonight. *Tomorrow, I will fly back to Jalalabad and get Asa to bring him to the caves*, he thought in triumph. *And he will sell for much money!*

For now, though, he would enjoy tonight. Tonight was about entertainment. Dastgir prefered hand-selecting the boys depending on which men were his customers. *Which boys would be best for these men?* The total number of boys in the cave would range from twelve to thirty overall. Tonight, fifteen boys were in the cave, seven of which would be used for tonight's entertainment. Dastgir stood at the den entrance and watched the boys as they waited in a semi-circle around the fire.

Dastgir smiled in greedy delight, looking at the boys.

Out of the circle of boys Dastgir heard a voice—a confident, strong voice from the group that echoed off the rock walls. It was a boy named Jamil. Jamil was a tall, gangly boy, the oldest of the group at 12 years of age.

"You, there!" He heard Jamil yell, pointing to a young boy. "What is your name?"

Dastgir recognized Jamil's ability to get the most out of the younger new boys brought to the caves. Jamil had taken on the role as an older brother and mentor to get the most out of the boys—and stand up for them, if needed, risking a beating of the rattan.

*He still has some fire to him,* thought Dastgir. *He keeps the others in line.*

Jamil looked down with empathy at the other boys, who were all about eight to twelve years of age. He was aware that Dastgir was watching him from a distance, so he kept his features and tone stern.

Jamil took after his father Farrin, standing nearly 6 feet tall wearing a plain red outfit with a black silk tie around his waist, and black vest. The other boys were plainly dressed in the traditional clothing, some with white vests on.

Jamil had been introduced to the world of the bacha bazi boys running with a few boys that performed, ignoring his parents' house rules. In the beginning, dancing had been an opportunity to make money for himself, and he had enjoyed it. It was only dancing at that point. But a few men he danced for in the beginning he now knew had drugged him—making him forget the acts of the men as they raped him, passing him around.

After about a year of dancing, he had been abducted by Dastgir. As he was faced with the truth of the life, he then realized exactly what went on with the drugs and the sexual promiscuity of the men who had given him money before.

Dastgir had moved him from place to place until Jamil ended up as a captive at the cave. He had now become jaded as a bacha bazi boy, having entertained the men for nearly two years. Jamil hated it here, and he despised the men for what they had done to him and the new boys that came and went. Boys with fear and despair in their eyes.

Jamil's heart ached for the younger boys in front of him, knowing all too well what will be expected from them.

"You, there! What is your name?" he yelled.

"Shafiq," the boy replied, looking down.

Another boy instantly stood up to Jamil's right. "And my name is Naseefa. We have been here two days now."

"We are brothers," Shafiq said. "He is only eight years of age. I am 10."

Jamil stood looking at Shafiq and Naseefa, trying to remember if he had seen these boys before. Over the years, being drugged had left Jamil with moments of temporary memory loss. Most of the group had been captives for some time now.

"Do not let Dastgir know of this," Jamil said, lowering his voice leaning in. "He will for sure separate you from your brother, for he fears retaliation." Jamil looked over his shoulder towards Dastgir. The two brothers carefully watched. "Do not agitate him."

The two boys nodded in fear. Jamil walked over to the dark corner of the den and picked up several tinkling bells for their wrists and ankles. He knelt down and started his pep talk, instructing the boys to stay focused with the art of dance.

"Do not to be afraid of the men that will be trying to touch you. Just do your best to make a good impression," he said, feeling tired. He just wanted to escape, to leave this hell. But right now, that seemed completely unattainable.

Dastgir walked near the boys: They all slid back up tight against the rock wall out of fear of him. Moving closer to the boys, Dastgir stood over them with arms crossed and began pointing out the boys he wanted to perform tonight.

"You, there, come to me," Dastgir said with a stern voice. One of the boys stood and came to his side. After selecting three more out of the group, he came to the seventh and last boy: Shafiq, the eight year old and youngest of the group.

"Come to me," Dastgir commanded. Shafiq was frozen in fear. Tears could be seen welling up in his eyes, and he sat against the cave wall with his arms wrapped around his knees, rocking back and forth.

"Take me," the boy named Naseefa yelled, jumping up with confidence. "I will dance in his place."

Dastgir walked over to Naseefa, staring coldly through him. "Why do you offer yourself for this boy?"

"I have seen him dance and he is no good. I will show you I can out dance all of them," Naseefa said with determination and a convincing smile. Dastgir looked down at Naseefa, sizing him up. *Who is this boy that challenges my decision?*

"Very well, if you dance well for Dastgir tonight, I will give you extra food. If not it will be the rattan," Dastgir said as he turned to Jamil. "Have them ready in a few minutes."

Jamil nodded silently. Dastgir then walked into the large cave where the men were gathered. The smoke mixed with the smell of sweat made his eyes burn momentarily. Most of the men had been here for hours, drinking the vodka mixed with fruit juices.

The big room was decorated with hanging twisted colorful curtains attached to the ceiling by both ends to create a looped sag, just high enough to walk under. The entrance to the big den was the highest point of the room. Further in, the ceiling sloped down towards the back. The den was 25 feet wide and 40 feet deep. Colorful large pillows in gold, red, blue, and green sat all around the floor up against the walls of the cave. Random small tables with candles that flickered making the room come alive.

To Dastgir, it was the most beautiful room in the world. It smelled of power, of money. He sat down next to Mawlawi Abdul Kabir, one of the area's most powerful Taliban leaders, some local businessmen sat nearby. The chief of police stood off in the corner, observing. A total of fifteen men passed around a bottle of vodka mixed with fruit juice as they continued getting intoxicated.

*This will be a good night, I must make sure these men are satisfied with my boys.* Dastgir thought with a smile on his face.

The den filled with a haze of smoke from hand rolled cigarettes that bellowed up into the darkness, disappearing into the twisted curtains above. The men anxiously awaited for the entertainment, the bacha bazi boys. The men began to cheer as the boys entered the den.

Jamil was in the lead. As the boys passed the line of men, they reached out, touching the garments of the boys, trying to touch the boys themselves as they cheered on with excitement and desire. Dastgir watched Jamil lead the boys to the far smaller end were they stood waiting their turn. With men on both sides, it created a small space down the middle where the boys would take their turns dancing.

Jamil would be first. Dastgir watched as a man with a sitar begun to play as Jamil started to dance with a tambourine in his hand. The bells around his ankles tinkled to the beat. He began a walk-shuffle in a straight line with the bells in rhythm slapping against his wrists and ankles as he reached the far end, then back again. Walk-shuffle, walk-shuffle. Jamil then did a spin with his arms outstretched, moving up and down the small aisle opening. Jamil was graceful, all the while keeping beat to the music.

Dastgir watched as the men were mesmerized. Since Jamil was the oldest, he definitely had skill. But his youth was fading, which made him a little less desirable to some of the men.

Mullah Abdul Kabir leaned in to Dastgir.

"So Jamil has been with you for some time now. He is beyond the lick of a goat's tongue to remove his facial hair," he commented, smiling and looking at Dastgir, intentionally trying to agitate him.

Dastgir stared out at the entertainment, trying to contain his temper. *This Mullah is not one to challenge*, Dastgir thought.

"It seems your boys have lost the desire to be with such powerful men," the Mullah continued. "Jamil is a young man now, old enough to hold a weapon and fight at our side."

"Jamil will be done with dancing when I decide," said Dastgir cooly. "But I do have a new boy, a beautiful boy of whom you have never laid eyes. This boy is mind blowing. It took a lot of time and patience to bring this one in, but he will be available only for the most money offered, and all will have a chance."

"So, where is this boy?" Mullah inquired, licking his lips. "Is he not here tonight?"

A second boy begun to dance with a tambourine above his head passing close to the men as they leaned over touching the boy, clapping, cheering him on.

"I have him with Iffy in Jalalabad at this moment. Tomorrow, I will be bringing him to the cave for all to see." Dastgir sat back rolling a cigarette, waiting to see if Mullah would take the bait.

"If this boy is what you say, I will have one of my men fly me back to witness this beautiful boy. You have my interest now. What is the boy's name?" Mullah inquired.

"Asa," Dastgir spoke.

Both men gazed back to the entertainment and started to clap to the rhythm of the music. More boys danced. Dastgir, pleased with the Mullah's interest, knew he would pay excessive amounts of money for a talented boy. Having the Mullah the most powerful man in the area interested in Asa was exciting. Dastgir smiled with a cigarette dangling from his lip as he energetically clapped, watching Naseefa dance with high kicks and erect back as the men cheered louder. Dastgir was pleased.

The entertainment went on for hours. Dastgir finally glanced over and motioned for Jamil to leave the den, leaving the boys to further entertain alone.

Jamil knew what would now happen next. Feeling sad, he headed for his den. Jamil had earned the privilege of having his own sleeping quarters. Walking down the cave walkway, he stopped to look out over the lake—iridescent, beautiful. Back in his den, Jamil lay down. The den was small with only a few pillows and a threadbare worn blanket. Laying down on his back, he could hear the music and cheering that echoed throughout the cave.

*I should've left all this when I had the chance back in Kabul, but the money for dancing seemed so good,* he thought. *But I must devise a escape soon, or I would rather die! I must make it home. It has been too long now.*

Jamil began to weep quietly in the darkness. Exhausted from the day, Jamil drifted off to sleep dreaming, dreaming of home, missing his mother and father, and especially Asa.

Hours passed when a sudden noise woke Jamil. Lifting his head slightly off the pillow, he heard loud distant laughter towards the main den where the boys entertained. The music had stopped, and muffled laughter could be heard from some men in one of the dens. Jamil heard a stern command from one of the men, but Jamil was not able to make out what was said.

Jamil heard the voice of a boy, followed with loud weeping. Jamil covered his head with a pillow to block out the the boy's cries. Jamil swore someday he would find a way out.

# CHAPTER 6
# ASMAR

Rattled from the night's events with confronting the Taliban, I stood in the wooded area just meters from the Taliban village with my men. We could see the sun start to rise ahead of us.

All my men were accounted for except for Sal and King. We'd found Hakeem huddled in the rocky outcropping, visibly shaken, but we'd spent most the night in search of Sal and King. All Hakeem could recall was King pulling away from him and the shots not more 100 feet from where he stood, he guessed. He also mentioned the Taliban soldier he'd seen briefly before the man disappeared.

We searched around the area in the semi-darkness of dawn, but all we found was a few spots of blood. Still no sign of an actual human. Heavy-hearted, I made the decision to press on. I was sick with the thought of the possibility of losing one of my men so early in the mission. I could only hope Sal would find his way. We all concluded it was King he went after; they had been a team. They must be together still.

As the sun broke, we finally cleared the thick tree line of the lower elevations leaving the two villages behind us. We stood together shoulder to shoulder, taking in the vast mountain range before us. Our breath was visible in the cool mountain air as we exhaled the carbon dioxide. The mountains were beautiful, going up high in elevation to the white snow caps 14,000 feet and higher, glowing blue-white from the bright sun's reflection with clusters of tall pines peppered in.

I was worried that the missing Taliban soldier that eluded us last night would alert the other Taliban in the area.

"What direction are we headed?" I said, looking to Hakeem.

"We are north of Asadabad. Our guide will meet us near the next village over called Asmar," Hakeem, said recognizing this area. "It has been sometime since I have been here."

Grabbing the gear, we followed Hakeem in a northeast direction. The wind began to pick up. We hadn't walked more than a few miles when we spotted off in the distance what look to be a shadow: a man lying on the ground.

As we approached cautiously, I was horrified at what I saw before me. Sal and one of the Taliban soldiers lay just a few feet away from each other, boots nearly touching. Surrounding the bodies, there was a large area of blood—a thick crimson red saturating the frozen ground where they lay.

King was draped over Sal, transfixed on us from 30 feet out. The closer we got, King began to bare his teeth. We could see King's left ear was almost completely gone from what was probably a shot he took last night. Dried blood turned black down the left side of his face as if he had been in a bloody battle.

"Damn It! Sal, our brother," Big Joe knelt down near Sal, head in his hands.

"The Taliban soldier must've come up on Sal." I could see his rifle at his side. "Sal managed to take out the Taliban in his last moments."

It hit all of us hard so soon into the mission.

"Come here, boy," I called out, trying to coax King off Sal's body. He just laid there protecting Sal from anyone, starting to growl.

"Here you go, boy," Big Joe said as he reached in his left chest pocket and pulled out a piece of beef jerky, extending his arm towards King.

King tipped his head back sniffing at the air. Big Joe tossed the beef jerky at King that landed just inches away from his head. King still refused to move.

"Poor boy, the bond is that strong that he refuses the food," Tex said in astonishment, looking over at us. "What now?"

"We stand shoulder to shoulder and slowly walk towards him," I said, getting up from kneeling. "King has lost a lot of blood; he's scared and confused. We just move in as a large object—that should make him back off."

We stood shoulder to shoulder moving towards King, forcing him to back off Sal with a loud growl. King lay back down a few feet away, watching every move we made. We stood over Sal in silence, putting our arms over each other's shoulders.

Kneeling next to Sal, I took his hand and said a prayer. "Lord, here lies a great man, a honourable soldier, our friend. Sal made the ultimate sacrifice. No greater love than to lay down your life for your friends. We take comfort knowing he is home with you Lord, without pain, as you hold him close. Amen."

We stood in silence for a moment. I then removed all identification from Sal: dog tag, pocket ID, name patches—putting it safely in my uniform. King moved in closer, lying back down. Big Joe stood over the Taliban soldier as he started kicking at the stiff body.

"You son of a bitch," Big Joe yelled into the cold mountain air.

I laid my hand on Big Joe's shoulder, trying to comfort him. "Big Joe, get that shovel we brought. Let's get Sal buried here," I said, making my voice even and steady even in this hard moment.

It took about an hour to dig the shallow grave in the cold, frozen ground. It began snowing, the light layer of fresh fallen snow laid a soft fluffy carpet over the entire area.

"What about the Taliban soldier?" Ben asked with his rifle slung over his right shoulder.

"Let the wolves and crows take care of that piece of shit!" Big Joe said overcome with emotion.

The blood-saturated ground lost its battle with the ensuing snow layer, as if the bloodbath had never happened. With Sal's body hidden in the ground, I stepped back—angry with Sal for not following his order to stay back with Hakeem. *Had he followed that order, Sal would be with us now*, I thought. The fight to have King on this mission could be in vain without Sal.

I looked over at King and noticed he was just staring at the frozen ground. It was as if he just wanted us to move on so he could sniff out Sal's body in the cold shallow grave, get close to him, grieve.

"I pray this will be the worst of it. No more loss of life", I said, looking over at Tex and Big Joe. All were transfixed on the spot where Sal lie.

I looked back up the mountain as the snow whipped and swirled around us, creating eerie snow shapes in the wind. We are heading into what could be a bloody battle. All of our years of training and experience were being tested. *Will any of us make it?* I wondered.

"Let's move out," I said. We couldn't afford to stay here, because we had no idea if the Taliban would be back to the village soon.

As we headed out, King refused to leave Sal's grave sight. We coaxed him in vain; the bond with Sal stronger than words could express. He just laid there with his head down on his front paws, watching us with sad eyes. If we approached, he growled.

We couldn't wait any longer. I was worried that we would lose time after such a hard moment, and we needed to keep up the pace so that the mission would continue to go as expected. First, we had to call in our coordinates tonight, we needed those drones watching our backs just in case. Also, we had to meet the guide tomorrow.

"What is our timeline to the rendezvous spot?" I asked, looking over at Hakeem.

"Just a partial day's journey northeast of here," Hakeem pointed to his left. "Our guide will meet us near the next village."

"Grab that sled. We'll be suiting up for the higher elevations soon," I ordered with a wave. With my heart feeling heavy, we marched away from King and Sal. Every step felt like torture, but our mission had to keep going.

The foothills took on a steeper grade as we marched in the direction of the rendezvous point. After a couple hours, the snow line came into view. Concerned about our day's trek and the daylight for foot travel, I knew we needed to make a lot of progress.

Finally reaching the snow line, we stopped to switch into our white snow gear. I looked off at the terrain in the direction of Asmar through the binoculars. The mountain appeared to make a vertical drop between here and the village, approximately 100 meters out. My best guess was that we could make Asmar in a few hours.

Suiting up, we started the trek in the direction of Asmar. The time was 16:22 as the mountain air dropped the temperature into the teens. I glanced at the altimeter gauge strapped to my wrist, observing the green glowing readout displayed us at 900 feet elevation.

It was nearly an hour into the trek when we came to the edge of the precipice I'd noticed earlier. Looking down the precipice, it appeared to slope down at a grade of 5.8-5.95 degrees or so: manageable enough.

"Are you sure this is a good idea?" Hakeem commented, nervously looking over the edge while holding onto his hat jostled by the blowing wind.

"Hakeem, I want you in the middle," I said. "Big Joe, you last. We'll need your strength to keep us anchored as we descend down the slope. Everyone, secure that rope around your waist. We have 50 meters of rope. It's just enough for you five secured. I'll have to free descend."

Looking down the slope, I noticed the terrain was littered with boulders jetting out of the fresh snow. *Not any chance of an avalanche,* I thought.

Slowly working our way down at a steady pace, I was leading the way in a zig zag trek. The others stayed close to me. Working around the boulders, and at times waist deep in snow, made the trek slow moving. Finally, we made it to the valley, making the trek a bit easier. We took off our ropes and began wading through the deep snowy valley.

Hakeem, trying to keep pace with the rest of the men, slipped— and he let out a cry of pain. "Shit! What did I do?" Hakeem sat in the snow, rubbing his ankle in pain.

I walked back kneeling in front of Hakeem, loosening Hakeem's boot on his right foot. "You twisted your ankle. It's swollen up pretty good," I said. "Damn it, Hakeem!"

"I will be fine, I can keep up, no problem," Hakeem commented weakly, starting to stand on the ankle, then suddenly dropping back down, grimacing with pain.

"I can help him," Tex said. "All we need to do is get to the other side of this valley, and then it's a straight shot. Right?"

"Yeah, let's keep moving," I said as he loosened the rope from around Hakeem's waist. Tex wrapped his arm around Hakeem's waist, slightly relieving some of the weight to his ankle as Tex and Hakeem trailed the rest of the men through the small valley.

The snow drifts and the boulders made the walk difficult as we finally reached the other side of the valley.

*Thump-thump-thump!*

It was then we heard a helicopter off in the distance. We froze.

"Shit!" Big Joe said, looking up the precipice.

"Quiet!" I ordered. "What direction are they headed?"

The men all listened intently, breathing heavy from the walk.

"It's coming this way," I said. "If they have thermal imaging mounted cameras, they will pick up the body heat as a group. Spread out now!" I ordered.

The men quickly spread out. The copter flew overhead. It hovered above us a few seconds, shining a spotlight towards the top of the precipice, then moved on, making passes over the slope below.

"Difficult to pinpoint the direction they are headed." I tilted my head back and forth, suddenly realizing the copter was headed in King's direction below.

"They are establishing a grid search. Shit!" Tex said.

"This valley just saved our asses, this time," I said. "They'll be back. We have to stay one step ahead of them. Let's get out of this valley and find that rendezvous spot."

Re-adjusting the gear, we started the steep climb up the other side of the valley, finally reaching the top of the precipice. I spotted a few twinkling lights of the next village not far off through the pine trees. Looking at the time, I felt relieved that we were just missing the coordinance to be radioed in by a few hours. The starry night allowed for us to see the village clearly in the distance fifty meters ahead. There were rudimentary trails leading off in several directions into the small village. According to the maps, approximate population of Asmar was just over 7,500. Other than an occasional dog barking off in the distance, all was quiet. I lead the men along the outer edge of the village, we all kept close as we skirted the small village perimeter.

Hakeem was nearly being carried by Big Joe. His twisted ankle had gotten worse. We passed along the backside of the village near a few huts as we continued. The mountain's elevation to our right appeared steep and aggressive in the direction of the caves.

I spotted a few of the local men herding goats into the village. I knelt down behind a small rock fence, and the others followed my lead as we waited out the goat herders.

*Just another 200 yards and we will pass the village,* I thought. Darkness fell as the sun slipped behind the mountains. Our trek would pass Asmar, then east in the direction of the higher elevations. I spotted two massive clusters of pines ahead. The two clusters nearly touched and formed a circle—a wall of pine trees offering the perfect shelter. *Perfect spot to camp.*

"Here! In these pines, we'll bed down and make camp," I said, pointing towards the open area.

The day's events had been exhausting and emotional with the loss of our brother Sal, as well as King. The cluster of pines towered over us as the men tiredly made camp. We started to dig out small trenches in the snow deep enough to lay in, but just below the surface, offering protection and warmth from the cool night's weather.

After establishing the nightly watches, I decided to take another GPS reading. This would be the only radio contact till the mission was complete. If the Taliban had been monitoring radio transmissions, I wanted to falsify our exact location by a simple adjustment in our coordinates to put us down the slope. If we were being tracked, this would give us days lead.

It was time to radio HQ. The distance between my current location and base was just over 129 miles. Weather was good for the radio transmission tonight.

"Mike here," I said into the radio.

*Click...click...click...*

More static could be heard, then a faint voice.

"Go ahead, I hear you." It was Sergeant Bacon back on base covering the graveyard shift.

"We are at the rendezvous spot. Over." *Click.* "One man down, Sal. Over." *Click.*

"One man down?" the sergeant repeated. "Did I hear you correctly Mike?" *Click.*

"Copy. Engaged in enemy fire in lower elevations. Sal is gone. We are at rendezvous spot. Here is our GPS coordinates. Please confirm. 35.031978 lat 71.356137 long. Over." *Click. Click.*

"35.031978 lat 71.356137 long. Over." *Click.*

"Moving on tomorrow with our next guide. We will have no communication from here on out. Drone passes must begin tomorrow. Over." *Click.*

"Roger that. Copy! Take care and godspeed!" *Click.*

I turned to face my men. Silence fell over the camp in the star filled cold night, the smell of pine was strong. I turned back to look up at the mountains. My thoughts started running wild again.

*I have failed my men, Sal's family back home,* I thought. *But I can't allow this to cloud my vision of this mission. I've got to focus on getting to the caves. What will we find when we get there?*

# CHAPTER 7

# ZALEAH

*Images danced in my head. I was underwater, looking up towards the surface. Blurred distorted faces above gazed down at me, and my lungs burned for oxygen. I heard a woman's voice, beautiful and soft...*

Startled, I came out of my sleep, sitting up wide awake. I noticed that on the south side of the camp near the opening of the pines, Hakeem sat facing a stranger almost knee to knee. I could make out that they were speaking in Sindhi, a language common in Pakistan.

It was just after sunrise as I looked around the camp for the men. Ben, Antonio, and Big Joe could be heard in muffled conversation just outside the pine trees. Tex was sitting near his makeshift bed.

I stood, adjusting my snowsuit.

"Hello, my friend!" Hakeem said, noticing I was up. He slowly stood, hopping a bit from the twisted ankle as he turned to face me.

"This is a person I have not seen in sometime," Hakeem said. "This is my sister, Zaleah. She will be your guide."

Zaleah stood and bowed. I bowed back. She was dressed in a pure white snowsuit detailed with white hand stitching. A white camouflage turban wrapped around her head that partially covered her face and eyes. A slight gap at the top of her snowsuit just below the chin exposed a Balochi woman's undergarment for cold weather. Looking down at her feet, I noticed a pair of women's snow boots, light cream color with white laces. Her weapon of choice was a .300 Win Mag with a high powered scope. The gun appeared to have been custom painted white.

Her size alone was my immediate concern. She might be well

versed in the mountains and caves in the area, but she couldn't be much more than a hundred pounds. Even though she was covered from head to toe, with only her dark brown eyes exposed, her eye contact was direct and deliberate. It was hard to tell if she preferred guiding us or shooting us at this point.

Just then Ben, Big Joe, and Antonio walked through the tree branches, slipping through the small opening between the two towering rows of pines. The long pine needles grabbed at their white snowsuits with a *zip, rip* noise as they passed through.

"Oh! So you have met our guide," Big Joe said sarcastically. Hakeem, Zaleah, and I stood next to each other, facing the three men as they approached stopping directly in front of us.

"Mike, can I talk with you?" Big Joe asked as he turned and walked a few feet away. Tex stood up from his bed and followed us.

"I'm concerned about this so called guide," Big Joe said, talking quietly.

"Look," I said. "I'm a little shocked, too, but I trust Hakeem's decision. Their family all grew up here. This is his sister, and she knows this area well. We are aware that her other two brothers went to the dark side, taking up with the terrorists. But he has never mentioned anything but good things about his sister."

"What other choice do we have?" Tex said. "It's not like we can pick up the phone and dial in a new guide."

"I'm still not convinced," Big Joe said.

"So, what will it take?" I said as we stood together looking over at Zaleah.

"It's as if she knows we are talking about her," Tex said softly out of the side of his mouth.

Zaleah had been watching us. Suddenly, she stepped forward.

"Oh, shit! She's walking this way," Tex said.

The rest of the group watched her as she came towards us. She came to a stand directly in front of Big Joe, staring up at him. She looked like a child at 5 feet, while Big Joe stood with his hands on his hips, looking down at her from his 6'5" frame.

Zaleah look directly into Big Joe's eyes. "So, you doubt I am the correct one for this journey?" She asked, nearly toe-to-toe with Big

Joe. She spoke in an accented English, but confidence could be heard through her soft, calm voice.

"Well, I guess I have a few doubts, if you don't mind me saying," said Big Joe looking down at Zaleah.

"I know these mountains well" Zaleah said stepping back from Big Joe while looking at the faces of the men. "I am here for my brother; he has mentioned your mission. I have hate for the men you are going after. I have my own personal vendetta for these animals that caused years of pain to my village and myself personally. My own eldest brother lost a child to this bacha bazi boy trade. I have waited years for this opportunity."

Big Joe hesitated. "I mean, you may have the heart and knowledge for the trek, but—"

"But!" Zaleah said with a stern tone. "You don't! So what do they call you? Big Joe or Big Dummy? All brawn and no brains. A typical oversized gorilla."

Looking around, I noticed the men laughing. It was a true David and Goliath moment, and we all were intrigued with what the outcome would be.

"Well, I just don't want the extra responsibility when things get heated up," Big Joe said nervously, looking for support from the rest of us and getting none.

Stepping back from Big Joe, Zaleah removed her rifle from her shoulder, handing it to Hakeem, and took a fighting stance. Crouching low, she extended her arms out in front of her as she removed her gloves, exposing her fists, motioned for Big Joe to come at her.

With his typical car salesman grin, Big Joe handed his rifle over to Tex. Looking around at the men, he casually stood just grinning, not knowing what to expect.

Out of nowhere, Zaleah spun around, jumping up and kicking Big Joe in the chin. She came down with her stance low to the ground, spinning around again with one leg extended taking Big Joe's feet out from underneath him.

Big Joe lay sprawled out on his back. Zaleah continued her low stance, moving around him like a cat. Standing up, Big Joe brushed off the snow, rubbed his chin, and put his fists up in front of his face as he rushed her.

With quick reflexes, Zaleah stepped to the left and gave Big Joe a hard hit to his solar plexus with her right hand in a tight fist, dropping him to his knees. Gasping for air, Big Joe rolled over onto his back while holding his stomach.

"Okay, okay, I'm convinced!" Big Joe said with a strained whisper, trying to catch his breath.

Zaleah knelt down next to him. "What is it you say, Big Gorilla?"

"Would you *please* be our guide?" Big Joe, said sitting up and wrapping his arms around his knees. Looking up at the men with an embarrassed grin, he slowly started to get up. "I knew she would be a great guide. Perfect for the job."

The men all broke out in laughter as Zaleah helped Big Joe up to his feet. They shook hands.

"We should gear up, but I have concerns of Hakeem and his twisted ankle," I said, standing with Zaleah and Hakeem while the men starting packing up. "The way back to Kabul is a good two-day journey, taking him back down the mountain."

"I agree, my brother, you should stay here for a few days and get your strength back." Zaleah said with much emotion to her voice.

"But you must be quiet," I said. "Blend in and don't bring attention to yourself, don't mention anything of this mission. Do not trust anyone!" I was concerned about Hakeem's nervous nature. The knowledge of the mission in the hands of the Taliban would be dangerous.

"Don't worry about me," said Hakeem. "I can manage."

"Tex, bring those maps over here," I said. Tex brought over the topical maps, spreading them out on the ground over a bivvy bag. The group gathered around Zaleah, as she knelt down, pouring over the maps and pointing out the two best options for the journey.

Zaleah looked over the maps. "I estimate a two-day journey, weather permitting. We have two options. The first option we have offers a much easier terrain to navigate, but it will leave us exposed. It has a vast open range where you can see for miles, not much for cover. The second option will test our strength and endurance with more challenging grades to deal with, rocky terrain, and possible snow slides. It is more difficult, but it would give us more cover from terrorists."

We discussed for a moment, but we all agreed the second option would be best. It was clear that Zaleah was knowledgeable of the mountainous terrain in this sector.

"Is this your first ascent in that sector?" I asked Zaleah.

"When I first heard of this cave used as a refuge for the terrorist, I wanted to find it," she said. "Many have heard, but never confirmed. I decided to go and see for myself. It took days before I spotted the cave opening. I nearly gave up." Zaleah sighed heavily, speaking as if she was reliving that day. "Then three terrorist guards spotted me from a hundred yards out and started shooting at me. I was shot clean through my shoulder. I ran and jumped off a rock ledge. The drop seemed to go on forever. I thought I was going to die. I landed in a pine tree twelve, thirteen meters up. But God was watching over me that day. As the sun was low in the sky that evening, I heard the men below looking for me. I stayed hidden in that pine tree for a day and a half before I worked my way down. If not for that landing into the pine tree, I would be dead."

"That's quite the story," I said.

"What can we expect for enemy engagement?" Ben asked, looking down at the maps.

"This area has become more active with terrorists, and we must be always alert," Zaleah commented while standing. "I cannot say more than that."

It was time to head out. The men all lined up to say their goodbyes to Hakeem. One-by-one they embraced him, expressing their sincere friendship and respect for him.

"I want to talk with you," I said as I grabbed Hakeem by his arm, walking him away from the rest. Hakeem stood waiting for me to speak, clearly in pain but trying to remain strong.

"Here, I want you to take this." I handed Hakeem a small envelope. "Just in case things go to shit, give this to my Commander."

Hakeem looked down at the envelope, then back to me. Tears welled up in his eyes. Hakeem and I had established a great bond and trust over the years, and the reality hit that this could be it. Our last meeting.

"I will do this for you, my friend," he said. "But it brings me great sadness that I cannot be with you and my sister. I would rather die with my friends then not to know of the dangers you will encounter: I pray you survive your journey."

Hakeem took the sealed envelope as we embraced for a long moment. As we did, I slipped two hundred American dollars in Hakeem's left vest pocket. I knew that Hakeem would not accept it out right.

"Here, I should give this back to you," Hakeem said as he pulled out the 9MM from his waistband. He was still carrying it from the night at the Taliban village. Hakeem stood holding it, waiting for me to take it. I stood just staring down at the gun.

"Just keep it," I said, pushing the gun back at Hakeem. " You might need it on the journey back to Kabul. Until then, rest and lay low."

Hakeem agreed to stay hidden in the pines until darkness fell over the village.

Walking over to Zaleah, Hakeem put his hands on her shoulders "Here we just meet for the first time in years, and now it is difficult to say goodbye: I will pray for you and the men."

Zaleah stood looking into the eyes of Hakeem, placing her right hand on his face. "I love you, my brother. When I return, we will have time to be together once again."

We set out on the arduous trek with Zaleah in the lead. We followed the tree line up the mountain, trying to stay as hidden as possible. It was a bright sunny day as we slipped on our goggles, protecting our eyes from the blinding sun. Hakeem stood observing us as we moved up the slope. An hour passed, and he and the distant village of Asmar disappeared from our sight.

# CHAPTER 8

# KING

Two large male grey wolves were hunting along the treeline in search of food in the freshly fallen snow. At nearly 100 pounds each, both wolves ran with their noses to the ground. They'd caught the scent of a rabbit just ahead. With winter moving in, they were forced into a steady diet of rabbit and smaller rodents that temporarily satisfied their insatiable appetites.

Spotting a rabbit next to a tall pine tree, the two wolves made chase. Catching the rabbit was easy for the two as the rabbit was snatched up by its hind legs. The two fought over the meat, tearing the rabbit in half with a pop, and a burst of blood as they gulped it down in seconds.

Just then, they picked up another scent as they stuck their noses up high in the air—the smell of carrion upwind. Death was off in the distance.

After nearly two days without food and eating snow to stay hydrated, King's instincts for survival became overpowering. The piece of beef jerky Big Joe had tossed at him the other day was just under the fresh layer of snow.

Standing over Sal, King shook the snow off his fur and began sniffing out the beef jerky a few feet away. He gulped it down in one piece, snow attached to his nose. The hearing loss from the gunshot the other night was gradually returning. The dried blood on his coat was licked off clean, leaving just a small crust of blood that attached itself around the jagged wound on his left ear where he was shot by the Taliban soldier.

The wind over the last few days had partially disturbed the loose snow and soil over Sal. Part of Sal's right hand and face were exposed as King stood over him. Staring down at Sal's face, King let out a loud whimper and began licking at Sal's face, feeling the cold flesh with his tongue. Sitting down he glanced off in the distance towards the mountains where the men headed a few days ago.

Suddenly, King caught movement out of the corner of his eye. There were two wolves running towards him full speed. They spotted King and slowed down. They cautiously approached King.

King bared his teeth, making a stance between Sal's body and the approaching wolves. The two wolves kept their distance as they began to circle around King from 20 feet away—sniffing the air in attempts to get a scent.

King instinctively charged the two wolves. The two wolves teamed up: one luring King away from Sal's body, and the other quickly moving in on Sal biting into the stiff frozen exposed hand. King noticed the wolf pulling at Sal's flesh and charged back, lunging at the wolf, biting hard into his back right leg. He ripped out a piece of flesh and the two wolves retreated.

The two tore off in the direction of the rest of the pack not far behind. Hungry and exhausted, King monitored the horizon in all directions. The wind gusts created snowy white-outs in the distance that obstructed his view.

An hour or so passed since chasing off the two wolves. Suddenly, he saw the two young males returned with another male and female wolf: the alphas. Standing together off in the distance, they begin to slowly move in together. The wounded male that King attacked earlier stayed back as the other three moved in silence towards King.

The pack got within 20 feet as they spread out surrounding King. The dead flesh smell was intoxicating to the beasts, making them salivate. The alpha male bared his teeth and stared with his cold yellow eyes.

King, noticing he was surrounded, took a stance near Sal's body. King bared his teeth, his hair standing up on his back as he crouched ready for an attack. The dog could sense the big alpha male would attack first, just 15 feet away. The female moved in on King from the rear. The other two wolves inched closer towards King, making him back up a few steps.

King looked back and forth at the two males in anticipation of an attack. The alpha male and younger male moved in from the front left and right, while the female moved in from the rear; she was looking for an opportunity to sink her teeth into King's leg, crippling him.

King charged at the two males. They backed off momentarily, surprised by his show of force. Quickly spinning around, King eluded the female as she lunged at him from behind. King stood his ground facing her, and she backed off. The three wolves started to move in a circle counterclockwise. King watched them closely as he kept moving his head back and forth—focused on each wolf as they moved in closer, preparing for another attack.

King was ready for the fight.

The two male wolves distracted King as the female came from the rear. King sensed the attack coming from her and was ready for it. Inching forward towards the two males, King taunted the female to come closer, extending his right back leg. He felt her close as he spun with all his strength and leapt straight up, making her miss. He then came down on top of her, sinking his teeth into her neck as he shook the back of her neck violently ripping at her flesh. The female wolf pulled away in pain, yelping.

The two males moved in. King's face was bloodied from the attack and caught the full force of the alpha male colliding with him. They were both entangled in each other, sharp teeth finding their targets. King managed to muster enough strength to push the alpha male away; both backed off, breathing heavy.

The momentary standoff allowed the other two males to move in and attack King from behind. King knew he didn't stand a chance. There was no choice. Weak and tired from the fight, King took off running towards the mountains with the three males in chase.

He started his way up the mountain. Hungry for meat, the wolves stopped chase as they headed back. Easy pickings were their desire, not a full chase and fight. King stopping at a rocky lookout up the slope looked back one last time. In the distance, he witnessed the savages tearing at the flesh of Sal.

With a whimper, defeated King looked up the mountain, then back to the wolves. He sniffed the ground. It was no use staying with Sal. Sal was truly gone. King knew his only chance was to find Mike and his men. His survival instincts kicked in as he took off in a half-run in the direction the men.

# CHAPTER 9
# FREEDOM & CAPTIVITY

Farrin made his last rounds at the hospital before leaving for the day, wiping the sweat from his forehead with his handkerchief as he signed off on the last patient. The demands of the sick and wounded forced him to put in 12-14 hour days with the understaffing at the hospital.

Signing out for the day, Farrin thought of Rachel. They spoke daily before he headed to the hospital. With the time difference, Farrin would usually call her in the morning. She seemed more relaxed back in Minnesota around family. Farrin constantly reassured her that he had a good feeling with Abdul on the search for their boys.

Farrin felt the vibration from his pager that was clipped to his right hip pocket interrupting his train of thought. Stopping in the hallway outside the first operating room, he glanced down and recognized the number. It was Abdul. Farrin walked over to the nurses station, punching in the call back number. He was anxious to hear what Abdul had to say; any news was better than the waiting, and it had been days with no updates. The house was a lonely empty place without the boys and Rachel.

Abdul answered immediately.

"Hello!" Farrin said, speaking into the phone while looking towards the main lobby.

"Is this a good time?" Abdul asked.

"Yes, yes. Do you have something?" Farrin tried to contain his anxiousness.

"I have inquired from a few of my sources in Kabul, and it seems we may have found a trainer who works with the boys. His name is Iffy. We have been in Jalalabad following up with the leads. We have gathered this information and think they are training the boys currently near the Pashtunistan Square."

Farrin was silent. His mind was caught up in the emotional excitement that his Asa, his son, could be alive and coming home soon.

"Are you there, doctor?" Abdul inquired

"Yes! Yes!" Farrin broke out of his thoughts, snapping back to reality.

Abdul continued. "As soon as they find one location of a hiding place, they move the boys to another new location, making this group particularly hard to track down. This is as close as we have ever gotten to the hidden location where they hold the boys captive. If they suspect anything, they will be gone in a flash."

Farrin was trying to keep up with what Abdul was saying, leaving him in a state of semi-shock. "How soon will you have confirmation of Asa's whereabouts?" he asked. "Could it be possible you would have the location soon? I Could make the drive there, assist you in anyway?"

"Just stay put," cautioned Abdul. "This is what we do. I promise I will be in touch if anything changes."

After Abdul finished talking with Farrin, he slid his cell back into the front inside pocket of his jacket. It had begun to drizzle. Lighting the stub of his cigar, he looked around, observing the thinning crowd. They had been tracking Iffy all day, close to the scent of something big. He could sense it. Abdul sat under a tent used by a retailer for cover as the rain poured down on Jalalabad.

Then Abdul spotted Sam, his associate, moving fast towards him from down the alley. At 18 years old, Sam's birth name was Samama, but he prefered just Sam. A Pakistani, he was a slender, tall with short black hair and dark brown eyes. He was smart and tough, having lived most his life on the streets or in captivity. He was almost the complete opposite of Abdul in every way in looks and temperament.

"He's coming," Sam said, partially out of breath coming to a quick stop in front of Abdul. Abdul noticed over Sam's shoulder the man that fit the description working his way towards them, looking to be in a hurry.

Abdul motioned to Sam to hide quickly as they both ducked behind a rack full of colorful garments. "This is a good position," Abdul said. "Let's stay close behind him."

Iffy came within feet of them as he hurried down the wet street. Abdul tossed his lit cigar to the ground as they both moved quickly to stay close, watching as Iffy rounded the next corner, crossing over to the other side. The National Police passing in a Humvee nearly ran Iffy down in the middle of the street, causing him to slip in the greasy mud. Abdul and Sam stepped back out of sight up against a building as the Humvee sped along with no concern.

They both stayed put, watching.

Iffy got up and cursed out loud, shaking his fist at the National Police, his entire backside covered in the wet mud. Abdul and Sam looked at each other, both grinning. Iffy was half walking, half staggering while wiping off the greasy mud from his backside as he started to pick up his pace. It was only a twenty minute walk until he finally slowed down, periodically glancing back.

"He must be getting close," Abdul whispered. For a second, they lost sight of him as he went around another corner going to the right. The rain started to let up. Abdul, peeking around to get a glimpse, spotted Iffy just entering what appeared to be an old rundown mosque across the street. From here, they couldn't spot any windows.

Abdul looked over to Sam with a wide grin showing all his teeth. "We found it!" Abdul said. "I know this is it!"

"What's the plan?" Sam inquired all the while looking at the mosque.

"A stake out," Abdul blurted out. "We wait and see who comes and goes. If this is the building they use for holding the boys, we should see some activity. It will be dark soon. Let's head back. We will take turns monitoring the movements starting tomorrow. This door must be watched continuously until we have a definitive answer."

Five years ago, Abdul had a son who was 10 years of age. Abdul had been out working with his son for the day as a vendor selling jewelry and gifts from around the area in Kabul. In a blink of an eye, his son vanished. Abdul and his wife were crushed, knocking on doors looking for him. Other vendors teamed up in the search with no luck.

With some education, Abdul had wanted to pursue a career in law and decided to take on the search full time while his wife and friends continued his jewelry business. The pain they endured of the loss was the fuel that motivated Abdul to keep looking. He became talented in his abilities as a investigator. Over four years passed, and with Abdul's relentless efforts, never giving up, he finally tracked down the ring of men that had organized the abduction of his son. To his great sadness, he'd found his son was being held as a sex slave for a rich businessman.

Late one night, Abdul had broken into the guarded home in the brave rescue of his son. He was able to not only free his son, but three other boys. In the process, he was shot in the right arm—nearly bleeding to death on the long trek home while being pursued. Sam was one of the boys he'd freed that night. Sam has been a loyal employee—like a son now at the age of 19. Abdul placed the other boys with families, Sam with no family to be found was taken in by Abdul and his wife.

Having found and rescued his son, Abdul had decided to pursue a private investigative career in the helping of others. He'd gone back to school and learned everything he could about law and investigation. His wife had run the jewelry business, and they'd worked diligently together in the rescue efforts of other children, although their jewelry business was the front for their investigative activities. They'd always managed to keep out of the vengeance of the terrorists, but Abdul knew that could turn at any moment. His life was worth the risk in helping others.

For now, Abdul and Sam had been camped out from across the mosque for two days. The first night of the stake-out, Abdul had walked around the building. They'd noticed only two windows on both ends of the mosque off the ground a good 10 feet.

For now, they'd set up a food cart as a front loaded with fresh fruit and vegetables from around the area that had been selling well over the last few days. It was blocks away from the street market areas where most the locals and tourists shopped. No movements had happened other than Iffy coming and going. No boys or men had entered the mosque.

Abdul's coffee mug sat on the rail of the food cart; it steamed smoky in the morning sun. Sunrise in Jalalabad in late October was usually around 6am, giving 11 hours of daylight. The days slowly grew shorter over the winter months. Abdul waited for Sam, who was due for today's watch duties.

In the quiet of the morning, Abdul drifted off, thinking of his own son. It had been over a year now since he'd been found. Just to save one boy now would make all his hard work worth it.

*I just know Asa is here,* Abdul thought while sipping his coffee. *I know it.*

Knowing all too well how Farrin and Rachel have had their world turned upside down with both their sons missing, Abdul thought of how difficult it would be if he had to inform them that he had failed in finding their boys.

From around the corner walked Sam, snapping Abdul out of his train of thought. The hate Sam had for these men that had abducted other boys and himself as well drove him to learn all he could from Abdul.

"Anything?" he asked, slipping on a pair of sunglasses and looking towards the mosque.

"Not yet," Abdul replied, while taking another sip of his coffee.

"How much longer are we going to monitor before we go to Plan B?" Sam asked.

"Until we know without a doubt, we will not leave a minute sooner," Abdul replied. The warm morning sunrise on his face felt good in the chilly morning air. "Iffy still hasn't shown up yet this morning. If Asa is in there, there is a good chance he is alone." Abdul stared at the door of the mosque.

"I am tempted just to go knock, just to see what happens," Sam said with frustration in his voice.

"We can't risk it. Patience!" Abdul said. "Something will happen soon enough."

"Here we are not more than 20 feet away, and we wait with our hands tied," Sam said with frustration, taking another sip of his tea.

Overhead they heard a low flying helicopter as it momentarily blocked out the sun. Abdul looked up and felt a cold chill running through him. But it passed. Helicopters came and went occasionally— it was nothing to be worried about.

It was getting late in the morning as Abdul and Sam removed their light jackets as the day heated up. At this point, just a visual of Asa would suffice for Abdul. He removed a small photo of Asa in his front shirt pocket that had been given to him by Farrin at the first meeting. He was exhausted with the long overnight watches over the past few days.

★ ★ ★

"Asa! Asa! please open your eyes!"

Asa was curled up in sleep, but he slowly lifted his head, trying to focus on the two faces outside the half moon shaped cut outs to the cage. Rachim and Zaahid sat outside Asa's cage.

"We heard Iffy talking this morning before he left. Today, you will leave us! We beg of you to please help in our escape to freedom!" Zaahid pleaded. "There is only a short time before you leave. Please, Asa!"

"Yes!" Rachim jumped in. "Dastgir will be coming today to take you."

"Take me?" Asa sat up in the cage, feeling confusion. *What do they mean by taking me?*

"Yes, did you not know that you will be taken to the caves?" said Zaahid. "The caves where all the boys go? Did he not tell you that at the beginning? Today is the day."

"No. No. I was told I would dance here only. If I did well, they would consider letting me go." Asa now spoke angrily. But deep down, he knew the truth. *Dastgir lied! I should've never ever believed it.* Being good would not matter. Feeling suddenly overwhelmed with the turn his captivity had taken, Asa knew he had to help his friends. Maybe this was the only chance he had.

"Iffy will have you fed first. He will be distracted with Dastgir here. After eating, we will wash the dishes together. That is when you will have but just a moment to help us out the window," Zaahid explained. "You will help Rachim through the window first while standing on the wash basin."

"But the window is up so high. Are you sure I will be able to get you to the windows edge?" Asa was becoming concerned, especially with Zaahid and his bad twisted back.

"Sir," Rachim said earnestly, looking directly into Asa's eyes. "We have been wanting for this day for so long. I promise you that we will have the strength of many when that time comes. We will be gone in an instant. Please believe me when I say this to you!"

Asa looked into the eyes of both boys, unblinking as they awaited for his answer. If not for him, it could be many months before they once again felt the warm sun and cool rain on their faces.

"Okay," Asa agreed. "But you must help me in return. Once you escape, please, I beg of you to find my father and tell him where I am. Farrin Khan, he is a doctor at the Kabul hospital. Tell him I am being held captive, to please hurry!"

He saw their dull, lifeless eyes come to life as if they had seen God himself.

"We will!" they said. "We promise to help you, too."

Asa sat up, his adrenaline racing. "Now go to the backroom before we are caught."

*This is my only chance for help, I must be careful,* he thought.

They suddenly heard Iffy fumbling at the locked front door to the mosque.

"He's coming," Asa whispered loudly to Rachim and Zaahid, who were now crouched in the back room. He knelt in the cage, looking towards the door.

Iffy entered the room. "I'm very sorry, Asa. How careless of me to be late on your day of departure," he said, staring into the cage inches away. Asa could smell the liquor on his breath. "We must get you ready for your journey. We must hurry. Dastgir will be here soon."

*Maybe this is good. Iffy has been drinking,* thought Asa.

Iffy unlocked the cage. Asa crawled out of the cage, straightening up to stretch his stiff back. "Now go and have Rachim and Zaahid bathe you!"

Asa went to the back room, instantly looking up at the small window. Glancing over at the faces of Rachim and Zaahid, he noticed how nervous they looked.

"He's been drinking," Asa said in a whisper. The boys looked fearful. "No, no this is good. With his drinking, he will be off in his judgement!"

It was then that Asa noticed that the two had changed their clothes into clean crisp, white shalwar kameez outfits with brown sindhi caps.

"Now what is this you wear?" he said. "You must change back or you will be noticed. They will be suspicious."

"It will be acceptable," Rachim said. "Iffy likes it when we look good for Dastgir's return. If questioned, we'll express our honoring your accomplishment."

Asa nodded, removing his clothing. "Now bathe me quickly. Let us not anger Iffy."

★ ★ ★

Dastgir had taken the Russian Mi-24 Helicopter into Jalalabad, landing at a detention center that was run by the Chief of Police, one of Dastgir's best customers. The Chief of Police allowed a pass on Dastgir's activity, and he was able to use the large fenced area for a landing zone.

The Chief of Police welcomed him. They jumped into a Toyota Land Cruiser with a top mounted tripod 14.5mm KPV heavy machine gun at the landing zone. Two guards with black outfits, long beards, and black tunics wrapped around their heads accompanied them. The guards had rifles over their shoulders. The Taliban guards offered peace of mind when transporting the boys.

Razor fences opened, as they passed through the secure fenced area, then closed again. The drive to the mosque was just a short ten minute drive. Dastgir was anxious to get Asa and head back to the cave. Dastgir was always moving his training locations for the boys, trying to stay ahead of those family members that lost their boys to Dastgir, and who might be angry enough to get revenge on Dastgir or track the boys down.

Asa was a prize, and today was a good day to add Asa to his imprisoned inventory of bacha bazi boys.

The Land Cruiser came to a quick stop in front of the mosque as dust enveloped it in the late morning sun. Dastgir was the first out of the passenger's seat. The two guards immediately at his side stepping out of the back of the Cruiser.

As soon as they stepped out of the Cruiser, Dastgir gazed in the general direction of the street, which was full of locals. He then spotted the out-of-place food cart across the street.

*Hmmm,* he thought. *What do we have here?* Dastgir was immediately suspicious. He had been successful for years by noticing his surroundings, and he was not easily to be tricked by people who were always hunting him. Iffy hadn't noticed anything amiss, that was obvious. This made him even more furious. He motioned for the guards to stand outside. The Chief of Police followed him in. Storming into the mosque, Dastgir stood as he glanced around the large room, noticing the cage was open. Heading to the back room, he startled Iffy and the boys. They were eating what looked like a late breakfast.

Dastgir grabbed Iffy by his arm, nearly dragging him out to the front room. Dastgir went to the front door as he pointed to the food cart across the street.

"There," he said. "Have you not noticed that vendor?"

"I did not," Iffy mumbled a little. He was clearly getting over being drunk.

Dastgir gave Iffy a hard slap across the face. "That door must remain locked at all times!" he yelled. "And you are to notice anything that looks out of place!"

Iffy wiped a droplet of blood with his right sleeve from his nose from the hard slap.

"Do you not find it odd that he is this far from the market area?" Dastgir again yelled, still with a vice grip hold on his arm. "Go and have that cart removed this moment."

Dastgir then headed to the back room where the boys were waiting. He ordered for Asa to gather his things, tossing a small plastic bag in his direction.

"Now hurry!" Dastgir yelled. He was losing his temper. He followed Iffy out the door.

Abdul watched as the Cruiser drove towards the mosque. An un-recognized man with a white beard and black stripe running down it, the Chief of Police got out of the Cruiser and entered the building.

*The Chief of Police. Now this is an interesting twist,* he thought. *This is the first true activity we've seen. Something must be happening.* But it was also worrying. Having authorities like the police involved could complicate matters.

After a few moments, Iffy stormed towards them angrily. Abdul noticed Sam move towards Iffy, slightly getting between them. They were both trying hard to appear casual, but they knew that something was wrong.

"Sir, you must remove this cart immediately," said Iffy. "All vendors are to be in the market area. This is not good here; we have many wor-shipers that wish not to have the obstructing of our mosque entrance, and there is a crowd at your cart."

"I will not move! We have a good spot here with many customers," Abdul shot back, trying to seem defiant and harmless, but still stub-born. "There is not much going on in your mosque that I can see!"

"You will move, or I will move this cart for you!" Suddenly, Iffy grabbed the cart and started pushing it. Abdul, who was almost twice his size, grabbed Iffy—pulling him away by his arm.

The two Taliban guards and the Chief of Police quickly crossed the busy street. They aggressively grabbed the cart and Abdul. The Taliban guards moved in when Abdul and Sam started pushing back.

"Arrest this man!" The Chief of Police ordered the Taliban guards.

"Okay, okay!" Abdul relented. "We did not mean to cause a dis-turbance. We will move the cart immediately. We were only trying to make a little extra money." He smiled dumbly at Iffy and the others.

They seemed to buy it. Iffy tossed baskets of potatoes and onions on to the cart as he cursed at them. "Take your cart to the market where you belong!"

A crowd had formed as the locals voiced their distaste for how the Chief of Police and Taliban guards were handling this innocent food vendor. The Chief of Police and the Taliban guards looked around at a large crowd that formed. They all backed off, watching as Abdul and Sam pushed the cart down the street towards the market.

"We might of just had a small setback in our plan," Abdul said to Sam as they rounded a corner heading in the direction of the market.

Dastgir and Iffy were outside with the guards, Asa could hear some kind of commotion going on outside. "Now. Now is the time," Asa said urgently to Rachim and Zaahid "Keep watch, Zaahid."

Rachim stood on the wash basin underneath the window. The basin sat off the ground a few feet. Asa climbed up next to him, getting his balance as the basin shifted under the weight. Asa grabbed Rachim's foot. With all his strength, Asa pushed Rachim up.

Rachim's hand was inches from the edge of the window. He stretched, feeling the edge. "I'm almost there."

"Hurry, they will be back any moment," Zaahid said, looking back to the front room through the curtain. The commotion—whatever it was—was still going on outside in the street.

Asa gave one more push and felt Rachim's weight release off him. Rachim had made it to the edge. Rachim pulled himself up and squeezed through the small opening. He then turned to go out feet first. Face-to-face with Asa in that instant before letting go, he looked into Asa's eyes.

"You have been a good friend. I will miss you. We'll try to find your father, I promise you!" he said, as he disappeared through the window.

Asa nodded, tears in his eyes. "Please hurry!" The commotion on the street was dying down. "Quickly, come here Zaahid, they will be back any moment," Asa said with his heart pounding.

Zaahid, even with his twisted back, was a bit taller than Rachim as he climbed up on the basin. He managed to reach the edge of the window quickly, but his back lacked the strength to pull himself up.

Outside the window, Asa could hear Rachim calling softly. "Hurry! Hurry!"

Asa's heart was pounding. He looked around the room and spotted the footstool next to the table. He grabbed the footstool and balanced it on the unstable basin. This gave Zaahid an extra foot of height.

"Come quickly." Asa guided Zaahid up, and Zaahid found the window's edge—slowly struggling to pull himself up. With his back stiff and twisted, he had no choice but to go out head first. He disappeared through the window.

Asa heard a cry of pain as Zaahid hit the hard ground outside. He suddenly heard the door in front open to the mosque. He wiped the sweat from his face, grabbed the bag Dastgir's had given him, and slid through the curtain into the front room. He tried to seem as calm as possible.

It was Dastgir. He was clearly upset and did not notice anything else. "Come now! Hurry, we must go."

Taking Asa by his hand, Dastgir nearly dragged him outside the mosque to the waiting Cruiser. Asa looked around while holding his breath. Looking down the alley, he spotted Rachim and Zaahid holding hands and running as they vanished into the crowd. Asa smiled.

*At least my friends are free,* he thought sadly. *But I am not.*

Abdul and Sam were getting close to the market area while Iffy followed, shouting at them to move quickly.

"Out of the way!" Iffy suddenly screamed.

Abdul heard the sound of the Cruiser behind them in the narrow street. As he tried to move the cart out of the way, he turned and gazed into the Cruiser. There in the backseat sitting in between the two Taliban soldiers was what surely was the boy named Asa.

His stomach fell to the pit of his being. He had just missed rescuing the boy. He had just missed Asa!

Cursing, Iffy returned to the mosque and called out for his boys. If nothing else went right today, then he would at least punish his boys and have his way with them.

Nothing but silence filled the mosque.

Walking to the back room through the curtain, he noticed the footstool laying on it's side in front of the sink. The sink basin was dangling from the wall. Looking up, he noticed the open window.

Picking up the stool, Iffy threw it across the backroom, knocking over all the dishes from the table. Everything crashed to the floor. Iffy sat down at the small table and put his head down, pulling at his hair, his mind racing.

The boys were gone.

The Mi-24 Russian helicopter cruised along at 78 knots as it banked hard left. Asa sat with his arms wrapped around his knees for warmth, his feet bound by rope, trying to balance himself through the aggressive turn. He avoided eye contact with the two Taliban soldiers that sat across from him; their eyes were fixed intently on him, watching every move he made. Asa just stared at the Russian rifles on the floor of the cargo area, trying hard not to cry.

Three weeks had passed since Asa was taken captive. Asa's hopes of returning home had diminished each day that passed, and now it seemed hopeless. There was no way anyone would find him now that he'd traveled far away in a helicopter.

The noise was almost deafening inside the helicopter as the rotors cut through the air, the swoosh of the wind across the outside skin of the craft. Dastgir was sitting in the co-pilot seat with a headset on and watched as the chief of police navigated through the treacherous air thermals of the mountain passes. The weather turned cold and snowy at this altitude, making the ride unstable and rough.

Asa fought back tears. He had hoped the time would be close to seize an opportunity for escaping. It seemed as if he'd never feel the warm loving embrace of his mother and father ever again.

After leaving Jalalabad they had made an unscheduled stop to pick up another bacha bazi boy that was to be personally delivered by Dastgir to one of the Taliban leaders in the desert outside Jalalabad. Asa had observed the boy they picked up. He'd appeared to be not more than eight years of age: the boy was afraid, unaware of his fate. During the flight, the boy avoided any conversation and didn't make eye contact with Asa; he just sat and rocked back and forth looking down at the floor until they reached the drop-off point in the desert, a 30-minute flight away.

After touchdown, the pilot kept the rotors of the helicopter turning as Dastgir slid the cargo door open, lifting the frightened boy out. The boy briefly looked back at Asa with sadness and despair in his eyes. He was quickly led off by a Taliban soldier—who nearly dragged him from the helicopter to a group of waiting men that stood underneath a large camouflage netting that covered tanks and artillery.

Asa's heart hurt for the boy as he lost sight of him in the dust cloud as the helicopter took off. Heading into the mountains seemed to go on forever. Asa was getting anxious, especially after overhearing one of the Taliban soldiers mention it would be another half hour or so until touchdown at the caves.

Asa shivered. He was cold and wore only the clothing he had on in Jalalabad; the light brown shalwar kameez outfit and white pakol cap he wore was not enough for warmth in the higher elevations.

Looking out the small cargo window of the helicopter, he witnessed nothing but the vast bland whiteness of the sky. The last several weeks had made Asa grow up. He felt hardened from the abuse he had endured. He knew in his heart that there would be another opportunity some day to escape, but he might have to wait many months or years. He wondered what Jamil would do in this situation, but Jamil seemed so far removed from him now. It had been so long since seeing him that Asa was scared he would forget his face, his warm smile, his laughter.

The memories of his past life, his family started to slowly fade, becoming distant and blurred. They were gone now, and nothing could change that fact.

# PART THREE

## THE CAVES

# CHAPTER 1

# THE CROSSING

It had been three days since we passed through the Good Village, but it seemed like eons ago as I worked out the scenarios in my head in preparation of what to expect when we reached the caves. After leaving Asmar a day ago, the trek had begun to worsen with the thinning air in the higher elevations.The deepening snow line forced us to strap on our snowshoes.

I noticed that Zaleah, conditioned to this environment, was out in front about fifty yards. Big Joe determined to show Zaleah he could keep up with her was ahead of us. We all marched up the slope in a single line to minimize the tracks left behind.

I saw the dark clouds off in the distance in the direction we were headed. Zaleah estimated a two-day trek with moderate conditions remained if we continued to stay close to the tree line and rocky terrain as much as possible. To stay out of eyeshot of any Taliban that might be scanning the mountains. I took another elevation reading and learned that we were just short of 14,000 feet.

The time was 16:07, and I wanted to make camp as soon as possible in case the weather would take a turn for the worse for the evening. As I looked up the mountain with my binoculars for a plateau ahead to camp, I could see jagged rock formations ill-suited for setting up camp.

"Slow down, Big Joe!" Tex yelled, his words lost in the snowy mountainous terrain. Big Joe, with his determination to keep pace with Zaleah, was putting more distance between us.

"Look above." Tex pointed to the sky, spotting the first drone pass overhead with a bright flash of the sun reflecting off the fuselage momentarily. We watched as it headed up the slope, then bank to the right out of sight.

"About time they got here," I was concerned about that helicopter that had buzzed overhead outside Asmar. The drone should pass overhead two times a day, with the exception of bad weather and refueling until this mission was complete.

Zaleah was putting more distance between us as we struggled to keep her pace. She became nearly invisible in the blinding stark white terrain. Looking around, I noticed that the jagged rocky formations around us grew more pronounced. We were nearing the alpine zone where no trees could survive. I gave Big Joe and Zaleah a sharp whistle and waved my arms, motioning for them to stop.

"We need to pace ourselves," I ordered as we stood together near a rock ledge with a few of the men leaning against boulders to catch their breath. Zaleah paced back and forth, anxious to keep moving.

"We will have to locate a safe flat area to dig in tonight, the sooner the better," I said. "Let's continue for another hour or so, see what we find. That should give us enough daylight needed for making camp."

"I'm feeling a little woozy," Antonio mentioned as he bent over. "I need to sit and catch my breath!"

"Anyone else feeling light headed?" I looked around at the men. "You are experiencing acute mountain sickness; it should only last a day or so. Take your altitude pill! I don't need any of you losing focus, so keep up with the small sips of water. Our stop tonight will allow some time for the acclimation process to take hold. We need to continue monitoring our surroundings by keeping our eyes peeled for the Taliban. Don't get complacent on me now, we should make the cave tomorrow, God willing."

They all nodded silently.

"Zaleah, any idea if we have a plateau for making camp in our near future?" I asked. "Somewhere flat and stable for digging in tonight?"

"I do know of just a place," Zaleah went on. "There is a high point on this section of the mountain perfect for a camp. To get to the high point we must cross over one crevasse. It's a very dangerous crossing. Your men are slow and clumsy," she added with sarcasm as she leaned in to me talking in a whisper so the others wouldn't hear. "I hope they are mentally prepared and strong willed, because our trek will worsen."

"These men are as good as they get," I said defensively. "When the time comes, they will fight like warriors with hearts of lions. We've been together a long time—gone through so many battles that we can nearly read each other's minds."

"I believe you, but we just need the warriors to pick up the pace," she said with a grin.

Nearly two hours passed when suddenly Tex yelled. He'd spotted movement below to the left off in the distance. We all stopped and gathered around Tex, looking in the same direction through our binoculars.

Below, we spotted what looked to be two, maybe three Taliban soldiers a half day behind us down slope. They were dressed in white, nearly invisible to the naked eye if not for the black headdresses they wore.

"It appears they are on a different course heading east, away from us," Tex said, looking over at me.

"I know of that trail," Zaleah commented while looking through her binoculars. "We have nothing to be concerned of, that trek will pull them away from us. There are many caves and strongholds throughout this area."

"Yeah, I don't like it. Too close for me," Big Joe said looking over at Ben. "How do we know they haven't spotted our tracks? They could easily double back and catch us asleep tonight. Like shooting fish in a barrel. Could be that helicopter spotted us the other night confirming our direction."

"We won't do anything at this point," I said. "Our best bet is to keep moving. If they have radios, and most likely they do, we have no chance. This whole area is filled with Taliban, and we need to stay invisible at this point."

We kept moving, trudging slowly and deliberately up the mountain.

"We are close to the plateau where you want to camp for the night," Zaleah said, pointing a finger up the mountain in the direction of a flat area. "There to the right of that rock formation; it's just another thousand yards or so. We still have to cross the crevasse. If we are unable to be successful crossing at that point, we will have a setback of time until we find a stable crossing point further down. The mountain with the shifting ice is dangerous and unpredictable."

The last 100 yards became more difficult in snowshoes and steep grade. The snowfall started, and increased in intensity as small frozen pellets whipped around us. We spotted the high point just ahead. Zaleah, out in front about 30 yards, suddenly raised her arm, motioning for us to stop. We were at the crevasse she had spoken of. Looking back to us, she instructed everyone to remove their snowshoes. The snow was knee deep as we stood at her side near the crevasse. Leaning over the icy edge of the crevasse, all we could see was a straight drop down in complete darkness. The bottom was not visible.

As we helped one another remove the snowshoes, strapping them to our backpacks, we then put on the crampon ice spikes. The wind driven snow pelted our goggles as we grabbed the rope. Zaleah walked the edge of the crevasse, looking for a solid crossing point. She'd noticed a small area where the snow and ice had made a small ice bridge from one side to the other. The distance to the other side at this point was only three meters or so.

"This spot looks the best," Zaleah commented while removing a stick from her backpack. Looking for stability and the strength to hold the weight of each of us, she meticulously poked at the crossing point.

"This is good!" Zaleah said to me. "Once we are securely tied together, we will cross one by one. If one of us were to fall, we would have the strength of the others to pull them back up to safety."

Nodding, I kept my doubts to myself. I was worried most about Antonio with his effects of the altitude sickness.

"I will cross first," Zaleah instructed while removing her rifle and backpack and setting them to the ground in a snow drift. "The rest will cross, lighter men first. Big Dummy being the largest, will be our anchor and the last one to cross."

Big Joe began to securely fasten the rope around Zaleah's waist.

"So Big Dummy! Do I trust you to tie off a good mountaineering knot? Or do you secretly want me to fall to my death?" Zaleah commented, looking at Big Joe as they stood near the cornice at the edge of the crevasse.

"Don't worry, I was a sailor once," laughed Big Joe. "They taught us many useful knots, none of which I ever used, of course. I promise I won't use the slip knot today," Big Joe said smiling. He tested the rope giving it a good yank as he wished her good luck.

The rest of the men got in order according to their weight, and Big Joe secured the rope around each of the men's waist, making sure the rope was tight. Spacing between the men was 5 feet, leaving just enough distance between them to space out the weight on the ice bridge during the crossing. After Zaleah crossed, next it would be Tex, Antonio, Ben, myself—and Big Joe last.

Slowly crawling out to the ice bridge, Zaleah inched herself onto it on her belly, stopping to test it first. The loose snow over the ice bridge varied in snow depth, making her progress slow. The width of the ice bridge wasn't much more than 20 inches, and the thickness looked to fluctuate from four inches to six; Zaleah, small in stature, nearly filled the narrow space.

She finally made it to the other side. We all exhaled, feeling more confident that Zaleah made a good choice of location to crossover. One by one, the men tossed over their backpacks and gear before crossing.

Each man crossed without incident, and it was finally Big Joe's turn. With his size and weight, we pulled the rope tight from the other side, taking out all the slack and digging in with our boots. We braced ourselves in the event the ice bridge would give way. The soft powdery snow that had once covered the ice bridge was nearly gone from the men's crossing, leaving a crystal clear ice bridge. The thick ice distorted the dark icy blue crevasse below.

Big Joe inched his way out over the seemingly endless depth below him.

"You're almost there!" I called out encouragingly.

*Crack!* Big Joe was only inches from making it across when we heard a loud cracking noise. Zaleah reached for his hand to help move him along quicker. Finally reaching the edge safely, Big Joe stood up, brushing the snow off the front of his snowsuit.

"Damn! Nearly shit myself when I heard that crack," Big Joe said while loosening the rope and turning back to look.

"My gear! My rifle! Did you forget to grab my gear?" Zaleah said looking at Big Joe with her hands on her hips.

"Shit," Big Joe said. "I'll go back."

"No! Zaleah is the lightest here. She will have to cross back," I said looking over to Big Joe. "Now tie that rope off quickly; the snow is picking up and we're losing daylight."

The men lined up behind Big Joe, who was the closest to the edge. Kneeling down, Big Joe eased the rope out as Zaleah inched her way back across. Everyone held their breath, expecting the unstable ice bridge to go anytime. Zaleah reached the other side quickly as she grabbed her backpack and rifle, tossing them to the other side. She hurried back to the ice bridge. She knelt down on her knees, then to her belly to distribute her weight.

I could feel the tension in the air. The integrity of the ice bridge was gone, and she had to hurry.

"Hope it will hold," Ben said in a low whisper to Tex.

As Zaleah got within the last few inches, she reached out for Big Joe's hand. Big Joe was on one knee as he stretched out to grab her.

*Crack!* The ice bridge gave way. Zaleah disappeared over the edge into the darkness below, all we heard was silence, deafening silence for a split second, as the snow continued to fall heavy.

"Zaleah! Are you there?" I shouted down, trying to peer through the cloud of snow.

"Are you going to leave me here all day?" We heard her yell, her words lost in the wind driven snow. "I'm here!"

We felt her weight on the other end of the rope. The knot had held. All men pulled in unison and got her up to the edge. Big Joe lay on his belly, reaching out as he grabbed her by the arm, and pulled her up. There was nothing but darkness below her.

"Stopper knot!" Big Joe said while coming face-to-face with Zaleah as he pulled her up out of the black abyss. "It was a stopper knot!"

"What?" Zaleah said, breathing hard as she quickly stepped away from the edge.

"A stopper knot. That's what I always tie off with. I guess I did it right this time," Big Joe said, winking at her.

She just laughed nervously. "The Big Dummy knows something after all!"

"No more mistakes," I said, looking at the men, observing the buildup of snow caked around their goggles. "Up here, the simplest mistake will cost you your life, period. Got it? Now let's get moving. We've lost enough time."

Looking over to Zaleah, I noticed blood dripping from her nose. Reaching down, I grabbed a handful of snow and held it to her nose to slow the bleeding.

"Look there! Past that small boulder wall directly in front of us," Zaleah said pointing with her right hand while she kept holding the handful of bloody snow to her nose.

"You sure you're feeling okay?" I asked her. "That was a bit of a fall. Looks as if you dropped a good distance. Good thing you were close to the edge before the fall; any further out on the ice bridge with more rope would of created a pendulum effect, slamming you up against the side of that crevasse much harder. You could've of broken some bones."

"I'm fine. Don't worry," she said lightly. I could tell she was more shaken up then she let on.

With darkness falling, the temperature dropped as we finally made it to the flat high point. The wind and snow started to sting as it hit our flesh. We began to set up camp. For warmth and protection from the inclement weather, we created little igloos with a small rabbit hole openings to crawl into. When we were done, there were three igloos carved into the snow, big enough for two each. Big Joe and Tex were in one, with Ben and Antonio in the other, and Zaleah and myself occupying the third. Once inside, they were large enough to sit up in.

Exhausted from the day's journey, we patted the last bit of snow around the igloos, making them dense and preventing the cold to enter. Zaleah, still shaken and exhausted, was the first to turn in for the night without saying much. I went over the day's mistakes, hoping to learn from them as we continued on our journey. We all ate from our MRE food packs in silence.

With the men settled in for the night, I stood staring up the mountain. Deafening silence fell over the camp as the heavy snowfall lay down a thick heavy carpet of white. I heard frequent muffled voices coming from Tex and Big Joe's igloo, arguing over who got what side to sleep on.

I paused for several minutes, thinking of my wife and kids. *This is such a cold and unforgiving place,* I thought. *It makes me feel so far away from them. How I wish I could hold them, tell them how much I miss and love them!*

Looking out at the snow covered mountain alone, my mind was going in all directions with the mission, my family back home, the responsibility God had laid upon me. Finally, I crawled into the small opening of the igloo head first, removing the snowsuit and kevlar vest.

Looking towards Zaleah, I suddenly noticed in the low glow of a flashlight she'd placed on the other side of her that she was partially unclothed, facing away from me. I knelt there for a moment, staring at her back and listening to the wind-driven snow outside.

After my eyes adjusted to the low glow of the light, I noticed scarring on her back. Her soft, creamy brown skin was twisted with the ugliness of dark brown scars intertwined in her flesh. I felt as if I was intruding, but at the same time I couldn't look away at those scars. Zaleah had seen some harsh things in her life, and I wondered what her story was.

# CHAPTER 2
# WHITEOUT

"**D**o you miss your wife?" Zaleah asked in a whisper that was barely audible. With her back to me, she turned her body slightly to her right while waiting for my answer. The steam of her breath suspended in the air like a small vapor cloud in the flashlight beam.

She startled me with her question, which broke my stare.

"Yes, very much," I said.

I hadn't really thought about it until then that since we met in Asmar, she had been covered from head to toe with the exception of just her face. Her long, beautiful, shiny black hair cascaded down her chest, covering her breasts. At this angle with the light softly shining on her face, she looked like an angel with the dark features of a Pakistani woman. In a word, she was beautiful. I noticed below her right ear another thin scar that ran across the front of her throat that ended just below her right ear.

"How would she feel knowing you are here sleeping next to another woman?" she asked.

"Under the circumstances, she would be fine with it," I said, actually feeling the opposite and somewhat guilty. I slipped off my boots. The heat from our bodies had warmed up the igloo considerably. For warmth and survival in cold harsh conditions, it is a common practice to remove wet clothing, as the wet clothing quickly drains one's body warmth.

"I have heard that when married men are away from their wives for so long they get, what is it that you say in America, 'a roaming eye'? said Zaleah. "Are you a man with a roaming eye, Sergeant?"

"You have nothing to worry about tonight, if that's what this is all about," I said gruffly. "Now turn that light off and get some rest."

Zaleah reached over and clicked off the flashlight. I laid on my back, exhaling deeply from the day's trek; my hands were clasped behind my head, and I sat up to take one last sip of water.

We lay there in silence, hearing the gusts of wind. It was as if the wind outside was alive, trying to get at us through the small opening of the igloo with strong gusts. I noticed the opening of the igloo was becoming more covered in snow as the darkness claimed the mountain.

"You're the first man outside my family that has seen my scars," she said into the darkness. "How does it make you feel? Do you feel sorry for me?"

I was curious to know the backstory about her scars, I couldn't deny that fact. "How did you get them?" I asked.

She spoke her story into the damp darkness.

"When I was child, nine years of age, myself and Hakeem were sexually abused and beaten. It started with one of our brothers at first. Growing up in the Kunar Valley, we felt safe. We did well as farmers with the rich soil. But as the Taliban and Al-Qaeda began fighting in the area, they passed through our farming village almost daily. They would stop and rest, eating our food, taking what they wanted. We grew to hate them!

"My father and mother, strong and defiant, would stand up to them and often be beaten for their resistance. It was then that my two older brothers were convinced by the Taliban they should fight for the Caliphate. One day, we got up early for the harvest time and my two brothers were gone. Months passed. Then one day, they returned. My father and mother were overcome with joy that they had returned.

"But my two brothers were changed men. Their hearts were hard towards us. My mother pleaded with them to please stay, but they refused. My mother grew concerned for me and Hakeem's safety, and with much conversation she convinced my two older brothers to take us to safety in Pakistan so that we would be out of the fighting. A journey through the Hindu Kush would take three days, but they finally agreed to take us. My oldest brother was helping with the farming and stayed with my parents.

"That is when things got worse. My two brothers treated us as animals on the trek. I was surprised our brothers just didn't cut our throats instead of taking on the responsibility. We traveled with a group of three Taliban men and my two brothers. The second night of the journey, we stopped at a small cave in the mountains for the night. The men and my brothers drank until they couldn't stand. I awoke to one of the Taliban men holding a knife to my throat while the others raped me. I heard Hakeem let loose a muffled scream through a hand pressed over his mouth. The men took him outside and raped him, too.

"The next morning when they were asleep, I woke up and quietly went to Hakeem. Holding his hand, we slipped out of the cave, afraid for our lives with no idea which way to go. We walked for half a day in the snow, but the men caught up to us, they were very angry. My two older brothers were with them as they took us back to the cave. They knew I was the one who convinced Hakeem to escape, so they began to punish me. They tied my hands together and strung me up while each man took a turn cutting the flesh on my back. My older brothers could not be seen while I was tortured. They were cowards.

"They left me hanging there for the rest of the day. It was only my anger and hate of these men that kept me alive. Hakeem was bound by rope. He just sobbed, leaning against the cave wall. We were not fed, given very little water. On the third day, they argued whether to leave us or continue on to Pakistan. It was my two brothers that convinced them to continue on. How thoughtful, those devils! A great show of love, wouldn't you say?"

Zaleah paused. It was the first time she'd stopped speaking, and I was jolted out of her horrific story as if waking from a nightmare.

"So did they take you all the way to Pakistan?" I asked, turning to my left side facing her in the darkness.

"I remember that day so well, like yesterday." she said. "My brothers left us at the top of a plateau—at 12,000 feet in elevation, I guess—with Pakistan visible below us. They just left us to make it on our own or die. That was the last time I saw them.

"We managed to get down the slope, and we ate snow for hydration. But God was watching over us. Reaching Pakistan, we walked the streets with the rest of the other countless homeless children. We survived on the streets for a few weeks until some passing Americans patrolling the streets realized they have seen us almost daily. I guess we were in rough looking shape, so they took us to the Red Cross.

"Hakeem and I were inseparable. We now had our dark secrets and we told our story to no one. We confided in each other exclusively. He would have his bad days, I would have mine. It affected Hakeem much more. He eventually reconnected with my parents and oldest brother.

"But I swore that I would become strong and never be so weak again. I devoted myself to learning all I could about fighting and weapons. I did not care that I was a young woman. I became stronger of learning how to protect myself. But I haven't seen Hakeem or the rest of my family in a long time—until now."

She stopped speaking, and I couldn't figure out what to say. It was a horrible story. I swallowed hard, trying to focus on the wind outside that howled as if in sympathy for the pain my friend Hakeem and his sister had endured.

"And you, Mr. Mike, what made you decide to this course for your life—leaving the safety of America, a loving family, far from home?" Zaleah asked sliding in closer to me. I could feel her body heat.

I paused, not really knowing where to begin. *What did motivate me to commit my life to fighting for our country?* I thought.

"When I was only three months old, my father was a Sergeant in the Air Force," I began. "After re-enlisting, he was sent to South Korea to work as ground crew with a bomber squadron during the Korean War. It was just another day on the job for him. He loved his job and providing for his family back home in Minnesota. One day, there was an aircraft coming in for touchdown. His ground crew prepared for the recovery, but the landing was hard—causing a external fuel tank attached to the underside of the wing to dislodge. The fuel tank bounced across the tarmac and exploded."

I paused, picturing it, then continued.

"A large piece of hot metal flew through the air towards the ground crew slicing into to my father's main artery just below the groin. He bled out so quickly that nothing could be done. I was three months old when that happened. I always think about what my life would've been like had he survived that day. I guess between that and my uncles serving in the military, I just felt it a honor and privilege to follow in their footsteps.

"I just want good people to be free, to live in peace, to enjoy their families," I added. "The loss of thousands of American soldiers that have made the ultimate sacrifice for the protection of other countries can't go unnoticed. Terrorists who abuse children and the weak? I wish them all dead!" I said this with such strong visceral emotion that it scared me. It wasn't something I'd articulated before, and it was strange to be speaking to a foreign woman about this.

"I guess we are alike in some ways," said Zaleah. "I have hate in my heart for the spineless animals that have no regard for life in the killing of hard-working, innocent people. You do, too."

After that, we were both silent. There had been too many emotions and difficult subjects for one night. I finally drifted off to sleep...

In was the middle of the night as Big Joe turned over to his left side and came out of deep sleep with nightmares of the Taliban closing in, he was at the edge of his waking mind. No matter how fast he ran, they kept gaining on him.

"Tex! Wake up! I heard a noise outside," Big Joe shot up reached over nudging Tex's shoulder. "Something was walking softly in the snow, just outside our igloo."

Sitting up, Tex could hear it too. *Crunch, crunch...* There was definitely someone walking outside Tex was thinking with his eyes as big as saucers.

"Seems to be too soft of steps for a man." Big Joe said trying to peek out the snow covered opening.

"When it circles back to our igloo, I'm going to get a look-see," Big Joe said, positioning himself near the opening, gun in hand.

Quietly carving out a small opening in the dense snowpack, he created a small opening, and waited. The hole was still too small for a good visual. "Shit! I need to make it larger."

"There, again!" Tex said in a nervous whisper.

We inched closer to the opening on our knees, removing more of the snow pack. Finally, the opening was big enough to stick our heads through. Big Joe positioned himself at the opening partially sticking his head through with his rifle in front of him. "Your shitting me! I see what was making all the noise". Big Joe look back at Tex.

There, inches from Big Joe's face partially blocking the opening to the igloo, was the big furry head of King!

"It's King!" Tex and Big Joe said in unison with joy.

They both started to laugh, exhaling deeply, falling backwards into the small space with relief. King stuck his head through the opening and began to lick Big Joe's face. Both were filled with excitement and happiness embraced King. King, panting with excitement, gave a quick sharp bark as he continued to sniff out a piece of beef jerky in Big Joe's front pocket.

It wasn't long before everyone in camp heard the commotion and pushed through the snow caked rabbit holes to witness King tearing around the igloos like an excited puppy who'd found his way back home. My men were ecstatic. At least King was back, at least he had made it safely.

Sal would've been overjoyed.

Suddenly, there was a rumbling noise. The ground beneath us shook, and we all paused in our celebration of King's return.

"Do you hear that?" Antonio said.

The snow storm was winding down, but still it reduced our hearing and visibility for several yards.

We all stood looking in the direction of the rumbling noise down slope, waiting. But we heard nothing else.

"Sounded like a missile just went off," I said, looking over to the men. "Let's pack up camp. I'm not feeling good about this."

# CHAPTER 3
# THE PREDATOR DRONE

Sergeant Miller relieved Sergeant Bacon of his 12 hour shift at 0600 hours. Both have been a part of Officer Tucker's team for the last 3 years. Looking up to the wall monitors, Sergeant Miller grabbed a cup of coffee from the pot sitting on the shelf near his desk and noticed a break in the weather. Sipping his coffee, he stood observing the ground crew breaking down the tie down chains on the Predator in preparation for launch.

"Good Morning, Sergeant!" Officer Tucker said upon entering the command room.

"Morning, Sir!"

"Any changes in the weather?" Officer Tucker inquired while pouring a hot cup of coffee that steamed in the cold of the command room.

"Looks like the weather system is moving in a southeasterly direction. Later today, it should start to break up."

"Good! I have a meeting with the Base Commander in fifteen. I want that bird launched as soon as possible. I estimate they should be within a day's journey of the caves based on the intel from our source. Have the ground crew double check the Hellfire and Stinger missiles. As the men near the cave, they could have a fight on their hands sooner than we think."

"Yes, Sir!"

Sergeant Miller piloted the drone with precision, working the joystick as it lifted off the tarmac at 80 knots. The same weather system that affected Mike and the men had reached the base as rain. Sergeant Miller had to fight the wind gust buffeting the drone as it lifted off.

The drone quickly reached an altitude of 5,000 feet as it became more responsive, smoothing out just above the turbulent weather near the broken cloud deck. The flight would take a good hour, 140 mile flight to Mike and his men.

The images coming in from the drone's on-board cameras were clear and detailed as Sergeant Miller dropped altitude nearing the edge of the storm clouds where Mike and his men were dug in. With the weather system pushing to the southeast, Sergeant Miller made some adjustments with the flight direction. The weather became more zonal on the west side, allowing for the drone to fly at a lower altitude. Sergeant Miller started a grid pattern, keeping an eye out for enemy aircraft or Taliban on foot in the vicinity of Mike and his men.

The drone had a range of 675 nautical miles and could loiter for approximately fourteen hours. The ordinance crew on base had loaded two Hellfire missiles and one Stinger missile onto the drone. Stealthy and quiet, the drone could fly undetected for a total of 24 hours.

"Shit!" Sergeant Miller yelled as he pulled back hard on the joystick, taking evasive action. He yelled to the sensor, that was working the onboard drone cameras.

The monitor showed the red flare trail of a missile as it veered off to the left of the drone.

"Near hit to the port side," Sergeant Miller said with intense focus while taking the drone through a series of maneuvers, bringing her back around. "Until I get her around, I'm unable to confirm ground-to-air, or air-to-air enemy fire."

"Get a hold of Officer Tucker now!" Sergeant ordered the sensor.

Just then, Sergeant Miller spotted just below at four o'clock a Russian Mi-24 helicopter lining up for another shot.

"Officer Tucker is on his way, Sergeant!" the sensor said while setting the phone down.

The sensor watched as the Russian helicopter was flying at a high rate of speed directly at them.

"This one is loaded to the hilt!" The sensor said while pointing at the monitor. "Look! Two cannons, two four barrel guns, anti-tank missile bombs, and air to air." Sergeant glanced up briefly to look while making another series of maneuvers.

Officer Tucker and the base Commander burst through the door and walked quickly to the monitor.

"Where in the hell did they come from?" Officer Tucker asked in a high tone, looking over to Sergeant Miller.

"Not sure, Sir, but until I can lock with the Stinger missile, I just need to shake them first."

The room was tense as the men watched Sergeant Miller manage to outmaneuver the larger helicopter.

Suddenly, a clear low tone could be heard on the command center panel as the Sergeant Yelled out, "Got a lock, sir!"

"Fire!" Officer Tucker said as they witnessed the vapor trail leave the drone headed directly at the target. Seconds later, a fireball exploded at close range, causing the monitor on the wall to flicker.

"Hell yeah!" The sensor yelled.

"Take the drone down to a lower elevation, near the area you picked up the Russian helicopter. I have a feeling they were up to something. The fact that you never picked him up tells me they were in one of those deep valleys out of site, anticipating our arrival."

"Possible they might have dropped off or were picking up some troops," the Base Commander said, looking over to Officer Tucker that was stroking his mustache due to the tension.

"How far is this zone from Staff Sergeant and the men?" Base Commander asked.

"Not far," Sergeant Miller said focussed on the monitor while wiping sweat from his brow. "I would say a half day behind them."

"Look, do you see that there, just to the right?" The sensor said as he pointed to the lower right of the screen.

"Movement."

"Take her over in that direction. Hurry!" Officer Tucker ordered.

The drone dropped from 1,000 feet to just 200 feet in seconds as they scanned the terrain, flying at 60 knots.

"There! I see them! Looks to be eight men or so. See if we can enhance the image. Need to get a visual on these guys."

Sergeant Miller managed to position the drone in a perfect location, noticing the men below were Taliban soldiers. All the men in the group below noticed the drone buzzing them overhead. One of the Taliban pulled out a shoulder Stinger missile, taking aim at the drone.

"Pull up! Pull up! Now!" Officer Tucker yelled.

Sergeant Miller was already accelerating into a hard right turn so the sun was behind the drone, putting the sun in the Taliban's eyes. The stinger missile went wide of the drone. Miller brought the drone around over their heads, swinging to the left. The ground-to-air Stinger has a range of about 26400 feet, so he knew they needed to hurry and get in position before they had time to fire off another.

"Bring her around again! Take her to 2,700 feet and get a lock!" Officer Tucker ordered!

"In position, sir!" Sergeant Miller said, looking over to his sensor and the Base Commander.

"Commander," Officer Tucker said looking over to the Base Commander, waiting for the order to fire.

"Your team; you call it," the Base Commander said.

"Launch!" Officer Tucker ordered.

They all stood motionless as the missile left a vapor trail disappearing into the white vastness of the mountains below.

Leaning into the monitor, the men waited for what seemed an eternity. Finally, they saw a small explosion. A white cloud burst surrounded the impact area.

"Take her down. I need a visual," Officer Tucker said.

The drone made a pass over the target zone. All that could be seen was a deep crater and snow mixed with red blood.

"Enhance the image. Pass over again. I want to make sure we have taken out the whole lot," Tucker ordered.

After passing over several times, it was confirmed: no survivors. Sergeant Miller watched as the Base Commander and Officer Tucker stood staring at each other. He knew they were feeling relief and concern at the same time. They all sensed without saying a word that Staff Sergeant and his men had been spotted.

"Continue with the flyovers," Officer Tucker ordered Miller. "And stay very alert. We've have been found out."

"Yes, sir!" Sergeant Miller acknowledged, looking at the sensor.

This mission had just taken a very serious turn.

# CHAPTER 4
# ROAD TO KABUL

"Zaahid, Zaahid! Look! I see Kabul!" Rachim shouted.

Four days had passed after being freed from the mosque, and it was early morning. The sun was just peeking up from the blue horizon.

The two boys had started out on the 93-mile trek to Kabul on foot. Now, they could see the city of Kabul in the distance. Their promise to Asa was to be fulfilled by the boys in finding his father, the wealthy doctor in Kabul. When they find him, they would explain of the danger Asa was in.

Walking for two days in the intense heat had caused Rachim and Zaahid to nearly pass out from dehydration. It was on the third day that a farmer pulling an old wooden cart filled with fresh vegetable goods and a goat passing by had stopped to help the boys. He'd been heading for the market in Kabul.

Zaahid was asleep lying next to the goat for warmth in the cool morning air. He struggled to sit up hearing Rachim excited as the wooden cart traveled over the rough dirt road.

"What is it, Rachim?" he said groggily, but he didn't have to wait for his words to find out. He, too, saw the distant skyline of Kabul. "The city!" he cried, overjoyed.

An hour passed as they reached the outer east side of Kabul. This was the first time the two boys had been here. Kneeling in the cart with their arms over the wooded side rail, they were wide-eyed as they took in the new city. They observed the locals scurrying about, and a few passing military vehicles.

The cart slowed as it reached the edge of Chicken Street. Speaking in Dari the farmer turned back, motioning for the boys to get out.

"Merci, mamnoon." Rachim said— which meant, *thank you very much.*

"Khodahafez," the farmer said waving.

The boys stood together watching as the cart disappeared around the next corner. The goat gazed at the boys from the back as it pulled away.

"I am hungry. What are we to do for food?" Rachim said while looking around.

"Here, I have these," Zaahid said, pulling out four apples he'd taken from the farmer's cart with a big grin.

The two boys sat on a broken curb near the street down from the market—grateful for the small snack and trying to ignore their growing hunger pains.

★ ★ ★

It was 6:00am, and Farrin was already up with his morning workout. Classical music played through the earbuds as he was in full stride on the treadmill. His shift was to start at 7:00. It would be a week tomorrow since Rachel had left for Minnesota, it seemed so much longer.

Abdul had called just a few days ago, informing him that the trail had been lost, and that he'd seen Asa being whisked away in a Toyota vehicle. The pain Farrin felt could not be described. He stepped off the treadmill while looking at his watch.

The phone calls with Rachel had lessened, almost as if Rachel was putting herself in a cocoon, being far removed from this horrible part of the world that had taken her boys. He had not told Rachel of anything involving the loss of Asa's trail. Finding comfort in being in the States around familiar places and family, it was as if Rachel was beginning to think of Kabul as another planet. Farrin wondered if she'd ever return home again if the boys weren't found.

The sun was rising as Kabul came to life with the demands of the constant daily struggles of life playing out. Pulling up to his parking spot just a few feet away from the back doors to the hospital, Farrin flipped the switch on the dash of the MG—watching as the convertible top sealed tight.

Farrin looked over the white board filled with today's surgeries with a fellow surgeon. "Looks like a busy day," Farrin said as he glanced towards the lobby full of families anxious to save their loved ones.

The Head Nurse came over and stood next to Farrin. "Doctor, I need to talk to you immediately," the Head Nurse said in hushed tones, waving Farrin away from the counter.

"What is it?" Farrin tried not to show his concern.

"Early this morning when I got in, two boys off the streets were sitting in the lobby," the Head Nurse told him. "They mentioned they were looking for you. They said something about Asa and that they knew him. In their condition, I didn't take them too seriously—but anything about Asa, well, you never know."

"Really?" Farrin said quietly. He tried not to let any hope linger. With every hour, Asa seems further away. A mirage.

"You have a few minutes until your first surgery, and the boys are in the lobby," said the Head Nurse. "I brought them some bread and water a few hours ago. They look in pretty rough shape. You will spot them—they look pretty rough."

With his heart in his throat, Farrin walked the 30 feet to the lobby with his clipboard at his side, rounding the corner he looked around at the people in the lobby. Some sat, some paced the floor mumbling prayers for loved ones. As the glare of the morning sun shown through the large lobby windows, he spotted two ragged boys sitting together. Watching the two boys, Farrin noticed one sitting, while the other stood next to the chair. Both held the others' hand, looking extremely tired. The shalwar kameez outfits they wore were ill-fitted, dirty, and showing some tears.

Farrin walked over and stood directly in front of the boys. "Hello. I am Doctor Khan. My head nurse mention you boys have some news of Asa?" Farrin spoke in Dari, unsure of the language the boys spoke.

Both boys jumped to their feet, hugging Farrin, they wrapped their arms around his waist. Farrin looked around the room, confused and a little bit embarrassed.

"We have urgent news for you," the smaller one blurted out, Farrin noticed his missing right eye. "We have been told you are Asa's father. We traveled far to tell you, He is alive! He is alive!"

"He helped us!" the one with the twisted back said, tears filling his eyes. "He told us where we could find you."

Farrin felt his heart quickening. He sensed truth to their words. *Could it be that these boys truly have news of Asa?* "Come with me. We can go to my office," Farrin said as he took both boys by the hand, leading them down the hallway. "I need to hear your story."

Closing the door to his office, Farrin helped the older, bigger boy onto a small couch, observing his deformed twisted back. Sitting on the front of his desk, he saw that the boys were abnormally skinny— malnourished, maybe. He noticed scars on their bodies that hinted at some kind of violence.

"Can I get you some water? Food?" Farrin asked, looking down kindly at the boys. "And what are your names?"

Both nodded their heads eagerly at the thought of water, Farrin stuck his head out of the office door to call a nurse to bring some bread and water.

"I am Zaahid, and this is Rachim," said the larger boy. "Are you really a doctor, sir?"

"Yes," Farrin commented, with a smile.

"Asa helped us in our escape; he is alive!" Rachim said.

"Yes!" chimed in Zaahid. "If not for Asa, we still would of been held against our will at the mosque."

"The mosque in Jalalabad?" Farrin inquired, leaning in.

"You see, sir, we were taken as prisoners a few years ago, tricked by Dastgir and Iffy," Rachim started to tear up.

"We made a promise to Asa we would come here. He was very brave, and the punishment for such a thing would of been terrible. They are very evil men," Zaahid said as he stood and turned his back to Farrin while sliding up his shirt.

Farrin knelt down, noticing the gruesome bruises and welts on Zaahids back. It took his breath away.

"You too Rachim? Have you been subject to this abuse?"

"Yes."

"And Asa! My son?"

Both boys looked at each other, hesitating, then both looked into Farrin's eyes.

"Yes," they said simultaneously.

Farrin was overwhelmed with grief, so helpless with the weight of the news.

*Clearly these boys are sincere with this news, what now?* he thought. *Abdul mentioned the mosque.*

"Where is Asa now? Is he still at the mosque?"

"No, the day he aided in our escape, they took him away," Rachim said, standing next to Farrin—who was still kneeling in front of them."

"Where have they taken him?"

"He was with us for three weeks or so. Iffy had trained Asa to entertain for the men at the caves where they take all the boys."

Farrin just stared past the boys in shock of this news.

"They have moved him again?" Farrin said out loud.

"Your son, sir, is our friend and very brave!" Rachim said now, standing on the other side of Farrin.

"Did they hurt him? I mean, is he bruised and marked as you?"

"No sir. Iffy did hit him with the rattan a few times, but he is to be prized and protected."

Farrin dropped his head to his hands and began to sob uncontrollably for the first time since Asa's disappearance. He'd been trying so hard to be strong through this for Rachel the last several weeks, but finally all the grief and pain caught up to him.

Rachim and Zaahid wrapped their little arms around Farrin as he knelt sobbing.

"We miss our friend. We will help you," Rachim said in a sad tone.

Farrin stood wiping his eyes. "You boys have nowhere to go, do you?"

"No," both responded.

"You will come to my home, and you will stay with me," Farrin ordered. "I'm calling Abdul who is a private investigator, he might have a few questions for you, and if you will be so kind as to answer, maybe something good can some of this. You both have been very, very brave, and I will never forget this."

They began crying, too. "Paging Doctor Khan," Farrin heard as he held the boys close at his side.

# CHAPTER 5

# RACHEL

Rachel sat at the kitchen table while watching her sister, Rhonda, cook some macaroni and cheese for her kids. The trip back to Minnesota had helped her relax some, to decompress, centering her. Every night she would lie awake in bed with an aching heart and pray for the safe return of her two boys.

The clock above the kitchen sink window displayed 12:32pm. Rachel slowly lowered her eyes from the clock to the window just above the kitchen sink, noticing the trees in the front yard with the leaves turning color. Tall maples with bright red leaves and oaks drenched in dark red brown colors stood along the boulevard. They were lit up by the sun's soft filtered light shining through the leaves, making them dance with life.

This was her favorite time of year. Having grown up in Minnesota near the Metropolitan Stadium in Bloomington were they could hear the cheers of the crowds during Viking games. Her father was upset when the Vikings played their last game at the Met in 1981, losing to the Kansas City Chiefs 10-6. The following season they would play in their new home in downtown Minneapolis at the Metrodome. Rachel remembered her dad hated it. Only five-years-old at the time, she remembered how she and Rhonda would sit with their parents in their front yard on lawn chairs, with blankets on the ground and listen to the Vikings games on a old Motorola radio her dad had in the garage.

In the living room off the kitchen, Rachel heard laughter as Rhonda's three kids—aged 13, 9, and 7—watched cartoons on TV, giggling at a huge yellow hammer slamming down on a green monster.

It was then the phone rang out: a loud metallic bell sound that made Rachel jump. Rhonda grabbed the phone off the wall, cradling the phone to her right ear with her shoulder. Not missing a beat, she kept stirring the mac and cheese that steamed in front of her.

"For you, sis! It's Farrin," she said as she handed the phone over to Rachel. "Kids, lunch!"

Rachel stood from the table and went into the living room. She leaned over the blaring TV, turning down the volume.

"Hello?" Rachel said softly.

"Hi, sweetheart," Farrin said as if he was a million miles away.

"I miss you so much," Rachel said into the phone as she leaned against the wall in the hallway that led back to the bedrooms. "Please tell me you have some good news," she whispered. "I sure could use it!"

There was a pause on Farrins end. "As a matter fact, I do," he said, sounding weary. "I haven't spoke to Abdul now in a few days, but this morning two boys about Asa's age showed up at the hospital when I got into work. The two boys traveled from Jalalabad, and they said they spent a few weeks with Asa in a Mosque! The same Mosque Abdul mention, so it must be true."

Rachel let out sigh over the phone. "He is alive! What else did they say? Are you able to make the drive, go get our son?" Rachel said with excitement in her voice.

"Well, first I will try Abdul. He is there already in Jalalabad, and I can have him confirm if its true. If it is, I will see what he advises."

"I want to come home," Rachel said, wiping the tears from her eyes. Everything felt a little lighter suddenly. More hopeful.

"I agree. It's time for you to come home!" Farrin's voice came through over the phone. "So I went ahead and booked you on a flight for the day after tomorrow. An afternoon flight. I need you here now, and I miss you so much!"

"Okay," Rachel replied with excitement in her words. "Being here has helped me in so many ways, but I'm just ready to be back. I want to go find our boys together. I'm feeling much stronger now. Determined!"

"I love you. Look I have a full schedule today with surgeries," Farrin said. "Let's talk later!"

"I love you, too. God, I dread that long flight back, but I'm so anxious to be home!" Rachel said.

As she hung up the phone, new strength ebbed through her like the sunlight shining through the autumn leaves.

# CHAPTER 6
# THE VISITOR

Farrin had just finished with a 14-hour shift at the hospital. It was 9:45 pm as he pulled into the garage. Farrin headed towards the house wearing his light blue scrubs, carrying his briefcase in his left hand while he walked along the low lit cobblestone path to the back door.

He thought about his phone call with Rachel, and he felt a little guilty for not telling her the whole story. *As much as I want to tell her about Asa's possible abuse, I'm not ready to,* he thought. *She isn't ready! She will snap in two.*

Rachid and Zaahim spent their first night with Farrin. Samina was watching the boys while he was at work. With them here, he felt a connection to Asa through them—a new hope. Nothing could be certain yet.

Farrin glanced at his cell phone. He had hoped for a call today from Abdul, after he had left several messages for him. He wanted to let him know of the news from Rachid and Zaahim.

"I home—Rachim! Zaahid!" Heading upstairs, he passed the library that was still cluttered with Rachel's painting supplies and works-in-progress. Farrin decided to leave it the way she'd left it before leaving for Minnesota, a reminder to him of her every time he passed by. He could still smell her perfume in the library mingled with the wood and canvas smell from the stacks of wood frames around the library.

Standing at one of the windows in the library that overlooked the backyard, he watched as Samina was playing catch with the boys as the yard lights blared. Farrin could almost picture Jamil and Asa as he listened to their laughter, it was infectious. After spending some time with the two boys, Farrin had found out that both parents had abandoned them. They had no memory of their families.

*How sad,* Farrin thought. *Their families had no means to look for them, or they sold them off in the first place.*

"Come in now! It's getting late!" Farrin yelled as he went downstairs to the front step. They reluctantly rounded the front yard. "I want both of you to shower before bed!"

"I never want to leave this place!" Farrin over heard Zaahid whisper to Rachim while the two headed upstairs. Farrin put the boys to bed after their shower, the boys soaked in the freedoms they had been without for so long.

The sheer white drapes in the big bay window allowed a full view of the front yard and driveway. Farrin poured himself a scotch and walked to the front door to shut the lights off outside. He noticed a Jeep in the front roundabout driveway. Pulling the curtains to the left, he saw a man leaning up against the jeep just staring at the house.

Farrin froze for a moment, caught off guard. His thoughts immediately went to the pistol in the library. He ran upstairs and grabbed the pistol. He headed back downstairs with his heart racing. After slowly opening the front door, Farrin stepped outside while holding the pistol at his side, stopping on the front step for a moment while his eyes adjusted to the shadows. The strange man was still standing there, seemingly relaxed. Farrin noticed that he was an officer of some sort. He wore an American military uniform.

The unannounced guest introduced himself as Officer Tucker. "I don't think you will be needing that, sir!" Officer Tucker said while stomping out his cigarette in the driveway next to the front right wheel of the Jeep.

Farrin looked down the driveway and noticed the gate was open. "How did you open that?" Farrin asked. "That is one of the best security gates you can buy."

"We have our ways, sir. May I come in?" he asked while extending his right hand for a handshake. "I think you will be interested in what I have to tell you. I'm here on my own accord. I could use a stiff drink about now."

"Sure, sure, sorry. Not too often the military shows up at my doorstep. Come on in."

They sat at the kitchen table across from each other with Farrin pouring scotch over four ice cubes in front of Officer Tucker, hearing a *crack!* and *pop!* from the ice as the warm scotch hit the cubes. Farrin waited in silence taking another sip of his drink; the ice rolled around the glass with a tinkling noise.

Officer Tucker set his glass on the table, and Farrin poured another shot for Officer Tucker. Farrin watched as the officer slid his eyeglasses off and put them gently on the table on his right. Then he finally spoke.

"You've had two boys go missing, Jamil and Asa. I have some news of your boy, Asa."

"Asa?" Farrin sat up. "What is it you know about this? I mean, how do you even know he is missing?"

"As we speak at this very moment, we have a team headed up the Hindu Kush Mountains to a cave hide out used by the Taliban, where we believe your two boys could be held captive," said Officer Tucker. "This is supposed to be a top secret mission, and as you can imagine, I have disregarded direct orders to tell you this."

Farrin sat back in the chair. *So Rachid and Zaahim did mention the caves, the caves where they take all the boys!* Farrin was overwhelmed. *How do I find them now?* he thought while gulping down more scotch.

"I have followed your story since Jamil went missing. I know your a gifted physician, and I saw it in the local paper a few years ago," said Officer Tucker. "However, I had an informant call me a few days ago with interesting information he'd picked up recently. His name is Abdul Rehman, you see, I am part of his contacts for the missing bacha bazi boys. We work together with what intel we can get on this activity. I know you have retained him, and you have done well doing so."

"But how do you know Asa was taken to the caves?" Farrin said as he leaned forward.

"Myself and our forensics specialist on base, Brian, have been working in a covert capacity, you could say, for a few years. We've been working with some local sources that have provided some pretty reliable intel on some of the local boys that have gone missing and some history of the bacha bazi boys in this area. When I heard that it was your oldest boy Jamil that went missing a few years back, I became more interested, more proactive, and I'm positive the boys have ended up at the caves. Until now, we have had no idea of the location. We have organized a team with a guide that knows of this one cave, a very hidden fortress I hear. This has been the most promising news we have had in some time."

"Are you absolutely certain? Where are they now?" Farrin said, pouring them both another drink. "Tell me have you confirmation on Jamil? It has been several years now with no word." Farrin said with much emotion.

Officer Tucker leaned back in the chair. "I'm not 100% on Jamil, and I have tried to get word on him, but it's as if he just went off the radar. But Asa? We have confirmation on him from just a few days ago. Abdul said that he saw him in Jalalabad in a vehicle. We couldn't ID the driver and passengers."

"I can give you that information," said Farrin. "I have two young boys who showed up on my doorstep who have been living in slavery to those same men for years. They told me Asa sent them. They can help us identify who the men really are and how they're operating in the region."

Officer Tucker looked surprised. "Really? They will be helpful. For now, though, we have the best men we can offer poised to reach the cave," said Officer Tucker. "If anyone can get those boys out alive, they will. I will swing by when I have some news, so please don't try to find me. And I will speak to these two boys when we're ready to do so."

Farrin stood on the front step and watched as Officer Tucker drove away. He'd had too much information all at once. It was so much to take in between the boys and now this. Farrin gazed up at the moonlit sky, noticing off in the distance a falling star streak across the sky.

# CHAPTER 7
# THE REUNION

It was early morning as Jamil was working his way around the smaller east end of the cave. There was a small opening on this side that was never used, barely big enough to crawl through that lead to a dangerous ledge outside that sat 30 feet from the ground below, it was usually covered in snow over the winter months. As the temperature dropped outside Jamil needed to keep the generators fueled with kerosene—which provided heat and lighting to the cave.

The oily smell of the kerosene exhaust from the generators hung in the air in a blue haze that mingled with the damp smell of the cave. Jamil groaned from the weight of the two fuel cans full of kerosene, stumbling from the weight as he navigated the slippery boulders. The fuel cans tied together with a rope that hung over his shoulders.

On the larger end of the cave, there was an opening that eroded from years of the water slowly working its watery teeth at the granite stone, constantly eating away the walls of the cave structure, leaving jagged openings to the outside that allowed the sun's glow to pass through in the late afternoon. The sun light would momentarily reflect off the calm surface of the lake, casting bright sparkles that danced off the ceiling of the monolithic cave structure, casting a bright orange-blue glow for minutes as the sun quickly passed.

The generators purred fast and smooth with a oily hum. They sat directly across the lake from the dens and the main entrance. Jamil focused on his footing in the semi-darkness as he was just inches from the lakes edge.

As he neared the generators, Jamil thought about what he'd heard recently. Dastgir was headed back to the cave with another boy. Rumor had it this boy was very talented and special. The ensuing snow storm in the mountains had delayed Dastgir's return a few more days, and this would allow the extra time needed to prepare the boys and cave dens for the guests. Dastgir's parties could last for days, each boy going to the highest bidder. Jamil would be punished if his efforts didn't meet Dastgir's expectations upon his return.

*I must be careful of the two brothers, Naseefa and Shafiq, and try to protect them* Jamil thought. *Dastgir must not find out they are brothers.*

So far, Dastgir had not yet found out about the two boys. Often one of the boys in the group would snitch on another, looking for special treatment as a reward, so Jamil was concerned one of the other boys would tell Dastgir of their secret.

Jamil was often reminded of Asa as he watched the two boys interact. Their ages were similar to his and Asa's when they were last together years ago. Jamil's heart ached, thinking of how much he missed Asa and his parents.

*How could I have ever wanted to be part of this?* he asked himself, disgusted. *Money means nothing.* But then again, he had never known how organized this activity was until it was too late and he was trapped. Still, he felt such a self loathing when he thought about it.

Jamil strained as he poured the fuel into the generators, the other boys sat quietly along the lakes edge near the dens opposite side of the lake watching Jamil. Jamil constantly kept a watchful eye on the other boys while Dastgir was away. If any of the boys were hurt, or planning an escape, it was Jamil that would be punished.

Asa was cold and tired as he turned his head to the right to get a look out the window of the helicopter cargo space seeing if he could spot the cave they were headed to. The Hindu Kush came into view, snow covered and beautiful. They'd had to wait several days in order for the snow storm to clear, camping out at another mountain location until it passed.

Jagged towering rock formations jabbed out of the pristine white snow. Asa leaning over noticed a glimmer of light that caught his eye. A beautiful silver aircraft sparkled off in the distance. The sun made it momentarily glow a bright silver; it seemed to stay with them for a minute, then disappeared.

Asa blinked. *I must've been dreaming,* he thought.

It was then the pilot of the Russian helicopter slowed down, getting in position for the landing as he pivoted the front end away from the mountain in a counterclockwise direction. They gently touched down with a flurry of snow driven from the rotors. It partially blocked Asa's view as they landed on the precarious rock ledge 40 feet from the north facing main entrance.

The rotors came to a stop as the Taliban guards slid the door open to the cargo area. Dastgir, already out of the helicopter, lowered Asa down from the cargo hold himself.

Asa looked around, observing how high up they were, miles from anywhere in a desolate and isolated place. Looking towards the cave entrance he noticed an older boy standing partially outside the cave in the shadows, he was hidden from the daylight. Asa stared at the boy for a long time while Dastgir pulled Asa towards the cave entrance by his hand.

*This boy is familiar to me,* Asa thought to himself. That strange boy standing at the cave's entrance resembled Jamil the way he remembered him. *Could it be Jamil?*

Jamil recognized Asa immediately. *Asa! Asa is the special boy Dastgir had bragged so much about.* His stomach dropped. It took every fiber of his being not to run over and embrace him and protect him from Dastgir, to tell him how much he loved and missed him. Holding back his emotions was nearly impossible, but he *had* to do it. He had to.

Over the last few years, Jamil's heart had hardened into complete emptiness, devoid of any emotion. Upon seeing Asa in that second, he felt his heart immediately come back to life, filling up with the love he had for him. Jamil became angered at Dastgir in the way he forcefully escorted Asa to the entrance of the cave.

Asa now stood face-to-face with Jamil. Asa tried to pull away from Dastgir's grip and run to Jamil, to embrace his brother.

"Jamil! Could it be you? My brother! I have missed you so much!" Asa blurted out, choking on his words through his tears.

Jamil knew he must not have Dastgir realize this is true. "I have never seen this boy before," Jamil laughed, looking at Dastgir. "Is this one crazy?"

"Jamil! Jamil! It is me!" Asa said, surprised that Jamil would not acknowledge this truth.

Jamil slapped Asa hard across the face. "Get this boy away from me! He is starting to anger me with this lie!" Jamil yelled.

"How is it this boy knows your name?" Dastgir asked, questioning Jamil while jerking Asa back.

"I have been here many years now, with boys coming and going. Most have heard of Jamil the legend, a loyal servant to the great Dastgir. Please, take this boy away from me."

Dastgir seemed convinced for the time being, as he dragged Asa into the cave towards the holding den with the other boys. Asa was crying uncontrollably. It broke Jamil's heart to let him out of his sight, but he knew for Asa's protection it had to be this way, for now.

"I have supplies for the guests, get Naseefa and get those supplies unloaded now!" Dastgir ordered as he jerked Asa into the darkness of the cave.

Jamil hurt inside. *I hate Dastgir, I wish him dead,* he thought fiercely. It was time now to devise a plan and find a way to escape this hell with his little brother. But how? He must find a way soon, knowing that Asa would be subject to when the men arrived.

*He will be the prize tonight going to the highest bidder,* thought Jamil frantically. *If this happens, I will never see Asa again.*

He would save his brother if it was the last thing he ever did.

Asa was confined to the den with the other boys, with two guards just outside the den. The other boys gathered together, sitting on one side of the den. A few began to whisper with curiosity of Asa.

Asa was still sobbing, his heart hurting. He was so confused with Jamil's reaction to him. *Could it be Jamil doesn't remember me? What have they done to him?* Asa thought while he rubbed the sting on his cheek where Jamil had slapped him.

Asa then noticed the boys sitting across from him, staring with fascination. He dried his eyes with his sleeve.

"My name is Asa. I'm from Kabul," he said, trying to make conversation.

The boys just stared at him in silence.

Jamil's mind was racing with excitement. He knew Asa was smart, and together they would work together on devising a plan for an escape! For now, Jamil needed just the right moment alone with Asa to tell him how much he has missed him and ask for his forgiveness for striking him.

Tonight would be busy with the guests arriving, which should keep Dastgir and his guards distracted.

"Come, Naseefa! We must unload the helicopter!" Jamil said as he pointed to the stack of provisions.

Jamil and Naseefa quickly unloaded the helicopter. The provisions included fresh meat, rice, spices, fruit, raisins, vodka, and bread all brought in specially for the guests.

Jamil and Naseefa finished while resting on a crate of oranges, sweat dripping down their faces from the work they just finished. The cool, damp air of the den felt good as it rushed over them. Jamil wanted to share his happiness with Naseefa, but only when the time was right.

It was at that moment Jamil saw Dastgir out of the corner of his eye walking towards them. Dastgir extended his arm with a rattan in his left hand, he pointed towards the den opening, and ordered Naseefa out.

Jamil quickly sat up.

"This Asa, is he your brother?" Dastgir asked sternly. "I could see your demeanor change like I have never witnessed. Is this true?" He stared at Jamil as if looking into his soul.

"No," Jamil said, trying to sound convincing, all the while trembling on the inside—not for the strike of the rattan he was about to receive, but for wanting to protect Asa from this evil man. "No, he is just a another boy, afraid and confused."

Dastgir begin to pace back and forth in front of Jamil with his hands behind his back. Jamil kept an eye on the rattan in his left hand.

"I do not believe you. Take your clothes off. Now!" Dastgir shouted. Jamil jumped up and began removing his clothes. There he stood naked in front of Dastgir.

"You see Jamil, you have aged," said Dastgir. "You no longer have a monetary value to me. The men that come here want the younger boys. You have aged now, becoming only a servant to me. My boys bring in at least 10,000 to 200,000 American dollars. I would be lucky to get 100 American dollars for just a servant as you. Turn away from me now."

Jamil turned around, bracing for the strike of the rattan. He had been beaten many times before, his back displayed years of abuse.

*Snap! Snap!* Jamil stood defiant while Dastgir struck him till his back bled.

*Snap! Snap!* Again could be heard from the solid strike sound of the rattan as it cracked off his soft flesh. Tears came to Jamil's eyes as he started to buckle at the knees from the pain.

Dastgir knelt down on one knee next to Jamil, and began to whisper in his ear. "If I do find out this is your brother, it will be you Jamil that I will have to kill. Look out that cave; there are many places to dispose of you. Throw you to the wolves below. But Asa? Asa has a great value to me. You will do as you're told. I will be watching you very closely."

Dastgir turned away from him. The rattan hung at his side.

"He is not my brother," said Jamil firmly. "I promise you with all the life within me."

Dastgir took one more long look at Jamil. "Fine, If it is as you say, it is as you say. But you will not ruin this night for me, you understand? Or I will be rid of you and have Naseefa replace you! Now get those boys ready. This is a very important night!" Dastgir said sternly watching as Jamil put his clothes back on.

Dastgir pushed Jamil hard in the direction of the holding den where the boys were housed. Jamil's back was extremely raw, and he winced in pain. But he must do as told or he would never have the chance to get Asa and himself to freedom. He had to prepare the boys for the night's events. Jamil needed this time, especially now more than ever, he needed to stay close to Asa and make an escape plan so they could leave this hell behind and get home.

*What options do I have to get my brother and escape?* Jamil thought helplessly as he headed to the boys. *Maybe we could hide in one of the helicopters? Yes-Yes this should work!*

Jamil passed the two guards as he entered the den where the boys were being held. He needed to be with Asa alone just for a few minutes. Unsure how Asa would react to him after slapping him earlier, Jamil wondered what could possibly be going through Asa's head at this moment.

Jamil stopped for a moment just inside the den and looked around. He saw nine boys nervously sitting against the cave wall on the left: Dastgir's hand selected boys for tonight's party. The boys looked over at Jamil when he entered. Quickly, they all sat up, aware that the time was getting close for the entertainment.

Jamil looked around for Asa and noticed him sitting alone on the far right side of the den in the shadows far from the others, holding his head in his hands and staring down at the ground. He was unaware that Jamil, his brother that he missed so much, was staring at him from only a few meters away.

The mood in the den was understandably tense; the boys had fear of the unknown and what would happen to them tonight. The thought of all the boys subject to the abuse by the guests angered Jamil, but tonight was different, taking on a more serious turn. Tonight it would be his own brother that would be subject to the same treatment as the others, up for sale to the highest bidder.

Jamil hated Dastgir with all his being, he wanted his revenge! If not for him, none of this nightmare would be happening.

Asa had tried to remain defiant over the last several weeks, to never give up hope. He promised himself to always look and wait for a way to escape, to get home. But it was seeing Jamil earlier for the first time in years that brought back the thoughts of what he had been missing: family, home, the memories of Jamil at night, talking and laughing. The slap he'd received from Jamil cut deep into his confidence, making him feel empty, afraid, and alone.

He sat with his head resting on his hands, not caring anymore of what would happen to him here. *Nothing matters anyway*, he thought sadly.

Asa's thoughts were interrupted when he noticed two dirty feet inches from his own. Someone was standing in front of him. In a daze, Asa slowly looked up, and there he saw Jamil's smiling face staring down at him.

Jamil was looking around nervously. Kneeling down directly in front of Asa, Jamil put his finger to his mouth. "*Shhh.*"

Asa started to tear up, filled with emotion while staring into Jamil's soft brown eyes that he hadn't seen in years. Jamil slid his hands over Asa's, and pleaded; "Please forgive me my brother."

"I love you" Jamil said softly while wiping his tears away. "I have missed you so much! Please be strong. That is all I can say right now. I will find a way out of this. But we cannot visibly be brothers. They will kill us—they will kill me."

Asa nodded. "I love you my brother," was all Asa could muster overcome with emotion. But newfound hope filled his heart, a warmth and unwavering love of the two brothers that could never be taken away.

# CHAPTER 8
## FINAL TREK

We all sat dispersed around the camp in silence eating from our MRE food packs for breakfast. One-by-one, the men started preparing to pack up the gear.

"Look what I have!" Antonio said with a big smile as he walked towards us. Holding up King's white snow vest out in front of him, Antonio walked over and knelt down to strap it on securely to King with a couple quick snaps. King let out a bark, then began to pant excitedly.

My watch read 0630 hours.

Zaleah crawled out of the igloo and stood with her long black shiny hair cascading over the back of her snowsuit. She immediately began walking the perimeter of the camp looking out over the mountainous terrain in all directions while wrapping her long black hair with a white turban.

Big Joe and Tex scanned down slope with their binoculars. As the weather cleared, they could finally see off in the distance nearly a mile in all directions. Antonio set down a small container of water for King. King sniffed the water as he began to fervently lap at it.

So far, nothing had come of the strange rumbling sounds we'd heard earlier. But I knew it was now or never. We had to get going or risk our mission being exposed.

"There over that next rise is the cave. We are very close now!" Zaleah said with some anxiety in her voice. "We are only six kilometers or so away, just over that ridge. You can see just the top of the mountainous cave structure from here."

I walked over to her right side looking off in the direction of the cave. King followed and sat down at my right side.

"We should be there today, we must keep monitoring our surroundings very closely now," Zaleah commented while sliding on her goggles. "The Taliban will most certainly be keeping a watch around the clock for any intruders nearing the cave. This area is *very* well guarded."

"Movement below, Staff Sergeant!" Big Joe yelled, holding his binoculars with his right hand while pointing with his left. The men gathered together, looking down slope. I could see what appeared to be five Taliban about a half-mile behind us and heading our way.

"Ben, time to earn your pay," I said, motioning for Antonio and Ben to hurry. Ben removed his rifle from its protective case and quickly got into a shooting position.

"Looks to be 800-900 yards or so," Antonio said while getting into position at his side.

Ben, getting in a prone position, started to make the micro-adjustments on his high powered scope as the Taliban targets came into view. Antonio knelt down on one knee to Ben's right looking through the binoculars calculating wind direction, distance, and the grade of the slope below. They worked together in perfect unison.

"Wind left to right." Antonio relayed.

The wind gusts created momentary whiteouts, making it difficult for targeting the Taliban. Three Taliban were dressed in all white making them nearly invisible in the blustery weather, adding to the difficulty for a clean kill shot. The other two Taliban in the rear were dressed in heavy dark colored coats and black headdress. All five walked in line.

Tex stood near the ridge. "Antonio, you see that bend around those boulders they're headed for?" Tex said, pointing.

Antonio shifted his binoculars a couple degrees. The men below would open up momentarily to trek around the boulders, creating an opportunity for kill shots.

"Five targets to take out! And if I can't, the rest will scatter—most likely hide behind the larger boulders at that ridge," Ben said over the top of his rifle.

Zaleah suddenly plopped down to the ground to Ben's left with her .300 Winchester. "Why should you have all the fun?" She said while lifting her goggles to her forehead. She flashed a grin to Ben and Antonio. Ben looked back over his shoulder at me.

"You good with this, Ben?" I said, looking down at Zaleah, who was already in the progress of making her adjustments.

"Why the hell not?" Ben said sarcastically as he looked back through his scope.

"Well, whatever you decide to do, we have a only a couple seconds until they hit those boulders," Big Joe said, looking through his binoculars.

King, lying down on Antonio's right, began to growl and bear his teeth.

"You take out the two in the dark clothing," Ben instructed Zaleah. "I'll take the other three leading in white."

Everyone went silent. The five Taliban soldiers had rifles strapped over their shoulders, the middle one had an RPG. I knew if not taken out now, they most likely would have radios. We must have these five clean kill shots.

Antonio gave wind direction, distance, and grade to Ben and Zaleah. Antonio started a countdown to when the Taliban would spread out passing the boulders. Both Zaleah and Ben were motionless, getting into their breathing rhythms, and waited.

"Three...two...one," Antonio said calmly.

Rapid muffled pop noises echoed as both Zaleah and Ben with precision accuracy took out their targets. The five Taliban soldiers fell to the ground in a bloody pink mist, motionless. Zaleah quickly stood, looking through the binoculars. Ben exhaled deeply and looked over to Antonio for confirmation while remaining in position.

"I see movement from the one in the center, sir," Big Joe said looking over to me. "The one asshole in the middle."

Ben looked through his scope looking for a clean shot. The other four bodies were positioned over him preventing another clean shot. It was then they saw him slowly crawling out from under the bodies only a couple meters away from a large boulder.

"If he makes that boulder for cover and has a hand-held radio, we will have every Taliban in this sector coming down on us," Big Joe said.

Another pop noise was heard as Zaleah squeezed off another shot, just missing him and hitting one of the dead Taliban.

"Gholona!" Zaleah cursed in Dari while raising her fist.

"Shit! That's a half-mile down slope. We need to take him out now," Tex said as he watched the Taliban soldier slowly crawl to the boulder for cover with only his legs visible now.

With a growl and a quick bark, King tore down the slope, running at full speed. We watched in amazement at the speed and determination King had in his weak condition. The snow drifts blocked our view of King momentarily. Taking only minutes to reach the Taliban soldier, we witnessed King dragging the soldier back out from behind the boulder by the throat with the man futilely trying to fight him off.

Ben quickly got back in a shooting position. "I have him in my sights!" Ben said as he was getting ready to take the shot.

"No, hold up, this one is for King," I said. "After all, it could've been that piece of shit that took out Sal the other night, as far as we know. With his keen sense of smell, he must've picked up something."

We all stood and watched silently in awe at the strength and ferocity as King violently shook the Taliban's head back and forth with a vice-like grip on his throat. The man went limp with King still clamped down on his throat, his sharp teeth sinking deep into the soft flesh as the life drained out of the Taliban soldier. King finally let go.

The Taliban soldier's bloodied head dropped to the ground. King looked up to us with his face covered in blood. Everyone stood quietly, looking through their binoculars waiting to see what King would do next. It was then we witnessed something we never would've imagined: King lifted his right leg and urinated on the dead soldier, then took off at full speed back up the slope towards us.

We all cheered! We loaded the gear and leveled the temporary igloos as to not leave a trace for the Taliban that would pass this way. Even the five dead bodies of the Taliban soldiers were disposed of over the edge of a small crevasse.

It was at that moment off in the distance directly ahead that I spotted a bright flash of light that reflected off an aircraft. Then it was gone. I knew the base Commander and Officer Tucker were watching over us silently.

It was late in the day when we finally made it to the cave mass; the clearing sky displayed a bright orange setting sun that shone brightly to the west. It would be a cold night. We took in the massive cave through our binoculars from only a kilometer away. We observed the huge cave structure from the south side, ominous in appearance, looking to be impenetrable.

"God, I hope you're right on this" Tex said, overwhelmed with the size of the structure.

"What the hell? How are we going to get to the ledge?" Big Joe asked, with a piece of beef jerky sticking out of his mouth while looking through his binoculars.

"When I discovered the cave a few years ago, I was able to get to that ledge by climbing a huge pine tree going straight up ten meters or so," said Zaelah. "The pine tree is positioned tight to the cave wall. With God's blessing, we can only pray that the tree is still there. Even with the tree, we will have the Taliban guards keeping watch all around this area."

The moon began to rise over the Hindu Kush mountain range beyond the cave in the eastern sky. Thin wispy clouds drifted in front of the moon like delicate opaque curtains trying to hide a vulnerable naked moon. Darkness consumed the last gasp of daylight. The base of the mountain was directly in front of us. The terrain ahead offered no trees, or boulders for cover. This entire south side was flat and open, and we could easily be spotted in the white snow that surrounded us.

We slowly proceeded closer to the base of the cave on our stomachs, spreading out a few meters from each other in the fresh snow in order to reduce our body heat field in case the Taliban had night vision binoculars. King stayed at my side and was alert.

Suddenly, with a low growl I felt King's body stiffen, he tried to stand as if he wanted to take off spotting something off in the distance. Holding his lead tight, I then saw two Taliban patrols walking the perimeter of the cave.

The tall pine Zaleah mention still stood. The branches extended out, touching the cave wall ten meters up. Holding up my arm, I motioned for Ben to follow me first as we worked our way to the pine tree. I wanted Ben to be in position under the large pine first while the others made their way to the tree.

The large branches of the pine spread out 15 meters across just above us. The smell of the pine filled the cold mountain air. Ben stepped out from the group with his binoculars and looked in the direction where we'd spotted the guards. He observed them walking in the other direction 50 meters away from or location. It was too risky to attempt a shot.

"Here we are. This is where the Snow Leopard mission has lead us," I said, looking around at the faces of the men and Zaleah. "We have traveled nearly five days now, our fight inside this cave. The men in that cave would love to do nothing more than torture us before chopping our heads off. And if the bacha bazi boys are here, we have to be cautious and methodical in our approach. Without Sal here to handle King, we need to keep an eye on him and make sure he does as he's commanded. If he does not do as commanded, he will become a liability, putting us all in danger. Even with the fact that Sal and King have been a part of this team for the last year, I will give the command to remove King if necessary. The safety of my men, Zaleah, and the boys in the cave are my priority. So, here is the plan."

"Zaleah will go up the tree first. With her proving to be one hell of a shot, this will give us two excellent marksmen to work with. One-by-one, the rest of us will follow her up the pine every five minutes to the ledge. Big Joe, I want King clipped to your side on the climb up. Tex and Antonio will work together, getting our ammo boxes and gear to that ridge. Ben will be the last up just in case any Taliban make their way back to our location."

My team nodded. "But before we began, we first need to remove our white snow gear." Looking around, I spotted a couple boulders up against the mountain to stash the snow gear. The men removed their snowsuits, rolling them up in a tight ball to hide them out of sight near the boulders. Zaleah wore her dark balochi winter outfit with a black headdress. She wrapped the tails of her headdress around her face with just her eyes exposed. Even from a few yards away, she would blend into the cave's darkness perfectly. All that was visible was her white Winchester .300 rifle.

"Now, just a reminder," I whispered. "I do have my radio, but it is to be used only in the event we need a fast exit strategy—only as a last measure. Now, get hydrated, get that face paint on, and let's go kick some ass," I said while extending my right arm out, the rest followed, laying their hands on top of mine. "Kick Ass!" we said in unison. We quickly applied tactical face paint and prepared to become as invisible as possible for the cave environment.

"Where is the small access to the cave?" I asked Zaleah as she was just getting ready to climb the pine.

"The smaller cave opening is on this south side just to the right down that ledge, from where we stand. This opening is very small, so no heavy gear on as you pass through. The ledge from here to the small entrance is approximately 100 meters."

"Shit. Are you saying we need to traverse that ledge with King strapped to me the whole damn way along that treacherous ledge?" Big Joe asked with frustration.

"Good news is that the ledge widens as we progress towards the cave's access, enough for two men shoulder to shoulder to walk," Zaleah said, reassuring us.

Zaleah adjusted her rifle strap and swung the rifle around her right shoulder. She looked back at us, and then she was gone, disappearing into the darkness above.

Zaleah quickly reached the strongest branch nearest the ledge, 30 feet up. The branch was slightly higher than the ledge by several inches. Pulling herself out onto the branch as far as she could, she hung on tightly while looking to the left and right, making sure there were no guards nearby. In order to reach the ledge, she needed to push off while stretching out to reach the ledge, leaving her momentarily airborne.

Taking a deep breath she pushed off, hitting the side of the cave hard, slipping on the narrow uneven ledge, nearly losing her rifle. She stood quickly, wiping a droplet of blood from her nose. She pulled out her infrared binoculars and looked down the long ledge both ways, trying to pinpoint any movement in both directions.

Slowly, she worked her way along the ledge, which was barely wide enough for the width of a large boot that forced her to lean into the cave wall to steady herself. She kept inching her way down the ledge away from the pine tree. She thought she heard movement ahead, but she wondered if her nerves were just playing tricks on her. Looking back the way she came, she noticed the pine tree was no longer visible. She looked down over the ledge to the ground below, then back ahead.

In the crisp clean mountain air, she could smell cigarette smoke ahead. *Could it be I just missed a Taliban guard?* She stopped and positioned herself into a shooting stance, prepared for anything, listening. Nothing. Further down the ledge, with her heart racing, she could smell the cigarette smoke again.

There! She spotted a Taliban guard ahead; he was standing in the recess of the cave wall. The cigarette smoke bellowed out from the nook. Looking down, she noticed that between the guard's boots, she could make out the barrel of his rifle. He had no idea what was coming.

*I must be quiet, just a little closer...*

Now, just a few feet away, Zaleah knelt down, feeling around the ledge for a small rock. Finding one, she tossed it just past the recess, bouncing off the cave, the guard quickly stepped out with his back to Zaleah curious of the noise. Zaleah raised her gun.

*Pop!* The muffled gunshot was followed by a gasp from the Taliban guard as he fell over the edge, hitting the boulders below. She heard the snap of bones as he laid draped over a large boulder 30 feet down.

As I reached the ledge, I saw Zaleah extending her hand out, pulling me in. "Anything?" I asked, looking at two black holes for eyes.

"Yes," she pointed down the ledge. "One Taliban down."

Even though I couldn't see her face I could swear she was smiling. "Good!" I said. "Until all the men are topside, proceed in the other direction towards the cave entrance. I want to make sure we are clear to that entrance."

Looking over the edge, I spotted Tex working his way up the tree a few feet away. The ammo box tied to his back made his progress slow. Just behind him was Antonio.

Zaleah looked down the ledge ahead of her. The reflection of the moonlight bounced off the fresh white snow below, offering a full view of the ground. Just ahead of her she spotted another Taliban guard working his way towards her along the ledge. Getting into her shooting stance, she was ready for a clean shot. Just as she was ready to squeeze off a round, she heard men's voices down below.

Quickly lowering the rifle, she moved up tight against the side of the cave, peering over the edge. She spotted two other Taliban patrolling below. With her heart racing, she could see the one guard on the ledge coming up fast on her. She decided not to take the shot, concerned of giving her position away. She retreated quickly back down the ledge, she heard the men's voices just below her.

Remembering that she'd passed a small boulder just a few feet back, she hurried back to it. Hiding behind the boulder, she watched as the two Taliban patrols below worked their way towards the pine tree where the Americans were. Quietly removing her rifle and setting it down on the ledge, she reached in her right boot and pulled out a razor sharp knife.

The Taliban guard was tall, and Zaleah noticed his rifle in his hands. At the exact moment when she saw his eyes, she jumped up on top of the small boulder and plunged the knife deep into his throat.

The Taliban guard struggled with her while holding his throat, blood pulsating out between his fingers. Zaleah could hear a gurgling noise as she was dragged down with him from his weight, she struggled to keep his body on the narrow ledge.

She heard a few muffled *pops*! from below. The two Taliban patrol guards she'd seen below dropped to the ground. *Good, the American shooter hit the targets!* She was relieved.

The team worked in unison getting all men to the ledge—so far, undetected.

# CHAPTER 9
# RECON

"Sir, I have two enemy aircraft below at two thousand feet," Sergeant Bacon said, leaning into his monitor. He'd taken over the shift from Sergeant Miller. The drone flew undetected, high above the enemy helicopters. "It looks as if they are headed in the same direction of where that Russian helicopter landed earlier. Mike and his men are just outside the cave."

"Let's monitor the situation. If those aircraft are headed to that cave, we can only hope there will be a full house of Taliban tonight." Officer Tucker said while looking at the wall map marked with swirls, circles, and lines that denoted the men's progress, with his face inches away, as he adjusted his glasses.

Sergeant Bacon banked the drone to the left.

My watch displayed 22:17; Even with minimal rest for his crew the last few days we were wide awake and alert. The entire area around the cave was under surveillance with the Taliban guards patrolling tonight in pairs.

"Let's stop here!" Big Joe said while unclipping King from the harness."There is good solid footing on the ledge now."

Zaleah was out in front, as the group cautiously worked their way along the snowy ledge. We were prepared for the enemy at any moment. The icy cold silver moon shone brightly, offering some light along the ledge that trailed off into the darkness ahead. We were just a few meters from the cave entrance.

"Hold up! You hear that? Sounds like a helicopter not far off!" Tex said.

In the distance, we heard the *swoop-swoop* of a low flying helicopter towards the main entrance on the other side of the cave. I was becoming anxious to get inside. This was a great opportunity to remove or capture a few Taliban. The intel we got from Hakeem specifically stated the Taliban had been using this cave as a safe haven. I just hoped our timing wouldn't fail us now.

Zaleah snapped her left arm up, motioning for us to stop. "There! Ahead," she pointed, holding up two fingers towards the cave entrance.

King started whimpering, tugging at the lead. *"Heel!"* Big Joe commanded King, giving him a hard tug on the lead.

"What is it?" I said in a low whisper as I looked back at Big Joe.

"Not sure, but King is anxious, like he picked up on something."

"Give him to me," I said while grabbing the lead from Big Joe. The closer we got to the entrance, the more King started in with loud whimpers.

"Damn it, King! Settle down." I whispered. King immediately sat down in front of the snow blocked entrance to the cave, wagging his tail. Kneeling next to King, I recognized this behaviour from our patrols with Sal. "I think he has picked up on an explosive device. Tex, bring that shovel over here. Let's take a look."

Tex removed the small compact shovel from his backpack and knelt directly in front of the snow packed entrance to the cave. Removing his gloves, he began feeling around the snowpack. The opening of the entrance did not appear to be much more than a few feet in height and width at this point.

"Anything?" I asked Tex. King was transfixed with every move Tex made.

"I feel it! A trip wire!" Tex said. Using the tip of the small shovel he scraped away thin layers of snow till he tapped on metal. An IED package.

"What's taking so long up there?" Ben said. "We will have a patrol passing anytime now."

I watched as Tex cleared the snow away from the explosive case. The explosive package was packed tight into a bowl shaped container, perfectly positioned to force the blast outward. Tex carefully removed the container, I could see in the moonlight that it was packed with pieces of metal. A dirty bomb! Tex and I just looked at each other, then to King. Without that hit from King, it would have taken out most our crew.

We collectively exhaled, thankful for King tonight. "Big Joe, this dog deserves a treat," I said.

Tex continued to remove the outer layer of the dense snowpack with the small shovel blade until he gave us the all-clear.

"Antonio, Big Joe, let's get that hole cleared!" I said, handing the shovel to Antonio.

Big Joe and Antonio were on their stomachs taking turns working at removing the snowpack from the entrance. Zaleah was right; the size of the opening made it difficult to remove the snowpack in such a tight area. Big Joe was the biggest, and with his wide shoulders he could barely wiggle his way in. The rest of us dispersed the loose snow along the ledge, careful not to allow any to drift over, giving our position away from below. All the while Ben and Zaleah stood watch.

"I'm there! I'm inside! I can see the inside of the cave!" Antonio said with excitement.

"Thank God," I said, looking out at the night.

"The entrance looks to be a good nine feet in length," Big Joe commented.

"Grab those ammo boxes, quick!" I said, looking into the dark hole of the cave. We started to feed the equipment through to Big Joe.

"Tex! Your next," I said. "I'll get Zaleah in before King and myself. Ben, you stay behind until we are all in."

Getting ready to enter the small opening, I knew this would be my last chance to change my mind in the commitment or not with King as part of our mission. But I couldn't deny the strong feeling I had that he would be an asset in the cave. King was looking at me with his head tilting back and forth.

"Let's go boy!" I commanded. King held his ground, he just sat there looking at the small opening of the cave, unsure.

"Hurry! I see one guard coming this way along the ledge!" Ben said as he leaned up against the cave wall, looking down at me. "Hurry!"

Turning around, I went in feet first, having to crawl backwards through the small opening as I tried to get King down; it was then I felt a hand on my left ankle, straining in the tight space I felt Big Joe had placed a piece of beef jerky in my left hand.

"Grab King, I'll pull you in by your feet," Big Joe said.

Sticking the beef jerky in front of King's nose, he immediately began to crawl on his belly towards me while Big Joe pulled me into the cave. King followed, unafraid of the tight space.

I noticed immediately the smell of the damp, dank air inside this massive cave. Looking around, I saw a fairly good sized lake created by years of snowmelt. I could see two campfires along the lake's edge on the other side directly across the lake. A strand of low-lit lights hung along the rock ledge. Pulling out my binoculars, I noticed several dens across the lake. The lighting reflecting off the lake created a turquoise color that reflected on to the cave ceiling

It felt good to be inside from the cold of the night. King sat next to me and remained calm while peering over a small boulder watching intently at the movement across the lake.

I heard a muffled *pop* from outside, and then Ben emerged into the cave through the small opening in a hurry. "Shit! I had that guard on my ass, I blew his damn head off" he murmured. I could see blood spatters on Ben's face.

We spread out, positioning ourselves behind scattered boulders just a few feet from the water's edge, assessing the environment. We all watched the activity across the lake. I spotted a tall bearded man and a boy near the lake's edge. The low hum of generators could be heard just behind us. The cave size alone could hold a hundred men, offering fresh water from the snowmelt. The caves were very secluded, the perfect stronghold for the Taliban.

"Ben, take a count of those men over there," I said. "I see some activity in the first few dens."

"I count a total of 11 men so far," Ben said, standing on my right in the darkness as he counted the men through the scope of his high powered rifle.

Zaleah crouched on the far left end of the group, taking in the activity in silence

"The third den down the ledge is where I see two guards," Zaleah whispered. "If there are boys here, those guards would be watching over them."

"We will sit tight and wait till they get settled in," I said as I looked down at my radio, noticing that I had no signal. "Let's wait it out. In the meantime, let's replenish our water from the lake. Big Joe and Tex, work you way down the far side of the lake past the generators and see what we have for options to cross to the other side."

"Sir, I have the final helicopter landing," Sergeant Bacon commented while watching as the Russian helicopter prepare to touch down on the rocky ledge. The wind had picked up outside the cave entrance, causing the helicopter to bounce off the ledge a couple times before safely touching down.

"The men?" Officer Tucker asked, looking over to Sergeant Bacon as he poured a cup of coffee.

"They are in the cave. I lost sight of them less than an hour ago. In the process, they took out one guard near the entrance. We were still able to capture the image of the dead guard on the thermal camera."

"So, that's it then. They are truly on their own until Mike radios in for an exit strategy," said Officer Tucker. "We can only wait now and see. I'll have to notify the Base Commander. This mission has certain rules of engagement that will be fluid, the Secretary of Defense is now involved, and looking over our shoulders."

A half-hour passed before Big Joe and Tex walked out of the shadows. Periodically, I could hear loose pebbles falling from the ceiling of the cave, hitting the water's surface of the lake with a small *ploop-ploop* noise. Small ripples interrupting the calm of the lake's surface.

Big Joe knelt down next to me with Tex on the other side.

"The lake runs all the way to the far end of the cave to our left, eventually draining out through an eroded rough opening," Big Joe said while looking through his binoculars at the activity across the lake.

"The lake appears to be low in most part due to the time of year," Tex said. "We could wade through the water on the far end to get to the other side, looks to be shallow on that end. The dens trail off towards the far end. Nothing for activity in those. Almost looks as if they are sleeping quarters. The far right dens near the main entrance should be our focus, I reckon."

It was at that moment we heard the generators behind us slow to a stop.

"Shit! Now what?" Big Joe asked, looking back.

The cave went quiet, so quiet that we could hear the men's voices across the lake echoing off the walls. Some laughter came from the main den where we noticed the rest of the Taliban were heading. The chain of lights slowly dimmed to blackness, leaving just the two campfires flickering in the darkened cave.

A loud voice rang out over the lake. "Jamil! Jamil! Get those generators running!" a tall man in a bright blue shalwar kameez could be heard yelling near the lake's edge.

I saw a young boy come out of the third den, running around the lake in our direction towards the generators behind us.

"This is a great opportunity for us with this boy. He will need to pass by us to get to the generators. We need to talk to him, see if there are any bacha bazi boys here," I said while standing up trying to spot the boy's position.

"What if he calls for help?" Zaleah asked. "We will have a fierce battle on our hands, and these men are all armed and thirsty for blood, especially American blood."

"I see him, he's quick!" I said watching him round the lake's edge. "Let's grab him on the return, let him get those generators fired up first. We don't need any of the Taliban guards on to us. Take cover now!"

We all spread out, waiting for the boy to pass. He came within inches of Tex. I held King down when the boy passed. King remained quiet, but I could feel his muscles tensing up. We watched quietly as the boy restarted the generators. They hummed back to life.

I looked over to Big Joe, motioning for him to grab the boy. We waited.

The boy jumped from one boulder to the next in a great hurry, he slipped over a boulder and fell, knocking over one of the ammo containers that made a loud metallic noise as it slammed against a boulder. Big Joe was on him with his massive hand covering the boy's mouth. We all looked in the direction of the men across the lake to see if they'd heard the noise.

Squirming in Big Joe's grip, the boy was obviously trying to yell. I switched on my tactical light so the boy could see the American flag on my left upper shoulder. In an instant, he began to relax.

"We are here to help," I said. "Do you understand me?" The others moved in.

The boy nodded his head yes, wide eyed.

"We need to talk to you. If we let you go, will you remain silent?"

Again, the boy nodded his head yes.

"I don't like this," Ben said. "If he is raised like the rest of the young boys in this region, you know he will call for help. They hate us."

The boy nodded his head no, his eyes wide with both fear and excitement.

"I need talk to him. We need to know what we are dealing with," I said, looking back to Ben. "Look kid, just nod for me. Okay?"

The boy nodded yes.

"Are there other boys here?"

The boy nodded yes.

"How many? Hold up your hands, and I'll count."

The boy held up a total of fourteen fingers.

"Shit! Fourteen? if we let you talk, will you remain quiet?"

He nodded yes.

Big Joe pulled out a knife and held it to the boys throat while removing his hand.

In his excitement, he started blurting out his name. "My name is Jamil. I'm being held a prisoner with my brother. Please help us!"

*Good, he speaks English,* I thought, although I was a little surprised at how well he spoke it.

"Look Jamil, we need to trust you. If what you say is true, we are here to help all the boys. What I need for you to do is to go back and pretend all is fine, find out how many men are here, what weapons they have, and then you need to get that information to us. Can you do that for us, Jamil?"

"Yes, yes, but how will I get this information to you? I will be missed if I am gone to long. Tonight we have to entertain for the men. Tonight they will offer money for each boy, including my brother!" Jamil said, tearing up.

I looked at the other men's faces.

"Any ideas?"

Zaleah chimed in. "All we need for him to do is signal us. First, how many men total, and second, what weapons they have."

"Hmmm. Jamil, we will be watching and waiting for the men to settle in. Will they be drinking?"

"Yes, they will have plenty of liquor. This I know. We have prepared a grand meal for all."

"You will need to find time to just get to the lake's edge, just over there," I pointed to the edge. "We will be watching from here. Hold up your fingers first to signal how many men, then the weapons. Are you familiar with weaponry Jamil?"

"No, I am sorry," Jamil said, looking around at the men's faces.

"OK, just hold your arms chest wide for the rifles, and extend your arms out wide if there are any RPGs. The RPGs have one big end, and they are much longer than the rest. Okay, Jamil?" I said as the boy was getting anxious.

The tall man in the white beard called out for Jamil in a loud commanding voice from the lake's edge. "Jamil, what are you doing? I do not see you! Come to me or you will be punished. NOW!"

"You see those two over there?" Big Joe pointed to Ben and Zaleah. "If you say anything of us being here to those men, these two can can shoot the balls of a fly. Understand?

Jamil nodded yes. "I will help you!"

The last they saw was Jamil running across the boulders as if he had wings on his feet.

# CHAPTER 10
# THE DANCING BOYS

Standing just outside the cave entrance, Dastgir dressed in a light blue full-length shalwar kameez, complete with a gold karakul cap. Dastgir watched as the first helicopter to arrive lowered itself to the ledge. This would be the first of two helicopters that would be arriving. Standing next to Dastgir were two of his guards. Dastgir's white beard swirled in the turbulence as it touched down on the narrow landing area outside the caves entrance.

Each Taliban leader would have his own entourage of men to protect them: cold blooded and ruthless in their attempt to protect their leaders. Dastgir would have to be accommodating and cautious with his guests tonight. Dastgir was expecting each leader to be accompanied by three or four guards each, estimating at most twelve men. Added to the count for the evening were Dastgir's current Taliban guards out on patrol, another separate dozen.

Dastgir stepped out to welcome Mawlawi Kabir, the first to arrive. The men embraced as Dastgir lead him inside the cave out of the cold night's air. "So, you have this beautiful boy tonight. What is his name? Asa?" Mawlawi asked.

"Yes, yes! Tonight he will be performing," Dastgir said while looking around for Jamil.

"This is good, I have heard he is a boy of much desire. If he is as you say, I have come prepared to make a great offer for him." Malawi said heading towards the main den, the music could be heard as the musicians tune their instruments for the long night of entertainment ahead. "Now let's drink! Where is that older boy?"

The group of men walked in from outside the main entrance. The helicopter taking off was barely audible from our position. We all crouched low behind the boulders and tried to ID the men being escorted in.

Blending into the darkness we watched quietly hidden behind a few boulders watching the group of Taliban soldiers near the main entrance. There was a larger den that sat to the left of the main entrance, several smaller dens ran along the ledge. The Taliban guards were surrounding a man as they walked in from outside. The men surrounding him made it difficult to ID him. We had information with us on the top Taliban leaders in the area, their backgrounds, what slaughter they have committed, and photos. The odds that these higher ranking targets might possibly be here tonight made my heart race.

"It's him!" Zaleah said looking through her binoculars barely able to contain her emotional rage, speaking in a loud whisper. "It's him! It's Mawlawi Kabir!" She immediately raised her rifle, and got into position for a headshot. "This man I recognize, he is a very bad man. He and his men have been through our village many times over the years, nearly killing my father one night, believing we were hiding American Soldiers. This man is the one who recruited my two brothers to join their Jihadic operation."

"So, if this is true, the other men arriving have to be high ranking Taliban leaders too," Antonio said, looking down at the list of targets from the last year in Tex's hand. "That explains why all the body guards."

"Hold up!" I said looking over to Zaleah. "This isn't the time for revenge. You'll get your chance later," I said while resting my hand on the barrel of her rifle.

"I recognize that name, Mawlawi Kabir. He is definitely on our hit list of terrorists we are looking for," Big Joe said looking over to Tex. Tex, shining his flashlight down spotted the information about Mawlawi Kabir being the number one target we have been after for the last year.

"It says here that Mawlawi, is one of the dudes that lead the attacks on NATO after September 11," Tex said. "He also helped in the hiding of Osama Bin Laden," Tex stopped reading looking over to me. "This is the dude we went after a little over a year ago, remember? He is the number one target!"

"Oorah!" Big Joe said, taking in Mawlawi Kabir through his binoculars. "We are going to have ourselves quite the party tonight!"

The six of us huddled in the darkness in silence, processing this mission, the odds that these men would be here tonight. This increased the ante of the mission. These powerful targets that have been eluding us for so long. The mission had certainly turned out to be serendipitous.

The other helicopter landed safely within minutes of each other as Dastgir welcomed Al-Zarqawi and Mullah Abdul. These two men were ruthless leaders, both seemed anxious. Wearing full black outfits they stood and gazed around taking in the size of the cave not being here for sometime. The men gathered in the main den, starting in with eating and drinking. Having not seeing each other in a while, they discussed the challenges they had with NATO and the Americans this last year.

"The technology of the Americans has been amazing, and we are forced to keep moving our locations," Al-Zarqawi said with cold stern words, looking directly at Dastgir. "Even now, I feel concerned of this location tonight. The great Dastgir with his dancing boys might of become, well...complacent, forgetful of the importance of such powerful men's safety. I think Dastgir's desire of money might be more important to him."

Dastgir's anger flared with the insult from Al-Zarqawi, and their eyes locked. Al-Zarqawi with his ruthless stare made Dastgir shutter inside, forcing him to look away.

"I have completed much business with Dastgir, right here at this cave many times, never with any concerns of my safety," Mawlawi Kabir said as he re-filled his tin cup of vodka-fruit drink from a large metal bowl that sat on a wooden table filled with liquor and food. "I'm sure at this very moment Dastgir has his patrols keeping watch outside. But let us forget our battles for tonight! We have boys to entertain us!"

"Hello, my brother," Jamil said, quietly flashing a big smile while standing directly in front of Asa in attempts to block the view from the other boys. He had to act completely fine, and he didn't want anyone to notice he was paying special attention to Asa. "Here we are together once again. Tonight you will perform for some of the most powerful men around."

Asa looked concerned. "Our mother and father have to be looking for us, Jamil. We need to get home."

"We will," Jamil said with confidence, trying to hide his fear and concern over everything: the Americans, the Taliban, and his brother in danger. He put the outfit over Asa's head and slid it down over him. "But we cannot act like anything is wrong. Tonight you will be dancing. I must tell you now that this could be very dangerous tonight. After the boys dance, the men will want a boy for himself, sometimes two. Dastgir is wanting you to be sold with the rest of the boys to the highest bidder. I have seen this many times before."

"Sold with the others?" Asa said fearfully.

Jamil nodded gruffly. The thought was painful. "I will be close to you watching over the entertainment. Before you begin the entertaining, Dastgir will want you to drink a small amount of juice. Hold that in your mouth until no one is looking, than spit it to the ground. The drink will have a drug in it. Do you understand?" Jamil placed a hand on Asa's shoulder, looking directly into his eyes waiting for his answer.

"I understand." Asa seemed to be trying to be much older than his small amount of years, Jamil noted.

Jamil knelt down in front of him, adjusting the outfit around his ankles. He glanced over his right shoulder, making sure no else could hear what he had to say. "Please say this to know one, but there are Americans here, at this moment."

"Americans," Asa whispered.

"The Americans will be watching, waiting for the right time to make a move," whispered Jamil. "Not sure what we can expect, but this is good. When that time is upon us, look to me, and I will tell you what to do." Jamil stood up from making the adjustments to the outfit. "Until then, dance like you have never danced, and we will pretend that nothing is wrong."

Naseefa ran past Janmil. "Naseefa, listen to me quickly," Jamil pulled Naseefa aside and told him about the drug Dastgir would have them drink before the entertainment, which was laced with ketamine. "Tell the boys to not swallow the drink Dastgir has prepared for us. Tell them to spit it out when no one is looking. This is very urgent tonight. Now hurry!"

Sitting up against a boulder near the lake's edge, I positioned my tactical flashlight with a red glow shining it down at my family photos. The rest of the men were spread out, positioned along the lake's edge gathering intel. It wouldn't be long and we would move in on our enemy. The closest man to me was Ben, who was keeping an eye out on my right a few yards away.

We decided we would wait for Jamil to give us the signal on the weaponry first, and the total count of how many men we would have to battle with. If at all possible, I wanted to capture the warlords that we had been after for the last year. Too much blood had been spilled, and I wanted these cold-blooded killers alive.

My watch displayed 0100 hours, and we'd decided to give it till 0200 hours. If no signal from Jamil, we would gather what intel we had from surveillance and establish a plan of attack. The small den openings made it difficult to get a full view of our targets inside, and I was still curious who the other higher ranking Taliban men were. After a long wait, I finally spotted Jamil across the lake, nervously pacing along the lake's edge in the semi-darkness. King sat up, sensing that the men's energy had changed. I spotted Big Joe and Tex walking out of the darkness towards me just a few feet away. Looking around, there was no sign of Zaleah.

"Come on, kid!" I said anxiously, looking through my binoculars. "Give us the numbers."

He would be signalling how many men first. Jamil held up both his hands that displayed all fingers. Ten men. Then he held up one hand, a total of fifteen Taliban.

"Almost three to one," Big Joe whispered. "Now what about weapons?" Big Joe said. "Probably just that Russian antiquated shit for rifles."

Jamil held up his arms chest wide, telling us they had Russian weaponry. But it was the RPGs I was concerned with the most. Jamil outstretched his arms widely, letting us know they had RPGs. I sighed. The stakes were high, and we had to make sure everything we did counted.

In an instant, Jamil was gone.

★ ★ ★

Zaleah held her .300 win mag rifle high above her head while cautiously crossing through the frigid water of the lake. The water was up to her waist as she passed within just a few meters of the eroded opening of the cave. She could hear the water flowing out of the cave opening, spilling out onto the jagged rocks below. With ten meters left to cross over to the other side of the lake, she could feel her legs beginning to go numb from the icy cold water.

Concerned for the boys, she was determined and anxious to cross over as quickly as possible. She had no interest in showing mercy tonight or in catching the Taliban for political reasons. Her hate for the man she'd recognized earlier tonight from years ago—Mawlawi Kabir, the man that had tortured her family—had her wanting her revenge. So she was going solo.

Zaleah knew the boys were here. But where? This end of the cave was dark, cold, and damp. Looking down at the water ahead of her, she was amazed how clear and blue it is. An iridescent glow lit the way ahead of her. The bottom of the lake was silty with a few scattered large stones submerged in the frigid water from years of erosion, making the crossing slow and difficult.

Zaleah reached the other side of the lake and pulled herself out the the frigid water by grabbing a small boulder on her right. Shivering, she positioned herself against the cave wall. She wrapped her arms around her knees to increase her body heat. Leaning forward, she looked down the rocky ledge to her left towards the main entrance.

From her perspective, the rock ledge leading to the main den went straight for 75 meters, she would have to be cautious. Looking through her binoculars, her hands trembled from the cold as she noticed two campfires on the far end near the main entrance. Three guards stood

THE VISTA

near the flames while extending their arms towards the heat of the fire. The dimly lit small lights that dangled along the cave wall were strung up along the walkway, ending about 100 feet from where she sat, leaving her in complete darkness.

After warming up from the frigid water she slipped her rifle strap securely over her left shoulder, she started to inch her way towards the main entrance—staying close to the cave wall. Her heart raced. Off in the distance, she could hear music coming from the main den as it echoed off the massive cave walls. The only light that guided her way was the blue glow of the lake as her eyes adjusted to the darkness.

★ ★ ★

Dastgir walked into the den where the boys waited. The boys were all dressed in their colorful outfits, wearing makeup and bells on their feet and wrists. He was pleased with Jamil for his good work tonight. In his right hand, he held a dented metal jug filled with the drug concoction, and he ordered the boys to line up. Giving each boy a small amount from a small tin cup, he smiled as they drank.

Standing in front of Asa, the last boy to drink, Dastgir knelt down with the tin cup in his hand. "You will be perfect tonight! I want you to drink of this, it will relax you. Now remember all that Iffy has taught you. Your hard work will be rewarded tonight! If you do well, I will see what we can do to get you home."

Asa took the cup from Dastgir and sipped the juice in while staring into Dastgir's cold eyes. Jamil standing nearby noticed Dastgir forgot the jug next to a small rock by some clothing, as he left the den.

Impatiently, Dastgir lead the boys into the main den where the men awaited impatiently. Upon entering, the group of boys were received with cheers and whistles from the men. The music momentarily stopped while the boys stood at the entrance of the den gazing around at the men in the smoke filled den, observing the lust and desire on the men's faces.

Dastgir motioned for Jamil to lead the boys through the small opening between the men to the back of the den. The three Taliban leaders and chief of police sat on a small platform on the right lounging

235

amongst the pillows, the guards stood near them as the boys worked their way past each man.

A few of the men reached out to touch the boys garments as they passed by, and the men sat up and started clapping to the music. The men were already taking notice of Asa in the rear as the boys walked past in single file, and they began reaching out trying to touch his face. Dastgir smiled with delight. He would be making much money tonight, he was sure of it!

Hours passed with each boy taking their turn entertaining the men. Jamil stood just within the den entrance watching as the sixth boy danced. The boy removed a silky yellow scarf that was wrapped around his neck as he began to tease the men with it, swirling it in front of their faces. This excited the men, and the air was electric with their shouts.

Jamil kept a close eye on Asa, who was standing in line with the other boys. He would be the last to dance, which gave Jamil some time to slip away. Looking over to Dastgir, Jamil noticed he was focused on his negotiations for the sale of the boys. He must hurry.

*I must get that jug of ketamine,* Jamil thought.

Sneaking out of the main den, he headed to get the pitcher left by Dastgir in the holding den. Looking out across the lake, he wondered where the Americans were and when they would make their move. His heart raced with excitement.

Hurrying into the den, Jamil grabbed the pitcher. It was still half full of the drug concoction. Running back out of the den, Jamil slammed into a guard just outside, spilling some of the concoction to the ground. Jamil froze.

"You! What is it you have there?" It was one of the Taliban warlord's bodyguard.

"It is just water for the boys," Jamil said calmly. "I was ordered to get it."

The guard stood directly in front of Jamil looking down at the pitcher, then to Jamil. "Hurry boy! Go!"

Standing outside the main den, Jamil peaked inside. Dastgir, standing with his back to Jamil, was in deep conversation with Malawi.

*Now. Hurry!* Jamil ordered himself, frozen in his tracks. He needed to go just a few feet in to pour the drug concoction into the the bowl of vodka juice on the table. The guards watched as Jamil poured the liquid from the pitcher into the bowl of vodka. Heart pounding, Jamil looked towards the guards and smiled calmly. They smiled back.

Asa was next to dance. Going over to Asa, Jamil leaned in. "I have good news. I put the drug in the men's drink. This, I hope, is enough to drug them."

"Good," Asa said. "I'm next, my brother, and I'm ready!"

Jamil stood watching Asa start with a spin and jump like no other boy he had seen dance. The men sat on the edge of the platform inches from Asa, transfixed as he performed for them.

"This boy Asa is as you say, he is incredible!" Jamil heard Malawi Kabir say to Dastgir. "I will offer 175,000 American dollars for him this very moment! But first, I would like to have a talk with him in private."

Jamil could see Dastgir hesitate. *He would never do that*, he thought. *Not before a boy is sold*. His stomach felt sick inside.

"I normally would not allow this," said Dastgir. "But you have been a good customer for sometime now. I will allow this, but hurry."

Malkawi walked over to Asa and grabbed him by his hand, pulling him away from the others taking Asa out of the den. Asa looked confused.

Jamil, unsure of what was happening, started to follow them, but Dastgir grabbed Jamil by the arm. "You will remain here, leave them. Make sure the other boys keep with the entertainment."

*No! Jamil screamed inside*. Everything was over if Malawi got Asa alone.

Asa felt petrified as Malawi walked with him down the ledge to one of the smaller dens. He wasn't sure what would happen, but he knew he'd rather die if this evil man touched him. Asa begin to resist, trying to pull away.

"Where are you taking me? I should be back with the others!" Asa said.

"In here, Asa, everything is fine," said Malawi in a soothing voice. "You can trust me. I will protect you." Malawi dragged Asa into one of the smaller dens. "Sit here next to me," Malawi said as he wiped the sweat caressingly from Asa's face. "You are a beautiful boy, and I will take care of you now."

Asa's heart pounded as Malawi leaned in to kiss him. Asa recoiled, feeling so afraid.

It was at that moment that a woman's voice could be heard coming from the darkness. "Leave him."

Malawi paused. "Who is that?"

A woman stepped into the den. She had a large rifle. She looked both fierce and beautiful, unlike any woman Asa had seen. He felt hopeful. Malawi trembled next to him.

"My name is Zaleah," she said. "You do not remember me, but I remember you. That is all that matters. You tortured my parents and our village near the river years ago. You seduced two of my brothers into your sick Jihadic group. I have been waiting all my life to find you, and here you are."

Zaleah stepped towards Malawi out of the darkness. Asa saw the white rifle pointed at Malawi from a few feet away. In a quick motion, Asa took advantage of the distraction and bit Malawi on the arm. Malawi gave a short scream, and in that instant Asa pulled away from Malawi.

*Pop!* Could be heard from her rifle. Malawi dropped to the ground, a perfectly placed bullet to his head just between his eyes. Wide-eyed, Asa was momentarily paralyzed as he stood looking down at the body, with blood splatters on his face.

"Come with me. Now!" Zaleah commanded, interrupting Asa from his trance. Zaleah grabbed his hand and lead him out of the small den, running back down the dark ledge with Asa at her side.

They stopped when they were out of sight in the deeper darkness of the cave. Kneeling down in front of Asa, Zaleah whispered. "My name is Zaleah, and I am here with the Americans! Are there other boys here?"

Asa was still in semi-shock, and he just stared down the ledge. "My brother, my brother! He said to stay close to him tonight," Asa mumbled with fear in his voice.

"Look," Zaleah said with both her hands on Asa's shoulders, looking directly into his eyes. "Are there other boys here? You must stay focused so we can get you and your brother to freedom."

"Fourteen boys," Asa said, regaining some focus, "Fourteen in total. Ten are entertaining for the men, and there are four more just down the ledge. They are in the second den to the end."

"Let us go to them," she said.

Zaleah and Asa entered the den where the four boys were asleep. The boys heard them entering, and some sat up while rubbing their sleepy eyes.

"It is fine," Asa assured them. "This is Zaleah, and she is here to help us to freedom!"

Zaleah stepped closer to the boys, speaking in Pashto she quickly explained what was happening. Quickly, she motioned for the boys to hurry out of the den.

*Click!* It was at that moment that they all heard the cold metallic sound of a rifle just inside the den. Asa saw that a Taliban guard stood at the entrance, his rifle pointed at the back of Zaleah.

# CHAPTER 11

# THE VISTA

"**N**ow listen up! Ben, I want you and Antonio positioned here so that you can take shots from afar." I rattled off instructions almost numbly. It seemed almost unreal, but we were ready. "I think we all agree this is the best vantage point for our overseer. The rest of us will cross the lake. Turn on your helmet mics, and let's make sure we all can communicate."

I spoke into the mic.

"I'm good," they all said in unison.

"We can only hope that Zaleah is on the other side assessing that side of the cave," I said. "We now know that we have 14 boys in total. I counted 10 boys going in to the main den where the entertainment will take place. This will be dicey with the boys and our targets in the same tight space of the den. Our first priority is to get these boys to safety. And the only way that will happen is to get as close to that main den without being spotted, then take out our targets."

"What about King?" Big Joe asked, holding King at his side.

"We're taking him across with us. King will be with us until the end. Now into the heat of the oven!"

We worked our way through the darkness over the boulders to the far end of the cave. The three of us were waist deep, crossing the lake in the frigid water. We passed the eroded opening of the cave that lead outside, nearly the halfway point. We could hear the water outside the cave cascading over the rocks below. Big Joe carried King on his shoulders above the surface, King remained quiet.

It was crossing the lake where I felt the most vulnerable as we waded through the frigid water waist deep. I had never been in such a tight spot, and the odds were stacked against us. But deep down, I knew if we just kept the element of surprise, we could triumph.

Jamil knew it wouldn't be long before the Americans would be going to battle with the Taliban. *I must find Asa,* Jamil was thinking. Heading down the ledge, Jamil passed a guard unnoticed. Jamil looked down, avoiding eye contact as he entered the small den where the men would take the boys for privacy.

Jamil went den to den looking for Asa, walking into the 2nd den, Jamil froze in his tracks. He noticed a shadow of a body lying on the ground. It was the body of Malawi.

Kneeling down next to him, Jamil noticed blood dripping from his forehead. *The Americans! The Americans must be on this side.* Jamil's heart raced. But where is Asa? Without thinking, Jamil grabbed the arm of Malawi and dragged him to the back of the den away from the light. He covered his body with a few blankets and pillows.

*This Malawi is testing my patience!* Dastgir thought while watching the boys finish up dancing. *This is when I need Asa here. I must see what the others have to offer for my prized boy!*

Looking for Jamil, Dastgir spotted him just entering the den. Dastgir waived him over.

"Go check on that Malawi. Tell him it is time to begin with the bidding of the boys! Go now!"

*This Malawi has angered me!* Dastgir was thinking, while noticing a slight behaviour change to a few of the men. *Could it be the liquor was too much tonight?* Dastgir dismissed the thought as he began negotiating with Al Zarqawi for Naseefa.

Zaleah and Asa watched in horror as the Taliban guard smiled, his finger moving towards the trigger.

Just then out of the darkness from outside the den a stealthy dark silhouette of an animal attacked the guard with a vicious growl. King!

Zaleah witnessed King violently attacking the guard. The guard dropped his rifle to the cave floor, and Zaleah swung around. She shot the guard in the face. King ripped at the throat of the dead soldier. Tex, Big Joe and I entered the den to see the spectacle.

"I thought I would have to save your ass once again!" Big Joe said, looking to Zaleah with a smirk.

"What is this you say, Big Dummy?" said Zaleah, trying to act casual about the close encounter. "It was I who reached the other side of the lake ahead of the great American soldiers."

I looked around at the boys' wide eyed faces. "We need to keep moving on our targets. It appears the party is winding down. I think it would be best to keep the boys here. It looks to be the safest place we have for now."

"This boy Asa tells me there are 14 boys!" Zaleah said.

"A few more than we all expected," I said. "We will all have to coordinate our positions and timing to get these boys all out in one piece. Not to mention our asses!"

I noticed that King had calmed down as he sat next to Asa. Asa began stroking his big furry head, being careful of his missing half ear. King gave Asa a few licks to the face. I knelt down in front of Asa and reached into my pocket. Pulling out Sal's dog tag, I put it over Asa's head.

"Here, boy, this is from a great man that was with our team," I said. "King was his closest partner, his good friend." Asa nodded solemnly. "This is what I want you to do: Stay here with King and watch over the other boys. King has a liking for you, and he will watch over you. We will go rescue your brother and the others. Stay hidden, and if you hear gunfire just stay put. We will return for you, okay?"

Asa just nodded with a big smile. He held Sal's dog tag in his right hand staring at it as he gave King a big hug.

"Time's ticking," Tex said in warning.

"Alright, let's move out! Ben, you copy?" I said into the mic. "We are headed to the party!"

"Copy," Ben's voice came through the mic. "I'm watching the main den, and the music has stopped. Still no visual of you."

We worked our way further down the ledge, coming within just meters of the main den entrance where the boys were dancing. The men's loud drunk filled voices could be heard.

"They are bidding for the boys to be sold," Zaleah said as we stood along the cave wall invisible in the darkness.

"What are you going to do about those two guards at the campfire? They have been there for hours. I can take them out from here," Ben said into the mic.

"No, no gunfire yet! We need to get closer, get into position. We need to ambush those two first without alarming the others. How far can you see into the main den?" I asked Ben while looking at the two guards at the campfire, who were unaware we were just feet away.

"A meter, that's it. We are ready for multiple kill shots. We need to pull as many of the guards out of the den as possible for me to get clean shots. We have your back, and we will wait for you command," Ben said.

"Look! There's that kid, Jamil!" Big Joe said. I saw Jamil walking past the guards near the campfire, passing us without noticing we were up against the cave wall.

"Looks like he is headed back to those smaller dens. What's he up to?" I said. I had to make a quick decision on whether to get him to safety now or later. In that moment, though, I noticed that the guards were now looking towards Jamil. The guards at the campfire had their backs to us with their rifles leaning against a small boulder.

"Now!" I motioned."Let's take those two guards out." I ordered Big Joe and Zaleah.

Big Joe and Zaleah moved in on them in the shroud of darkness, their razor sharp knives in position for the kill. Before the guards knew what was happening, they were sprawled out on the rock floor of the cave, their throats cut deep. Both Big Joe and Zaleah stood over them watching as the blood oozed out between their fingers. Zaleah spit on both the guards while mumbling a curse in Pashto.

We raced towards the bodies to get them out of sight quickly.

Jamil entered the den where Malawi was. *What should I do now?* he thought frantically. *If I come back without Malawi, everything is finished.* He paced back and forth, wondering how to fix the situation and give the pretence that nothing was wrong for Dastgir. Time was running out.

He suddenly heard movement outside. Quickly hiding behind a small boulder, he feared that Dastgir or a guard was looking for him.

Suddenly, two of the American soldiers entered the den with the two bodies over their shoulders. Jamil recognized the bodies as the guards outside at the fire.

"It's you, the Americans. I knew it must be" Jamil said, relief and excitement filling his voice.

"Quiet kid, you're coming with us," one of them said as they hid the guards' dead bodies in the den out of sight. "My name is Big Joe, and this is Tex."

"But I must find my brother Asa," Jamil said, still restless.

"Yes! Come with me," Tex took Jamil down the ledge to the den where the other boys were waiting. Jamil came face to face with Asa. Both boys held each other tight for a long time, feeling relief from whatever terrible events could take place. "We are going home, my brother," Asa said with tears running down his face. "We are going home."

"Look, we have other boys that need our help," said Tex. "You boys stay put no matter what you hear out there. You need to promise me you will stay here, understand?"

Jamil nodded as Tex disappeared into the darkness. Jamil knew that everything could still go wrong, and he sat in silence, holding his brother tightly.

"God, please be with them!" Jamil whispered into the darkness.

Tex and Big Joe came back from hiding the bodies of the guards, and they told me they'd moved Jamil to safety. It was a huge relief, but I knew there were more boys in the larger den. It was now or never.

Getting into position near the lake's edge, we moved in close to the den opening. We had a good visual of the inside to the den, and I noticed the boys were now lined up like cattle for purchase. The Taliban leaders were walking around the boys, holding the laced vodka drinks in their hands. Their sick desire for the boys could be clearly seen on their faces as the boys stood in fear. The men kissed their cheeks, while touching them provocatively. The Taliban guards stood defiant, watching over the Taliban leaders.

I saw the man with the strangely striped beard, and I recognized him immediately as the man we had chased in Kabul. It seemed like ages ago. He seemed to be negotiating with the men, but he looked agitated. Suddenly, he started walking out of the den's entrance towards the smaller caves. The man passed by us, heading towards the same cave where the dead guards bodies were hidden.

"Tex, Big Joe, follow him!" I ordered. "I want this one alive. He's running this sick show. Put him in the den with the two dead guards. Hurry!" Tex and Big Joe followed Dastgir.

Looking through the binoculars, I spotted the top two Taliban leaders that the US Military has been after for the last year. There they stood just meters away. My pulse quickened and hate coursed through my veins. I couldn't help but think of the brutality of human suffering they had inflicted on our American soldiers, not to mention their very own people.

*I was certain we had another leader, Malawi here, but I can't spot him at the moment.* I thought while looking at the faces of the men. *Maybe he is just out of sight.* "I see eight Taliban guards surrounding the leaders," I said, looking over to Zaleah. "If we could just get closer for clean shots. I don't want those boys caught in the crossfire."

"Where are Tex and Big Joe? What's taking them so long?" Zaleah whispered.

I whispered into the mic. "Big Joe, Tex. You copy?"

"We got him tied up tighter than a roast beef on Christmas Day ready for the oven!" Big Joe said into the mic. "We are headed back, don't start the fun without us!"

"What's going on?" Ben responded into the mic, overhearing the comments.

"Just hold tight!" I told Ben. "We've captured one of the targets; it's the man who brought this disgusting party together. I have Big Joe and Tex putting him under wraps. As soon as Tex and Big Joe return, the show will start!"

Out of the darkness, Tex and Big Joe emerged to kneel down next to Zaleah on my left. We were ready for the final attack.

"From here I can see the guards," I said as I peered through my binoculars one last time. "They are bunched together blocking my view of the leaders. Let's spread out to give each of us a clean shot perspective. There is the possibility of more guards, so when we take out this group of eight, let's quickly move in and get any guards left standing. I want those leaders alive if possible!"

"Copy that," Big Joe said, getting into a prone position lying just over a small ridge near the lake's edge. "Have them in my sight."

Leaning over to my left, I motioned for Zaleah to get ready. Without a helmet mic on, she nodded with a thumbs up.

"Ben, you copy?"

"Let's go already!" responded Ben impatiently.

"Here we go...Three. Two. One. Now!"

A rapid succession of gunfire filled the large cavernous space, reverberating off the cave walls. In seconds, the eight guards were sprawled out at the feet of the only two men left standing: the Taliban Leaders.

"Mike, get out of there, move it! To your right at three o'clock," Ben yelled into the mic.

A Taliban guard came out of the darkness from outside the main entrance. He was pointing a RPG grenade launcher in our direction.

"I don't have a clear shot! Move!" Ben yelled.

We scrambled back down the ledge taking cover up against the cave wall. A large flash could be seen in the darkness of the cave that momentarily lit up the cave as the Taliban guard fired the RPG. The rocket propelled grenade buzzed over our heads. Moments later we could hear the explosion at the far end of the cave—just to the right of the eroded hole opening.

"I have a visual of the shooter now!" Antonio yelled to Ben.

"Got him in my sights," Ben said calmly as he squeezed off a clean shot with deadly accuracy. Ben and Antonio watched the guard as he dropped to the ground, the RPG launcher rolled to his right.

We raced back to the main den to get the boys to safety as quickly as possible. Slowly rounding the entrance to the main den, I peered in. All I could see were the boys all huddled together, some crying. But they were unharmed. The rest of the team rushed behind me.

We looked around the large den for the Taliban leaders. Nothing. "Where the hell did the leaders go?" Tex yelled.

"Do you hear that? I said, "Sounds like a helicopter! Shit! The Taliban leaders are in the helicopter. Big Joe, Tex, get those boys to safety with the others. Be careful, we could have more guards outside that heard the commotion! Zaleah, come with me!"

We raced outside towards the ledge just as the helicopter was lifting off.

"Get to the ledge quick!" I yelled at Zaleah. We saw the blades of the helicopter going over the ledge dropping out of site, we could hear the helicopter below us as we listened to the groaning of the engine while it struggled to gain altitude in the thin mountain air.

It was nearing dawn. The sun was just coming up, offering a hazy shadowed morning sky in the mountains. Zaleah pushed me back out of the way as she laid down, getting into a shooting position. Looking off in the distance, we could see the helicopter as it began to climb higher in the sky a half mile or so away in front of us.

"I will not let those evil men get away!" Zaleah said as she lined up her shot, squeezing one off. She missed, cursing in Pashto. I watched as the helicopter was getting smaller and smaller off in the distance. Just as it did, it banked to the right, giving us full view of the side. With only the running lights visible, a momentary flash of the sun bounced off the fuselage.

"Take this, you devils!" Zaleah said while she took another shot. A moment of silence as we waited. Suddenly, a huge bright orange fireball could be seen where the helicopter once was.

"You did it! Holy shit, that was one hell of a shot," I said, looking over to Zaleah, who was still on the ground with her head on her rifle. The loud noise of the explosion passed over us.

Standing up, Zaleah turned to me, and we just looked at each other with grins on our faces. Neither of us needed to say a word; the feeling we both shared in that moment was indescribable.

"Mike! You copy?" I heard Ben's voice coming through.

"Yeah. We are heading in," I said into the mic. "I hate to tell you this, Ben, but I just witnessed the most beautiful shot I have ever seen!"

"Yeah! Don't tell me. Zaleah?" Ben asked.

"I'll tell you later. I need you and Antonio to work your way over to the other side of the lake. Watch your backs. It's a good chance we still have some guards out on patrol."

Zaleah was looking in the direction of the downed helicopter, and we both spotted the black smoke now rising from the unseen wreckage.

"Thank God we can finally head home!" I said.

For the second time on the this mission, I switched on the radio to call base. At first, static blared from the small speaker as I adjusted the frequency. Finally, I could hear Sergeant Bacon responding—a distant distorted digital voice.

"Staff Sergeant! I copy you. Over. Good to hear your voice!" Sergeant Bacon said with relief.

"Mission has been a success! Need our ride home ASAP!" I said as the thought of my wife and kids flashed through my mind. "We will need two cabs for this trip. We have 16 boys we will be bringing back with us. Over!"

"Copy. Just to let you know, the Secretary of the State has been monitoring this very closely. Ends up the media caught wind. We have the drone on its way to keep an eye on things until we can get you back to safety. Looks to be a 45-minute flight time. Over."

"Copy. Media huh? I just hope we can get these boys out before we have a media circus out here. We will be on the northside ledge!"

"Copy that! I will inform Officer Tucker and the Commander! Have a safe flight back. Out."

Walking down to the den where all the boys waited, Zaleah and I told the others of the downing of the helicopter with the Taliban leaders on board. It was disappointing that we hadn't captured them alive, but we still had one man who had organized this disgusting party confined: the man with the strange beard we'd chased off the storage sheds.

"I suppose we should go see what he has to say," I said. "We can only hope he is cooperative. It would be easier on him."

"Dastgir," Jamil blurted out. "His name is Dastgir. He is the man that takes the boys and has them sold. He is a bad man! He has held me here for nearly three years. I hate him!"

Jamil said these words with such vehemence that it took me off guard coming from someone so young. "We'll be sure he gets justice," I said to Jamil. "Tex, Big Joe, come with me. Ben and Antonio are working their way around. Let's go have a chat with our prisoner."

The three of us entered the den. Squirming up against the cave wall, we saw Dastgir bound with a rag stuffed in his mouth. Hatred and spite could be seen in his eyes. We stood over him for a moment as I removed the gag from his mouth.

"You don't know who I am, but I have many powerful friends," Dastgir said while trying to sit up, his hands bound behind his back. "You'll regret this."

"Shut the hell up! You're in no position to be threatening us," Big Joe said as he kicked Dastgir in the side. "You are now just a few powerful friends less. I would say...they are very well done and crispy at the moment, if you get my drift."

"Is this piece of shit even worth our time?" Tex said with hate coming from his voice. "Maybe we should just shoot him here!"

Big Joe stood there with his pistol in his right hand.

"Just wait a minute," I said. "We've got to get him back with us."

Just then, Jamil came up from behind us out of the darkness, grabbing the pistol out of Big Joe's hand. I saw the look of hate in his eyes, Jamil raced forward lifting the pistol at point blank range to Dastgir's face. He pulled the trigger.

It had happened so fast. In one moment, the once young teenager now stood looming taller than the grown man, gun in hand triumphantly. I felt shocked that a boy could act so violently. I had no Idea what this boy had endured, but I could see this was his own personal vendetta. "We won't mention Jamil's involvement," I told my team. "Jamil has been through enough. And maybe it was what Dastgir deserved anyway."

The mood of the boys was upbeat as we waited just inside the main entrance to the cave. Big Joe and Tex showed their fatigue after being up for nearly 24 hours, as they sat up against the side of the cave next to each other. Even Zaleah was showing some fatigue, sitting down next to Big Joe and Tex. The boys sat close together, with a few in quiet conversation. Jamil and Asa sat with their arms around each other, feeling safe in each others presence, and King was lying next to Asa with his head on his lap. Ben stood at the lake's edge keeping watch, still concerned about any Taliban off in the shadows across the lake.

I leaned up against the cave wall looking around at the men and the boys, thankful my men were still all in one piece—with the exception of Sal. It broke my heart to think about it. It had been a strange mission, filled with ups and downs. We'd rescued the boys, but we'd manage to take out the leaders, this would set back their regime at least for awhile.

At that moment, we all witnessed something we could've never imagined. The rising morning sun shone brightly through the opening of the eroded end of the cave. We all walked to the edge of the lake, witnessing the radiant beams of sunlight reflecting off the bright blue water of the lake. The reflection cast bright blue turquoise colors throughout the entire cave, and this place that was dark and evil just several hours ago was completely transformed. We watched as the sparkles danced to life on the cave ceiling, sparkles of light everywhere. It was the most beautiful thing I have ever seen.

Jamil stepped out a few feet in front of the group and turned facing all of us.

"This is The Vista," he said as he turned slightly to his right, pointing towards the eroded opening. "The Vista. That's what I have called it for years. My time here has been very long, and when the light came through for only a few moments most days. It was all I had to look forward to, an escape from the darkness that I had to endure living in this dark place. When the sunshine poured through The Vista, I felt as if God himself was with me, giving me hope and inspiration. It would last only minutes, but it was all I needed to keep strong."

The hair on my arms stood on end as I listened to his story, we all were transfixed listening, and the beauty before us. It was breathtaking. Other than Sal the mission was a great success, I felt at peace. It was at that moment that we all heard the welcome sound of the helicopters off in the distance.

# CHAPTER 12
# BREAKING NEWS

"Sis, did you see my black leather boots?" Rachel yelled from down the hallway from the back bedroom. Rachel stood over the bed as she arranged the items in her suitcase that overflowed with her clothes from the last few weeks.

It was 8:30 am on a Sunday morning, and Rachel's flight was on schedule to depart in 5 hours from the Minneapolis-St. Paul Airport. Her state of mind was good, and she was anxious to get home. The call she got from Farrin a few days ago had lifted her spirits, and she had renewed hope of finding the boys. Because it was early November in Minnesota, Rachel was concerned of a flight delay with snow predicted later that day.

"Here they are Rachel!" her sister yelled from the back porch. Her sister and brother-in-law had decided to skip church and spend the last few hours with Rachel before her departure, not knowing when they would have this time together again. Sunday morning football could be heard blaring from downstairs; Rhonda's husband Doug was taking advantage of a no church day to catch the Vikings versus Green Bay Packers game. The kids were upstairs in the living room off the kitchen watching the morning cartoons. Rhonda was working on a breakfast for them that included scrambled eggs with sausage, hash browns, pancakes, and toast.

Rachel headed into the kitchen, walking over to her sister and put her arms around Rhonda's neck. "I'm going to miss you! You don't know how good it has been to finally spend this time together. It's been too long." Rhonda and Rachel held each other with a few tears in their eyes.

"Don't make this any harder than it is!" Rhonda said, wiping her eyes dry while flipping the pancakes. "Maybe next time Farrin and the boys can make it. Did you hear from Farrin today?" Rhonda asked as she set the kitchen table.

"No. He mentioned he had 14-hour shifts all weekend." Rachel said while helping in making the toast. "I did try calling his cell, but no answer. I'm feeling so good. Funny how a little winter weather and family can clear the head!" She said with a giggle. "I'm so ready to get back home though."

"Mommy, I saw Asa on TV." Rhonda's 7-year-old daughter, Samantha, said, looking up at Rhonda in the kitchen with her big blue eyes.

"Honey, that's not nice of you to make things up like that!" Rhonda said while looking over to Rachel.

"That's okay, sweetheart." Rachel said with her arms out. "I miss him, too." She gave Samantha a tight hug.

It was then that Rhonda's oldest daughter, Ashley came running in to the kitchen. "Mom! Come quick! There is some breaking news! Come quick! Asa is on TV!"

Rachel and Ronda hurried into the living room. Hearing the commotion, Doug came upstairs, eyes glued to the TV. A breaking news alert on Channel 9 Minneapolis could be seen. The picture was a live feed being taken from a helicopter that appeared to be circling a snowy mountain in some remote area. The journalist could be heard broadcasting live. Rachel went to the TV and turned up the volume, kneeling down directly in front of the TV to watch the broadcast.

"We have confirmed that American soldiers have rescued 16 boys from this remote part of the Hindu Kush mountains that separate Afghanistan from Pakistan. It appears these boys have been held captive here by the Taliban. Good news is that they are alive and appear to be in good health."

The journalist was broadcasting from a media helicopter, his feed at times broken up. The camera was zooming in and out as the helicopter moved in closer to the rescue scene taking place. The faces of the boys and soldiers just outside the cave started coming into focus. Rachel was transfixed on the TV screen, her face just inches away as she watched the news unfold.

"Oh my God!" Rhonda said as she knelt down next to Rachel. "Is that Asa? Oh my God, Rachel! It is. I could spot that beautiful face anywhere." Rhonda put her arm around Rachel as they intently watched the news unfold.

Rachel felt like she was in her own world far off. She couldn't believe it. She stared at the screen, drinking it all in.

"We have more boys coming out of the cave," the journalist keep reporting. "It appears the ledge can hold only one military helicopter at a time. We will have to move back and let this rescue helicopter prepare for lift off with the first group of boys and soldiers. The second helicopter is out of camera view to our right getting into position to land. This is great news for these boys, and their families!"

Asa came onto the screen again. Rachel looked at Rhonda with tear-filled eyes. "It is Asa, Rhonda. It's him."

The journalist went on. "I have word that we also have a downed helicopter with some smoke rising from It. The downed helicopter appears not to be one of ours. This is a hostile area with many Taliban throughout the area. The military has confirmed the death of several Taliban members, but names have not been released. The second military helicopter is landing now," the journalist said with more static coming over the feed. "They look as if they want to get this done as quickly as possible, and the last few boys are headed out. We will swing around and see if we can't get a good picture for you watching this amazing breaking news moment."

As the camera zoomed in, there was the last boy coming out of the cave. Rachel froze. It was Jamil. Jamil saw the civilian helicopter as he waved into the camera with a big smile. Rachel could see Jamil's face as clear as if he was standing next to her in the living room. Her heart almost stopped. "Jamil! It's Jamil. Look how thin he is. I barely recognize him, but I know it's him."

Overcome with emotion, Rachel fell forward as she reached out and touched the screen of the TV. Jamil's face. Her sister's children just stood watching Rachel as the raw emotion came out of her through deep and guttural sobs. Rhonda held her in her arms. Doug crouched down and brought his arms around them both protectively as they all watched in shock. They sat there for what seemed like hours, crying and laughing and simply being in that strange state of disbelief and joy when something horrible is over. Rachel had never felt so free.

Finally, Rachel stood up, tears still streaming down her face. She smiled and laughed. She mustered up the only words she could manage. "My boys are coming home. Let's get to the airport. I'm not missing that flight for anything in the entire world!"

# CHAPTER 13
# THE FOLLOWING DAYS

The C-160 transport aircraft taxied down the tarmac, coming to a halt just outside the hanger. My men and the entire base were lined up in two rows as the engines of the C-160 cargo plane whined to a stop. All the men were dressed in their dress service uniforms and stood at attention just behind the cargo gate of the C-160.

I took it all in, and I was filled with deep emotion. We could feel Sal's presence as we watched the cargo gate of the C-160 slowly drop to the ground. Big Joe stood to my right, and Tex on my left. I had the lead of King in my right hand as he sat quietly panting in the warm morning sun. Looking to my right, I watched as the casket of Sal was carried out of the cargo plane by the Honour Guard. The casket was covered with the American flag as the Honour Guard walked slowly through the two rows of soldiers. "Taps" could be heard in the background.

Three days had passed since our rescue. After a good day's rest, we'd met with the base Commander and the Secretary of the State for a debriefing, going over the details of the mission and the Taliban leaders we took out. This little mission to rescue the boys had gained attention over the days of our trek, and it had reached the top of the command. The taking out of the top three Taliban leaders was big, and there was even talk of the Silver Star being given to the five of us. Ben would also get the well respected Marksman Badge, and the Purple Heart would be given to Sal's parents.

We stood and saluted as seven members of the Honour Guard fired three shots into the air in perfect unison. The Honour Guard passed through the men while we all stood at attention, watching in silence as they gently carried the casket to the hanger bay.

Tex, Big Joe, Antonio, Ben, and the rest of my unit surrounded the casket. King, sniffing at the casket, laid down next it as he started in with some whimpering. He knew this was Sal. We stood in silence, and the whole base behind us stood at attention in quiet recognition of this fallen soldier.

With all that was going the last few days, we didn't hear of Hakeem until a week after our return. The Base Commander informed us that he had made the long trek back from Asmar with his wounded ankle. After his ankle was strong enough to leave, he did, taking another route through the hills. Now he was back on Chicken Street.

My men were anxious to see Hakeem once again. Tex, Big Joe, Antonio, and I went out to find him.

After an hour or so, we saw him sitting outside a café with Zaleah. Zaleah was in her traditional balochi Pakistani outfit, but her beautiful face uncovered in the morning sun. She seemed to be glowing with happiness to see her brother alive and well. Zaleah had been treated with respect for her contribution from our peers for her determination and devotion to the mission; there was talk that Zaleah would be receiving the Presidential Medal of Freedom.

It was not customary in this culture for a man and woman to display affection in public, but these two siblings didn't care. They were oblivious to people that passed by, together and safe with each other once again. In that moment of watching them, I remembered the story Zaleah had shared with me on the mountain about the physical abuse the two had endured, left for dead by their two other brothers. It was their secret I vowed never to share.

Pulling the humvee around so they wouldn't see us, we all came up behind them. We surprised them with with huge grins and shouts of laughter. It felt good to be back on Chicken Street like old times, and it felt good to be with comrades who knew what it felt like to push oneself to one's limits and to have survived such a harrowing mission. These would be comrades and friends for life.

As we sat and watched Hakeem and Zaleah my mind wandered to my family back in Wisconsin. I had plans of taking leave in a week to go see them. It has been nearly 6 months, would I even recognize my kids? Over the years my men have become my second family. I knew that when I head home that I would always be thinking of my men, my brothers.

Rachel's plane was on schedule with a arrival time of 4:30 PM the next day. With little sleep on the flight, her mind was swirling with all that has happened the last few weeks, she couldn't contain her excitement. Her heart raced thinking that her boys are alive and home, she couldn't contain her excitement to hold both her boys once again.

She was nervous on what to expect from Jamil, what to say to him. It had been nearly three years since they were together, and those days before he went missing they had been doing a lot of arguing. She could only hope he had missed her as much as she has missed him. She loved them both so much.

Getting off the plane, she walked the tarmac to the entrance of the airport. Walking through the busy airport, she spotted Farrin with a huge grin. Standing at his side was Jamil and Asa. When the two boys saw Rachel, they ran to her. Rachel grabbed onto Asa and Jamil and held them tight.

"My boys, my boys," was all she could say, tears rolled down her cheeks.

The boys wrapped their arms around her as they cried with joy for the first time since she could remember. Jamil wiped away the tears running down her cheeks, and he whispered in her ear how much he had missed and loved her. Farrin stood a few feet away, taking in the three together once again, wanting to always remember this special moment.

Months went by. Farrin and Rachel Khan took all 14 of the bacha bazi boys into their large house, and they made it a personal mission to find good homes for each of the boys. Farrin had cut his hours at the hospital and was using his free time to begin to raise money for fighting against the sexual exploitation of the bacha bazi boys.

The Khans worked closely with the government to ensure things went well for each boy. After a few months, they were able to find suitable places for each of the boys, and some of the boys were even able to locate their blood relatives and families. As for Rachim and Zaahid, Farrin and Rachel decided to adopt them.

It was on a February evening in Kabul a few months after the rescue that Farrin and Rachel were sitting on the front step at their home watching all four of their boys playing soccer together in the backyard. Their family had grown. Rachel gazed out at the setting sun as she put her arm around Farrin, looking him directly in the eye.

"Honey, I've been thinking," Rachel said, running her hand through Farrin's hair and smiling playfully. "With all that has happened, I think we should move."

Farrin threw back his head and laughed heartily at the irony of the comment. "Maybe you're right," he said. They held each other close and thanked God for the blessings of family.

The End

*If you would like to further learn of, and help in the fight against this horrific, evil act of sexual abuse towards boys please contact the https://www.unicef.org/protection/*